John Evans is a pseudonym of Howard Browne, an editor and screenwriter as well as a detective fiction novelist. Born in Omaha, Nebraska, Browne worked in Chicago for fifteen years as an editor with Ziff-Davis gaining broad experience in pulp science and detective fiction. He left Chicago in 1951, eventually settling in California, where he wrote motion picture and television scripts. When he retired in 1973, he had been employed by virtually every major studio and had written more than one hundred television plays for series programs ranging from *Playhouse 90* to *Columbo*, and several films, including *The St. Valentine's Day Massacre* and *Capone*. *Halo in Blood*, published in 1946, is the first of his novels featuring private detective Paul Pine.

Otto Penzler, series editor of Quill Mysterious Classics, owns The Mysterious Bookshop in New York City. He is the publisher of The Mysterious Press and *The Armchair Detective* magazine. Mr. Penzler co-authored, with Chris Steinbrunner, the *Encyclopedia of Mystery and Detection,* for which he received the Edgar Allan Poe Award from the Mystery Writers of America.

HALO
IN
BLOOD

HALO
IN
BLOOD

— • —

JOHN EVANS

A Quill Mysterious Classic

SERIES EDITOR:
OTTO PENZLER

QUILL
NEW YORK

Library of Congress Catalog Card Number: 84-60848

ISBN: 0-688-03921-9

Printed in the United States of America

First Quill Edition

1 2 3 4 5 6 7 8 9 10

To the memory of
SIDNEY M. SPIEGEL, JR.
who, if he had written a book,
would have filled it with two words

HALO
IN
BLOOD

· 1 ·

That was the afternoon I drove out to one of the colonial modern homes in the Lincolnwood district to talk a nineteen-year-old named Sally Kurowski into giving up her job as housemaid and going home to mother.

I didn't have any luck in convincing her, but I didn't try very hard either. She had her own room, the work was light, the place was clean, and the man of the house didn't make any passes at her. It didn't take long for me to find out things were different in her own home.

As it turned out, we decided she should keep her job since she was of legal age and beyond the control of her folks. She agreed to drop her old lady a card to let her know the white slavers hadn't got hold of her. And that was that. It meant I wasn't going to get paid but it wouldn't have amounted to much anyway.

She insisted on making me a glass of iced tea and I drank it to be polite and went out into the hot June sun to where the Plymouth waited under a giant cottonwood at the curb.

I lighted a cigarette to kill the taste of tea and looked at my wrist watch. One-forty-five. My appointment in Oak Park was for three o'clock and I was a long way from there.

I drove south and crossed Devon Avenue into Chicago proper. After a couple of blocks I found a diagonal street that would bring me out onto Crawford Avenue. From there on it would be just a matter of ignoring the speed-ometer.

After a mile or so I spotted a traffic light at a crossing up ahead. It was red, against me, but the yellow came on while I was forty or fifty feet away. I kept going, figuring the green would show with room to spare.

It showed, all right. But I was pretty well out into the intersection before I realized the northbound cross traffic hadn't stopped for its red light. The lead car was a heavy Nash sedan, painted a nice genteel blue, and the driver was pouring it on to close the gap between him and the car he was following.

I said some words, hit my foot brake hard and cut sharply to the right. Tires screeched like cats on a fence, and I braced for the crash I knew was coming.

It didn't come. I dug my fingers out of the steering wheel and looked to see why it hadn't come. The sedan's front bumper was stationary no more than six inches away.

I was going to enjoy this. I put my head out the open window and opened my mouth to say a few well-chosen words . . . and right then I saw some things I should have seen before.

For one, the sedan's headlights were burning—as were the headlights on the cars lined up behind it. And every windshield in the line had a purple-and-white sticker on it—a sticker that read: FUNERAL.

There was more. On the west side of the intersection a park wheeler was getting off the seat of his motorcycle without any particular hurry. His black leather gauntlets were already tucked under his left arm and he was digging under his uniform coat for his book of traffic-violation blanks. The city of Chicago makes a few bucks every time some fatheaded motorist gets caught bulling his way through a funeral procession.

I did what I could: I swung my wheel still more to the right and tramped on the gas and lit out after that part of the parade already past the corner and well down the street.

For a minute there I thought I was going to get away with it. The cars behind me closed up to keep the line in tight order, and I didn't hear any siren to indicate the cop was going to make an issue out of it.

My idea was to swing out of line at the next corner and go on about my business. It was an idea to be proud of, particularly if there had been a next corner.

There wasn't. I kept right on rolling, through an open pair of ornamental iron gates in a red brick wall and onto a narrow, winding, crushed-rock roadway that cut a sweeping curve between rows of gravestones and monuments and mausoleums. There were trees all over the place: tall and heavy elms and cottonwoods and some oaks, and all kinds of bushes and vines. The grass was thick and it was green, and the trees and bushes had their June clothes on.

After a hundred yards or so, I eased on my brakes when the Buick coupé in front of me winked on its warning lights. The road wasn't wide enough for me to pull out of line and go on. I was stuck—stuck in the middle of somebody's funeral while the minutes ticked away and half a city stood between me and my three-o'clock appointment.

I cut the motor and leaned back and fished for a cigarette. There was only one left in the pack; I took it and crumpled the pack and tossed it at a gravestone. While I was finding a match the door of the Buick slammed shut and a tall, slender man in a dark suit and gray hat was standing in the roadway. He stood there a moment and rubbed a hand over his smooth-shaven face, then smoothed down the skirt of his coat and went over and prodded the right front tire with a shoe toe in an appraising way as if he was worried a little about the air pressure.

It wasn't until then that I saw he was wearing the turned-around collar of a clergyman.

Feet crunched against the crushed stone of the driveway and five or six men filed past the right side of my car on their way to the hearse. They were a good fifteen feet beyond me before it suddenly dawned on me that every one of them was a clergyman.

I said, "What the hell?" under my breath and finished lighting my cigarette. I slid over and put my head out the window and looked back at the cars lined up behind me. There were six, all different makes.

Except for the cars the roadway was deserted. I got a fresh pack of smokes from the glove compartment, dropped them into the side pocket of my coat and stepped out into the open.

The blue sedan was parked with its front bumper almost against my rear license plate. A man was behind the steering wheel. He sat slumped down in the seat with only a uniform cap and the upper part of his face showing. The eyes were watching me. They blinked a time or two, slow deliberate movements as though the brain behind them was tired.

Without hurrying I walked over to a rounded headstone in the grass bordering the far side of the driveway. Raised letters on the top read: FATHER. Weather had softened the contours of the limestone edges. I flicked away some of the dust with my handkerchief and sat down, stretched out my legs and breathed in some smoke from my cigarette. It probably was bad taste to sit on somebody's father, but no one yelled at me.

Up ahead maybe a hundred and fifty feet, things were going on. The hearse was drawn up near an open grave a few feet off the road where there were no trees or bushes. Twelve men were standing in a group off to one side and discussing something quietly among themselves. As near as I could make out, every man in the bunch was a preacher of one kind or another. Some carried Bibles or prayer books and there was a black robe or two among them.

The undertaker's assistants were fishing the casket out

of the hearse by this time. From where I sat, it wasn't much of a casket: one of these cheap pine black boxes that run about fifty bucks and aren't worth more than ten.

The assistants weren't wasting any time building up the solemn atmosphere you find at a run-of-the-mill planting. They hauled the coffin out quick and laid hold of the sides and ran it over to the grave like a butcher bringing a beef haunch out to the block. They got it set up on the slings ready for lowering and stepped back and took off their hats and mopped their heads.

A car door slammed near me and I turned my head. The man behind the wheel of the Nash was out of the car and coming across the road toward me. He was a little man, not more than five feet four, with a small wise face full of shallow wrinkles in skin the color and texture of gray sand. His nose was bigger than it should have been and was set slightly off center. His mouth was about the size of the quarter slot in a juke box. He was wearing a chauffeur's uniform of gray gabardine and the pushed-back uniform cap showed reddish-brown hair pretty much thinned out at the temples.

He came over with a casual slowness and tipped a hand at me and showed stained teeth in what might have been a smile and said:

"You're a hell of a driver, Mac. You got a extra smoke?"

I tossed him the fresh pack. He tore off the cellophane and one corner of the foil with quick nervous movements of his stubby fingers, took a cigarette, tossed back the pack and struck a kitchen match against a thumbnail. He blew smoke through his nose and flicked the matchstick into the roadway. He said:

"Yessir, Mac, you come prit near getting yourself smacked back there. Lucky I got good brakes, hunh?"

He wasn't tall enough to make me uncomfortable by standing there. He wanted to talk and I had nothing else to do right then anyway, so I said: "From the looks of things, one of the Twelve Apostles must have died. Why all the preachers for just one funeral?''

His chuckle wasn't loud enough to wake a cat. He put the sole of a polished boot against the headstone I was sitting on and ducked his head a little nearer to mine.

''You hit it there, Mac,'' he rasped. ''Yessir, you really picked a lulu to bust in on. I get in on a lot of these plantings—I drive for Reverend Clark of St. John's Lutheran. But this one, by God, beats 'em all. Just kind of take a look at what goes on down there.''

I looked. One of the clergymen was standing at the edge of the grave with his head bowed, probably saying a prayer although he was too far away for me to hear his voice. The rest were standing back a ways and watching him, their heads bared. The undertaker's boys were off to themselves by the hearse and one was sneaking a smoke. A couple of gravediggers in stained coveralls leaned on their shovels a few yards behind the mound of tan clay at the opposite side of the open grave. The only sounds were from birds among the trees and the occasional scrape of a shoe against the crushed-stone driveway.

''See what I mean, Mac?'' the chauffeur said heavily. He took a long drag at his cigarette, the smoke coming out ahead of his words like Indian signals. ''I ask you: what the hell kind of a funeral do you call *that?* In the first place, where's the mourners? A guy's got a right to expect his family to show up when the time comes to throw dirt in his face. All right, maybe he ain't *got* no family. Then his friends ought to come. But say he's fresh out of friends; then his neighbors or his landlord or the people he owes money to . . . *somebody* for Chrisakes!

''And that ain't all. I been to a lot of these things, like I said. But I *never*—not once, Mac—been to one where they was more'n *one* psalm-slinger to say the words over the stiff. Even two preachers would of been something to really talk about.

"But what we got here, Mac. I'll tell you what we got here. We got twelve—you hear me?—*twelve* of the Bible boys. Now what the hell? I ask you, Mac, what the hell? No guy could of led the kind of life that needs twelve Holy Joes to get him past them Pearly Gates, could he?"

By this time he was around to the knee-tapping stage. I put my cigarette under my heel and ground it into the grass and stood up and dusted off the seat of my pants. I said:

"It does seem a little overdone. But then some guys get funny ideas when it comes time to die. What's this one's name?"

He grinned like a marmoset. "John Doe."

I stared at him. "Is that supposed to be funny?"

"That's what the card on the chapel door said," he insisted, still grinning. "How do you like that?"

"It's a beaut, all right," I said. We walked back over to my car and I opened the door.

He said wistfully, "You ain't got a racing form on you, have you, Mac?"

I shook my head. "The horses don't mean a thing to me, friend."

He sighed. "I used to be a jockey up to when I got all this weight. I like to follow the gee-gees but the reverend don't like me to read the form. Hell, he don't like me to swear or smoke or nothing. I'm getting old before my time."

He plodded back to the Nash. I got back in my car and sat down to watch the rest of the funeral.

They finished up finally, just when my watch hit two-twenty. I was going to be late for my appointment, which is no way to treat a possible client, but there wasn't anything I could do about it. The twelve clergymen split up and went back to their individual cars, while the gravediggers started throwing clay back into the hole.

The hearse got under way and the line of cars was moving again. I held onto the heels of the Buick while we went sailing around the curve, through another iron gate in the cemetery wall and back out onto the street. At the next intersection the hearse and most of the cars turned off to the east; I swung west and lit out for Crawford Avenue. Out in the best section of Oak Park my client was probably wearing a path in his Oriental rug waiting for me to ring his doorbell.

Before I'd gone more than a block a siren went off behind me. It lasted only a second or two and then shut off, the way the cruiser boys do when they want your attention. I idled down and glanced at the rear-view mirror and there was a gray prowl car right behind me. The driver was motioning for me to pull in at the curb.

This was turning into a trying day, all right. I cut over to the side of the street and switched off the motor and sat there taking the Lord's name in vain but not out loud.

The prowl heap pulled in behind me and one of the three men in it got out and came over and put his head in at the open window opposite of where I was sitting. He was in plain clothes . . . about forty-five, taller than average and beefy through the shoulders. His face was gray and thin and a little too long, with too much chin for any claim to handsomeness. His narrow blue eyes were cold and direct and slightly contemptuous, as eyes are apt to be when they've seen too much, and he showed about the same amount of expression as the sole of my foot.

His name was Zarr—George Zarr, and he was a police lieutenant attached to the Homicide Detail at Central Station. I had met him for the first time when I was working as an investigator for the State's Attorney's office. Zarr had been a sergeant attached to the Robbery Detail in those days, and even though we were technically on the same side of the fence we just hadn't got along. He was given too much to slapping people around when it wasn't necessary, a little too much in a hurry to go for a gun. Still, he was an honest cop, and that will always excuse a lot.

I said, "Hello, George. What's on your mind?"

His eyes got even narrower and a scowl developed between them. "Pine, hunh? I might have known it. Who was your friend, shamus?"

"Friend?"

He put one of his big feet on the running board and pushed the gray snap-brim felt hat back off his forehead, exposing the thick black hair with streaks of gray over his ears. "Friend is what I said. You were at that cold-meat party. I spotted you coming out of the cemetery."

"Okay," I said. "You saw me. But the corpse was no friend of mine."

Right there was where he was going to be cunning. He put out his jaw a little farther and said quickly, "Somebody you didn't like?"

It seemed a shame for all that guile to go to waste. But I had no choice. I said, "Make it somebody I didn't know, Lieutenant."

He wasn't going to cherish that one either. He took out a cigarette and turned it over and over between a thumb and forefinger and kept on looking at me. He said: "You make a habit of going to strangers' funerals?"

I drummed my fingers lightly against the wheel. "What's the belch, friend? Am I supposed to have bent a law?"

"All I want out of you is answers."

I indicated that I was bewildered by all this.

"Who was he, Pine?"

"The stiff?"

"Yeah."

"Name of John Doe," I said. "But I don't believe that either."

"Who gave you his name?"

"A chauffeur to one of the preachers."

"How come he knew?"

"It seems the name was on the chapel door." I made a show out of looking at my wrist watch. Two-thirty . . . and clients as scarce as German generals named Cohen.

"Nice to have seen you again, Lieutenant. Now, if you'll excuse me . . ."

"How'd you happen to be in there?"

He was going to stand there and ask questions until I ran out of answers and if I didn't like it I could write to the newspapers. So I told him about getting into the procession by accident and why I had to stay there until the end. Minutes were important right then so I left out most of the details. I should have known better.

When I finished talking, he used up a minute or two more to finger his chin and spit in the gutter and put the cigarette he was twiddling into his mouth and get it burning.

Presently he said, "Notice anything peculiar about that burial, shamus?"

"Three things," I said promptly. "Four, in fact. There were no mourners; there were twelve preachers instead of one; everybody was in a hurry to get it over with."

He was staring at me curiously. "What's the fourth one?"

"This business of you being in a lather about it."

Red seeped up from under his collar. "Don't get me mad at you, gumshoe."

I lifted an eyebrow at him but didn't say a word.

"You going some place, Pine?"

"Now that you mention it—yes."

"Where?"

"To see a client."

"What's his name?"

"You wouldn't know him, Lieutenant."

"That doesn't answer the question."

"That question isn't going to be answered."

The two vertical lines between his eyes deepened. "What's the matter? He somebody I shouldn't know about?"

"I didn't say that."

"You're not saying anything."

"I'm going to keep it that way."

He tucked in a corner of his lower lip and looked at the ashes on the end of his cigarette. "I'm a nice guy to co-operate with, Pine. A private cop needs the police ever once in a while. Like when it comes to getting a license renewed, say."

I was sore enough by now to do a little sneering. "Don't scare me, Zarr. I learned a lot in those two years with the State's Attorney. Now kind of take your goddam hoof to hell off my fender. I'm tired of this."

We stared at each other. He put the cigarette back in his mouth and took a deep drag, then took it out again and dropped it to the pavement and stepped on it with the foot that had been on my running board. He said:

"Last chance, hot-shot. Who was the guy in that coffin?"

"John Doe. I told you that."

Zarr took off his hat and looked at the sky. He scratched his half-dollar-sized bald spot and put his hat back on his head. "Okay. . . . Maybe I'll drop in at the office and see you one of these days."

I said, "Any time, George," and stepped on the starter and drove away from him.

Several times I looked back. But I didn't see that gray prowl car again.

• 2 •

Oak Park is a suburb of Chicago. It lies directly west of the Loop and is a nice place to raise your kids. Or so I've heard. The residential sections run from not-so-hot to very fine indeed, with less of the former than most towns its size. There are trees and grass and flowers all over the place. The streets are sleepy streets, with maids pushing perambulators along the sidewalks and sprinklers whirring on the lawns and neat delivery trucks courteously giving you the right of way.

The address I wanted was on Kenilworth Avenue, a block or two south of North Avenue in the exclusive Fair Oaks section. It was a neighborhood where more than three houses to one side of a block was rank overcrowding. Some of the residences went in for Old World charm; some were modern as sulfadiazine; some combined the worst features of both and still managed to look as though nice people lived in them.

Number 1424 narrowly missed being classified as an estate. There was a tall green box hedge, trimmed as carefully as a movie star's toupee, fronting the grounds to keep out the stare of the vulgar passer-by, and there was an ornamental bronze gate set in an opening that led to the grounds beyond. About fifty or sixty feet farther along, a glazed-concrete driveway cut through the hedge, but it too was sealed off from the street by a pair of bronze gates that would swing back for you if your car was custom-built and had gold-plated headlights.

I parked across the street and got out and straightened my tie and moved my gray felt hat straight on top of my head so the gardener would think I was too respectable to sick the dogs on. Then I crossed over to the smaller gate.

I turned the handle and passed through and along a curving walk of gray sandstone flags, lined with bearded irises, that I could see was going to lead around to the north side of the house. There was enough lawn on either side of the walk to set up a golf course and the grass was thick and dark green and cut to the right length by somebody who knew his business.

There were no flower beds in the landscaped grounds at the front of the house to detract from the sprawling, two-storied gray-stone residence of John Sandmark. The place had a weathered look that was as comfortable and unobtrusive as an old hat. Beyond the driveway was a row of Lombardy poplars, all of a uniform fifty or sixty feet, that probably marked the northern boundary of the property. On the south lawn were three very big yellow oaks that dwarfed the house.

The entrance was on the north side, all right. But where there should have been a comfortably big porch, with maybe a swing or two, were three stone steps and a two-bit-size platform and an ornamental bronze railing to hold onto in case you came home drunk. The driveway curved out of sight behind the house and I never did get a look at the garage.

The door was narrow, arched at the top like a cathedral window, with a circular sheet of glass behind a bronze grille about head-high. I put my finger against a small pearl button in the pilaster on the right and heard three deep-toned notes that would have delighted Johann Strauss.

My wrist watch put the time at three-twenty.

A slip of a girl in a black cotton uniform under a frilly white apron opened the door. She had straight legs and black hair and black eyes and a face you'd call cute and forget about. I told her my name and she took my hat and put it on a hall table I could have reached myself and led me into a big square hall that went up two stories to a skylight. Twin staircases in redwood, with beige runners that matched the carpeting under my feet, curved gracefully to meet at the second floor. Between them, on the first floor, French doors led onto a terrace of gray tiles, beyond which a vast bed of scarlet peonies tugged at my eyes.

There were doorways leading off either side of the hall. The maid went over to one on the right and opened the door and said, "In here, Mr. Pine." I said, "Thank you," and walked through, and she closed the door behind me.

It wasn't the kind of room you'd call cozy. They could have put Rhode Island in there by squeezing it a little. The south wall was mostly French windows, with white metal Venetian blinds turned against the sun, and maroon velvet drapes as contrast to the patternless gray carpeting tickling my ankles. The west wall was books to the ceiling, with a ladder on wheels and a trolley to bring them within reach. The north wall was covered with soft gray-blue parchment, with three very good prints in blond-wood frames spaced to break the monotony above the stone mantel of a fireplace you could have broiled a mastodon in. Two long chesterfields in dark-blue leather stood back to back in front of the fireplace and there was a white bearskin rug near the polished copper screen.

Over near the French windows was a limed-oak desk not much smaller than a tennis court. The man in the blue-leather swivel chair with his back to the windows stood up as I came in. He waited until I pulled my feet out of the rug enough times to reach him; then he put out his hand and gave me a medium handshake and said:

"How do you do, Mr. Pine. I'm John Sandmark. I think you are a little late."

"I didn't mean to be," I said.

He indicated a chair next to the desk and waited until I was in it before returning to the swivel chair. He leaned back and put his elbows on the arms and laid the tips of his fingers gently together and looked at me over them.

Even sitting down he was a big man. Not fat, just big-boned and big-chested and with a head like a lion. His hair was coarse and thick and black, combed straight back to fight a tendency to wave. His face was square, heavy in a massive way that had nothing to do with soft living. His eyes were dark blue and they looked at you without apology. His nose would have been at home on an Indian chief and the large mouth under it wasn't much more than a straight line. You could have hung a lantern on his chin but not without his permission. He could have been forty and he could have been sixty. I figured fifty was about right.

When we finished sizing each other up, he said, "I appreciate your coming to see me, Mr. Pine. Would you care for a drink?"

"If you will join me," I said, in my society voice.

He bent and swung open a door where desk drawers should have been and pulled up a portable bar that operated on levers like a typewriter shelf. There were three or four decanters and a soda bottle and an electrical freezing unit for cubes. All it lacked was a brass rail and a barfly.

"Will Scotch do, Mr. Pine?"

"It always has."

He dug out a pair of highball glasses, poured respectable amounts of whisky from one of the decanters, added ice cubes and soda, put a swizzle in each and handed me one.

We murmured a polite word or two and drank. Mine tasted like something you could bribe angels with. There would have been no point in learning the brand; I couldn't have afforded it anyway.

I refused a cigar and took one of my own cigarettes

instead. He snapped on a gold lighter from one of his vest pockets and held it out to me with a hand that trembled about as much as the Cheops pyramid. After his cigar was burning right, he pushed a copper ash tray over where we both could reach it and leaned back and blew out a cloud of oily blue smoke and said:

"You are better than I expected, Mr. Pine. I don't know much about private investigators, you see, and I had pictured some sort of beetle-browed subhuman with flat feet, a derby hat, and given to talking from the side of his mouth."

I couldn't think of anything to say to that so I didn't say anything.

"Tell me something about yourself, if you don't mind. I'm not just being curious, I assure you."

"It won't take long," I said. "I'm thirty-one, five feet eleven, one hundred and seventy pounds. The dent in the bridge of my nose came from high-school football. I was an investigator in the State's Attorney's office until a change in administration gave me a new boss. He had a nephew who needed a job. I went into business for myself about a year ago."

His smile showed even white teeth that were probably his own. "I imagine it was a good thing for you, Mr. Pine. You impress me as a man who does not like to take orders."

"I've had complaints about that," I said. "Some of the complaints were probably justified."

His smile broadened. "At least you're frank about it."

A gray squirrel darted along the ledge of the terrace outside the windows, startling a robin who had been minding his own business. The robin said about what a man would have said under similar circumstances and flew off somewhere. I cut down an impulse to yawn and sampled my drink again.

Sandmark nodded as though he had made up his mind. He put his smile away and his glass down and said crisply:

"Mr. Pine, I have a daughter—actually a stepdaughter, although I legally adopted her when she was hardly more than an infant. Now she's grown into a very lovely and charming young woman and I love her very much. But . . . she has caused me some trouble and quite a bit of worry from time to time."

He stopped abruptly and looked past the top of my head at nothing at all and his lips went back to a tight line.

I said, "Is she in trouble again?"

My abruptness surprised him into looking at me. "I think so, yes."

"What kind of trouble?"

"A man, Mr. Pine."

"I see. How old is your stepdaughter?"

"She'll be twenty-five in two months."

"What form does the trouble take?"

He studied the ash on his cigar. "I think she intends to marry this man."

"You would object to that?"

He glared at me. "I most certainly would! I told you my daughter is very dear to me. I do not propose to allow her to make a mess of her life the way her mother did."

"I just asked," I said mildly. "Of course you realize your stepdaughter is of age. If she's hot to get married I don't see what can be done to prevent it."

He got a little chilly around the eyes. "I didn't send for you to tell me that, Mr. Pine."

"I'm sure you didn't," I said. "And while we're on the subject, just what *did* you call me in to do?"

People didn't talk to him that way. His face reddened and a vein began to throb in his temple and for a minute there I thought he was going to throw a thousand dollars' worth of desk at me. He took three or four deep breaths before he figured he could open his mouth without having a roar jump out.

Finally he said, "I want this affair broken off once and for all. And I want it done quickly."

"That sounds all right," I said, "and it can probably be done. But I'll have to find out whether I want to do it."

I got sneered at for that. "You're mighty independent for a workingman, I would say."

"You'd be right," I said. "There's no point in getting mad at me, Mr. Sandmark. I make my living by working at a business that has more bad smells to it than most. I try to avoid them. I don't know enough of the facts on this case to say anything one way or the other. If it's okay with you I'll ask some questions; if not, I'll say good-by and no harm done."

"What do you want to know?"

"What is your stepdaughter's name?"

"Leona."

"Sandmark?"

"Yes."

"Okay. What's her boy friend's name?"

"Marlin. Gerald Marlin, I think."

"You think?"

"She refers to him as Jerry. I've never met him."

"You mean she meets him only away from the house?"

"Leona isn't living here, Mr. Pine."

"Why not?"

His shoulders moved in the ghost of a shrug.

I said, "I'll have to know where she's staying."

He took some of his drink and set the glass back on the desk but kept his fingers around it. "Of course. She has an apartment at 1317 Austin Boulevard in Chicago."

"That isn't far from here, is it?"

"About a mile."

"How long has she been living away from home?"

"About two months."

"Is she employed anywhere?"

"No. Certainly not."

"Money of her own?"

"None to speak of. I give her an allowance."

"Mind telling me how much of an allowance?"

"A thousand a month."

"How long has she known this man Marlin?"

"Well . . . about three months."

"She know you have no use for him?"

"I make no secret of my dislikes, Mr. Pine."

"And she moved out because you didn't like Marlin?"

He sighed and his heavy shoulders sagged a little. "Leona is quite—well, headstrong. She is stubborn, willful, proud . . . and beautiful. She is very beautiful, Mr. Pine." Lines deepened between his eyes. "I've tried to keep her from being hurt. I'm afraid I haven't been successful. Her father's blood, I suppose. There have been some unfortunate . . . incidents."

I waited, but he set his jaw and said no more. If I wanted particulars I was going to have to blast for them.

"What were the incidents, Mr. Sandmark?"

"I don't think we need go into that." He was polite about it, but it was a frosty politeness meant to chill me into dropping the subject. But I put on my earmuffs and mittens and dug into it anyway.

"I like to be thorough, Mr. Sandmark. You want me to go to work for you. From what you have said, I'll be actually working for your daughter too—even though she doesn't realize it. But I won't be able to do a good job if things I should have known about keep popping up to confuse me.

"You say your daughter has had some trouble. A lot of nice people get into trouble. I don't expect to be in charge on Judgment Day, so I don't go around sentencing people for practice.

"The point is, your attorney gave you my name and, I suppose, recommended me as someone you could trust. Then go ahead and trust me, or ring the bell and tell the maid to fetch my hat."

It was a long speech for me and left my throat parched. Sandmark sat there without moving, looking at me from behind a stone face. I took a long pull at my highball that about finished it and put down the glass and lighted another cigarette from the stub of the first and waited. . . .

He smiled. I've seen wider smiles on a cue ball, but there it was. He took his cigar from a groove in the ash tray and put it in his mouth. His hand was steady as ever. He said:

"You'll do, Mr. Pine. . . . When Leona was sixteen, two years after her mother's death, she ran off with a boy in her class at high school and lived with him alone for a week in his parents' summer home in Wisconsin. Naturally I did not prefer charges. . . . When she was twenty she became involved with a married man twelve years her senior and was named as corespondent in the wife's divorce suit. I managed to keep that out of the papers. . . . When Leona was almost twenty-three she— I'll be frank with you, Mr. Pine—she had an affair with a criminal . . . a handsome devil who had served time for armed robbery, counterfeiting, operating a confidence game—I don't know what all. Fortunately no one ever found out about it because he pulled something shortly after he met Leona and was sent to prison for two years."

He sighed. "That's the worst of it. Although about three months ago I paid off six thousand dollars in IOU's— gambling debts at a place called the Peacock Club. I could have refused to honor them, of course, but there were some especially nasty threats made.

"Another time, just recently in fact, I was called down to Central Station to arrange bail for her. She had been arrested in a gambling raid. It so happened she had a gun in her bag at the time. . . . And only three weeks ago she came to me for money—quite a considerable sum. She refused to tell me why she wanted it. Leona has quite a temper at times, and there was something of a scene."

"Still," I said, "you gave her the money?"

"Yes. Yes. I have never been able, really, to refuse her a thing."

"How much did she want?"

"Five thousand dollars."

"You've no idea why she wanted it?"

"It is not difficult to figure out. Gambling fascinates her."

"It fascinates me too," I said. "But not five thousand dollars' worth."

There was pain in his fine eyes—pain and a fierce pride. I finished my drink and sat there holding the glass, thinking about what he'd told me. Presently I said:

"It isn't pretty, but I've heard worse. Much. What have you against this Jerry Marlin, Mr. Sandmark? Why shouldn't your stepdaughter marry him—if that's what he intends to do."

His jaw stiffened and his thick black brows came together in an uncompromising line. "Because he is the same type of man that has hurt Leona before: a wavy-haired, smooth-talking, flashily dressed young man with no visible signs of support. Eventually I would have to buy an uncontested divorce for her, and you can be sure the price would be considerable."

I said, "I understood you to say you'd never met him."

"I was never introduced to him," Sandmark said grimly. "I managed to avoid that. At first he called for Leona on several occasions and I caught glimpses of him. I didn't need any more than that."

"How old a man is he?"

"Hard to say. He might be twenty-eight and he might be thirty-five. Somewhere between those figures I'd say."

"How would you describe him?"

He thought for a minute. "Around five feet ten, a hundred and sixty pounds, slender build, narrow face with small features and an olive skin, black eyes set close together, black hair with a wave in it, and I don't like his taste in clothing. . . . I'm afraid that's the best I can do."

"You did fine," I said. "I feel as though I went to

John Evans

school with him. Do you happen to know his address?''

"No."

"Any of the places he might hang around?''

"No."

"You don't think he works for a living?''

"If he does it's probably something outside the law.''

"All right,'' I said. "I think I get the pitch; correct me if I'm wrong. You want me to dig into Marlin. You want something on him that will be strong enough to turn your stepdaughter against him. And if I can dig up something that will put him away for a few years, you'll like that a lot.''

We stared into each other's eyes. The fingers of his right hand tapped softly against the chair arm. Very slowly he said, "I see that we understand each other, Mr. Pine.''

"Maybe not too well,'' I said. "There's always the possibility Marlin is okay. Some people can't help how they look.''

His smile was as bleak as the Siberian steppes. "I'm not engaging your services to prove Marlin is a suitable match for my daughter. I want this romance cut off at the roots and I don't give a damn how it's done.''

I looked at the empty glass in my hand and said, "I don't go in for framing people, Mr. Sandmark.''

He didn't say anything although I waited to give him the chance. I said, "I'll look into it. It will cost you thirty bucks a day. That includes expenses; I don't like to make out expense reports. Is that satisfactory?''

His eyes were still watching me and his smile was still cold. "There will be a thousand-dollar bonus if you get the proper results. I would like you to remember that.''

I nodded and let him see a face as expressionless as his own. "That's nice and I can use the money. I'll work to earn it, too, but no harder than the original thirty a day would cover.''

He didn't say anything to that. I put down the glass and took out another cigarette and turned it in my fingers.

I said, "I gather that I'm to stay away from your daughter on this."

"Unless it can't be helped," Sandmark said quietly. "Certainly she must not know what I've engaged you to do."

"Have you a snapshot of her I can have? It might help."

He pushed back the swivel chair and stood up easily and went over to the bookshelves on the west wall and took a dark leather album from one of the lower shelves. He leafed through the pages, found what he wanted, pulled it loose, put the album back and came over and tossed a small glossy print face up on the desk in front of me.

While he was getting into his chair, I picked up the snapshot. It showed a girl in shorts and a sweater against a background of bougainvillaea and pepper trees. She was fairly tall for a girl, I judged, and slender with a kind of curved slenderness. She had at least two excellent reasons for wearing a sweater and her legs were probably good for walking too.

I got around to her face finally. It was a little too angular for perfect beauty maybe, but I was satisfied. She was wearing a lot of hair in a shoulder-length bob with a swirl on top. She had a good forehead and narrow eyes, wide-spaced, and a thin aristocratic nose. Her mouth was small and nicely shaped, with the lower lip a little fuller than it might have been. It would be fun to nibble on that lip. She was looking sulky, so I couldn't see her teeth; but I would have bet she didn't have gingivitis.

I said, "It's a nice picture. Too bad it isn't in color."

In a faraway voice he said, "Her eyes are gray-blue, like her mother's. Her hair is reddish-brown—the kind they call chestnut, although you don't hear that word much these days."

I took out my billfold and tucked the snap into one of the pockets and put it away again. "All right, Mr. Sandmark. I have enough to start on. I'll telephone in a report in a day or two. Unless you prefer me to make them in person.''

I stood up and so did he. "The telephone will do. Meanwhile you will want some money.''

He took a black pin-seal wallet from an inner coat pocket, counted out three fifty-dollar bills and handed them to me. It meant taking out my billfold again but it was worth it. I refused a second drink although it hurt me to do so and he pushed a button set in the desk's edge. The same maid opened the door, waited while I shook Sandmark's hand, and led me into the smaller hall and gave me back my hat.

She put me gently out on the small porch and closed the door. I walked slowly down the path between the irises, through the bronze gate and out into the street.

The Plymouth was still parked at the opposite curb. That surprised me a little. Considering the neighborhood someone might have had it hauled away to the dump.

· 3 ·

I was opening the car door when a big black custom-built Packard convertible coupé with its top down swung around the corner on two wheels and came down the street toward me with a soundless rush.

A girl was behind the wheel—a girl in a green-linen tailored sport dress out of *Vogue* and a ribbon to match in her shoulder length reddish-brown hair. There was a brown leather bag of golf clubs propped in the seat next to her. She came up even with me and swung the car's nose into the Sandmark driveway entrance and applied the brakes.

It was none of my business. I slid in behind my own wheel and put the key in the ignition.

"Say. You there."

As a voice it was probably all right—a little husky but clear and not too high-pitched. If there was a queen-to-commoner quality to the tone the convertible probably justified it.

I ducked my head and looked out the window. The girl was swung partially around in the seat and staring over at me.

"You," she called. "In the Plymouth."

"Okay," I said. "I hear you."

"Come over here a minute."

There would have been no point in refusing. With that head of hair she wasn't likely to be anybody other than Leona Sandmark. I had been told to stay away from her, more or less, but nothing was said about this kind of situation.

So I got out of the Plymouth and walked over to her. She had a cool, impersonal expression on her lovely face, the kind of expression installment collectors get used to. She flicked me with a glance and said:

"Pardon me, but did you just leave this place?"

I suppose I should have taken my hat off and stood there clutching the brim like a share cropper being interviewed by the mistress of the manor. You could see it was what she expected. Instead I pushed my hat back and hooked my shoe over the fender apron and gave her a leer and said:

"I hate to admit it, but I can't quite place you. You're not the Smith's second maid, are you?"

She straightened up as though I'd laid a cadaver in her lap and her face turned as red as a slaughterhouse floor. "Well, I *beg* your——"

"My mistake," I said. "You don't have to apologize."

John Sandmark had been wrong about her eyes. They were green instead of gray-blue and right now they were hot as twelve passes in a crap game. "I suppose you're trying to be funny!"

I shook my head mournfully. "I guess I'm not very good at it." I turned around and started back. "Well, it was nice seeing you."

"Please don't go. I'm—sorry."

The lorgnette was gone from her voice. I came back and said, "Okay. Maybe I made a mistake. Is there something you wanted?"

She managed to push out a smile but it was the hardest work she had done all day. Her face seemed a little less angular than the snapshot indicated and the lower lip wasn't quite as full. But there wasn't any doubt that she was Leona Sandmark. Her dress was pulled up well above her knees and I could see two generous lengths of suntan nylons and a strip of skin the color and texture of new ivory.

I might have been looking at the radiator cap for all she cared. She said: ''There's no need for either of us to be rude. I only wanted to know if you just came out of 1424.''

I glanced over at the double gates of the driveway. ''From the looks of the place it would be nice to come out of.''

She took a quick breath and her chin rose a degree or two. ''Would you mind answering my question?''

''Is there any reason why I should?''

Her left hand jerked against the wheel as though she had been on the point of smacking me across the chops but managed to control herself at the last moment. She tried to stare me down but my conscience was clear and she was the first to look away.

She said, ''All right. I'm Leona Sandmark, and I live here. I know my father is worried about something. When I saw you coming out I thought maybe you had something to do with—with—well, with what he is worried about.''

''What's he worried about?''

''I don't know.'' She seemed to have cooled off some and her eyes were more blue than green. ''I hoped you could tell me that.''

''You made a nice try,'' I said. ''It's been swell meeting you, but I have to go now.''

I was on the point of turning away but she reached out and caught hold of my sleeve. ''No . . . wait! You're keeping something from me, I can tell. What did you want with my father?''

I looked down at her fingers. They were very pretty fingers: long and tapering and without the knobby knuckles you see on so many feminine hands. She wore no rings and the skin was tanned and clear. I let my eyes move slowly along the softly rounded bare arm to her shoulder, to the V of her neckline, to the poorly hidden panic in her face. Right then she looked older than twenty-four has any right to look, older because she was scared to death. It flickered in her eyes, it pulled at the corners of her mouth, it beat in the pulse of her throat.

"Look at it this way, Miss Sandmark," I said gently. "If I had anything to hide from you, I'd have given you some smooth little story about being an insurance man, or something, long before this. By looking at it that way, you'll see that my business in the neighborhood must be something that couldn't possibly be of any interest to you."

Her hand slipped slowly from my sleeve as doubt began to replace fear. "Then you're not—a police officer?"

I shook my head gravely. "No, ma'am."

"But you did call on my father?"

"I give you my word, Miss Sandmark, so far as I know I've never laid my eyes on your father."

"Then, damn you," she snapped, "why didn't you say so to begin with?"

She slammed the tip of her golf shoe against the starter and the hundred and twenty horses tried to kick the convertible's hood over the hedge. It made me jump back. Not that Leona Sandmark noticed. The hell with me. I wasn't important any more. Maybe I never had been.

She kept her eyes straight ahead and began to jab savagely at the horn button. But it was one of those musical horns and the sound matched her mood right then like pink ribbons on a prize fighter.

I could have hung around and pouted. Instead I went back across the street and climbed into my car. While I was stepping on the starter, the driveway gates folded back and the convertible roared through and out of sight ahead of a swirl of blue exhaust smoke.

I drove south and east until I was back over the line into Chicago, at Jackson Boulevard, then directly east to the Loop. It was getting well into five in the afternoon, but I had a job to do and now was as good a time as any.

By the time I parked the car and put away a sandwich and malted milk at a Walgreen drugstore, six o'clock

had rolled around. I picked a red-streak edition of the
Daily News off the stand at Jackson and Wabash and
went on to where I spent the sitting part of my days.

The Clawson Building was twelve stories of tired red
brick between a couple of modern skyscrapers on the
south side of Jackson Boulevard, just west of Michigan
Avenue. It had been put together before the turn of the
century by an architect who must have figured he wasn't
going to be paid. There were gargoyles on the cornices
and one in the superintendent's office. The halls were
dark and forever smelled of lye and damp hay. The
offices had businesses in them: one business to each
office and the kind of business that made very little
money or none at all. I fitted right in there.

I had a reception room and an inner office on the eighth
floor, with a window in each. There wasn't anyone sitting
on the secondhand leather couch or in either of the two
chairs, and the magazines on the reed table were just as
the cleaning woman had left them the night before.

I unlocked the inner office door and went in and tossed
my hat on one of the two brown metal filing cabinets in
one corner. There were a couple of envelopes under the
mail slot and I picked them up, put them on the desk
and went over and opened the window a crack from the
bottom. Two flies and a little air came in behind the
sound of streetcars from Wabash Avenue. I pulled back
the golden-oak swivel chair and sat down behind the oak
desk and snapped on the lamp and spread out the newspaper.

The article was under a heading on a three-column
box near the foot of the first page.

UNIDENTIFIED MURDER
VICTIM GIVEN UNIQUE
FUNERAL

It was my funeral, all right. Some rewrite man had
really enjoyed himself putting that yarn together. It seemed
that about thirty days earlier some floater had been sapped

to death in a room at the Laycroft Hotel, a flea-trap on West Madison Street in the heart of Chicago's Bumville. Nobody could identify the corpse and the name on his registration card was illegible, so it ended up at the morgue and lay on ice for a month waiting for some relative to come along and claim it. Nobody showed, however; and about the time the coroner's office was ready to bury the body in the Oak Forest potter's field, an anonymous letter had come in. The letter instructed the coroner to turn the body over to any undertaker for interment after chapel and graveside services of a religious nature. Money accompanied the letter—enough money to pay for a cemetery lot and the cost of the funeral.

If there was any excitement over the letter, it wasn't enough to get the story into the papers. Since the corpse had got that way by being murdered, the police probably kept the letter quiet, hoping the murderer, or at least the anonymous philanthropist, would show up at the funeral.

Nothing like that happened; but when twelve clergymen, each of a different denomination, arrived to officiate at the services . . . brother, there *was* a commotion! Each clergyman produced an unsigned letter engaging him to run the show, and each was going to run it, come drought or flood!

A few tempers got strained before the boys worked out a deal, but it was finally decided that each was to have a turn at officiating—both at the chapel and at the cemetery.

Anyway, they got John Doe planted, dusted off their hands and went back to their churches. Then somebody—not necessarily one of the turned-collar boys—tipped off at least one city editor and things started to buzz. You could bet your umbilicus the newshawks weren't through digging into the puzzle. Circulations have been upped on stories that started on a tamer note than this one.

By the time I finished the article I knew why Lieutenant George Zarr of the Homicide Detail had asked so many questions. Well, he could ask somebody else. I had my own living to make.

I folded the paper and put it in the wastebasket and set about earning the money John Sandmark had paid me earlier in the afternoon. The envelopes from under the mail slot were just a couple of bills. I pawed them into the middle desk drawer, dug a Chicago telephone directory out of another drawer and flopped it down on the desk pad.

There were six listings under the name Marlin. None of them was Gerald or Jerry, and one was a company. That meant five numbers to call.

I pulled the phone over in front of me and, one by one, called all five. Among them was one Jerry Marlin, but he was nine years old and doing his homework, so I passed him up.

That was that. I put back the receiver and lighted another cigarette and twiddled my thumbs over some thinking. Then I reached for the phone again and dialed a number I didn't have to look up. It belonged to an unlisted telephone in a six-by-eight cubbyhole at the Criminal Courts Building out on Twenty-sixth and California.

". . . H'lo."

I said, "Harvey?"

"Yeah."

"This is Paul Pine."

"Yeah."

"Still a one-syllable guy," I said. "How've you been Harvey?"

"Okay."

I gave it up. "How about a little help, pal?"

"Okay."

"You ever hear of a gee named Marlin—Jerry Marlin?"

"No."

"Check up on it, anyway, will you, Harvey? I'll hold on."

"Okay."

I propped my feet up against the edge of the desk and
leaned back and waited. A wilted breeze slipped in through
the open window and riffled the leaves of the Varga
calendar, and the brunette in the red bathing suit wiggled
her hips at me. She was wasting her time. An elevated
train screeched on the Van Buren Street curve two blocks
away, a faint thin screech like the E string on a violin.

"Pine?" said the receiver against my ear.

"Yeah, Harvey. Anything?"

"Nothing on him."

I sighed. "Okay. Thanks for trying."

I reached out and pressed the cut-off button and took
the telephone standard on my lap and dialed police headquarters at Eleventh and State. It took another fifteen
minutes of talking and waiting—mostly waiting—to get
the same answer Harvey out at the State's Attorney's
had given me. Mr. Gerald Marlin was as clean as a
commencement-day neck. Under that name anyway.

I thought some more, a little sourly this time. If I was
going to find out what kind of jamoke Marlin was, I had
to start by finding him, where he lived and what he did
for a living. There were three million people in town.
Finding one of them who wasn't in the phone book or
on the records of the local law could get to be quite a job.

In my line of business I was used to being called on
to find people. But my clients usually supplied former
addresses, a list of friends, former jobs: information that
made locating the missing person mostly a matter of leg
work.

All John Sandmark had given was a name, a description that would fit a lot of guys, and orders to break up
a romance. Of course, I could always pick up Marlin by
tailing Leona Sandmark around until she met him someplace. But I had instructions to stay away from her, and
in the circumstances, it was probably the better thing to
do. She had spotted me outside her stepfather's home;
if she found me underfoot a second time I could get

pressured off the case. I made my living by staying on cases.

I went back over my talk with Sandmark. By the time I finished there was an idea or two within reach. I blew on them and polished them up a bit and discovered they were pretty good ideas. So I took my hat off the filing case and locked the office door and went out to see a movie.

·4·

It was a clear hot night, with half a platinum moon hanging above the Chicago Avenue water tower and a blanket of gasoline fumes settling over Michigan Avenue. I turned off at Huron Street and parked halfway down the block from Rush and walked around the corner to the Peacock Club—a night club that drew most of its clientele from the powdered-shoulders and white-tie crowd.

I let the doorman open the door for me and went into the glittering foyer. It was empty of customers, and beyond the arched entrance the semicircular rows of white-clothed tables showed only a few diners dotted about the empty dance floor. Only part of the orchestra was on the stand and they were playing quietly, almost to themselves, with most of the brasses loafing. The time was nine-forty-five.

The bar was off to one side behind a glass partition from ceiling to floor. It was a long straight hunk of what looked like mahogany, with rounded corners and, at the far end, a redhead in a black evening dress behind a twenty-six board under a light with a green glass shade. A narrow mirror ran the full length of the shelving behind the bar, with a mural above it that was mostly nudes. There wasn't much light, but then there never is in places like that. The only customers were four men drinking together just inside the door.

I climbed onto the red-leather top of one of the chrome stools halfway down the bar and the nearer of the two aprons unfolded his arms and drifted over.

"Your order, sir?"

He was a compact little man, put together with the neat precision of a Swiss watch. His black hair was plastered down above a small white face with a brief nose and a mouth like a pencil mark. His small narrow eyes didn't really see me.

"A dry Martini," I said.

He put it together with the economy of motion of an old hand at the game. When he set the glass in front of me, I said, "Marlin been in tonight?"

Now he saw me, but nothing else changed in his face. He put two narrow stubby-fingered white hands on his edge of the bar and leaned forward with polite attentiveness. He said, "What was the name, sir?" His voice had a peculiar false brightness to it that was going to grow into nastiness if I let it.

I didn't intend to let it. I said, "The name was Marlin and it probably still is. I asked you if he had been in tonight."

His lips curled back but he wasn't smiling. The light wasn't strong enough for me to see what was in his eyes but I knew what was in them just the same. He said, "I don't think I've seen you around before, sir."

I turned the stem of my glass slowly between a thumb and forefinger and waited for him to say something more or move away and say it to somebody else. He had told me all I wanted to know.

He straightened up stiffly and moved a few steps down the bar and found a towel and wiped off a section of the already immaculate wood. He studiously kept his eyes away from me but he was conscious that I was still sitting there. I sipped at my drink and lighted a cigarette and looked smugly at myself in the mirror behind the bar.

When I turned my head again the barkeep was talking into a telephone. It didn't last more than thirty seconds. He put back the receiver and turned his head quickly and saw me watching him. It made him jump a little. For a moment or two he was very busy doing nothing important, then he sidled along the bar to where I was sitting and smiled tightly and said, "Shall I fill your glass, sir?"

"Not until I empty it," I said.

"Yes, sir." He found another towel and wiped off some more of the bar in my vicinity. Two girls in bright evening dresses came into the bar with a tall thin guy with a long neck. They sat down a few stools to my left and called over my new friend and ordered cocktails. They never got cocktails any quicker than those, and all the time the barkeep was keeping one eye on me.

I finished my Martini and he had hold of the glass before it had time to make a ring on the wood. "Another, sir?"

"Relax," I said. "I won't run away."

He stood there, holding the glass and smiling his tight smile. I took out my wallet and gave him a bill. He put the glass under the bar and went over to the register for change.

It took him twice the necessary time to get the proper change together. He came back and was counting it out carefully for me—something no experienced apron would ever do—when a medium-sized man wearing a tuxedo came into the bar, looked around quickly and came over to me. The barkeep got the stiffness out of his fingers and face, gave me the rest of my change without counting and moved away.

The man said, "Pardon me," in a soft voice and I looked around at him. He was five or six years older than I, with dark hair turning gray at the temples, pointed ears and a face like a tired fox.

"It's a good thing you didn't take any longer getting here," I said. "Your stooge had his nails just about gnawed down to the elbow."

He looked me over carefully before he said, "You wanted to see Mr. Marlin?"

"Not that I recall," I said. "I asked if he had been in tonight, that's all."

"You know Mr. Marlin?" His politeness was acquiring an edge.

"We have a mutual friend, I believe."

"Yes?"

"You wouldn't know him," I said.

He put a long-fingered hand into the jacket pocket next to me and said, "This isn't the best place to talk. Come with me, please."

If he had a gun in there it didn't mean anything. Only a hophead would do any blasting where we were and he wasn't a hophead. I was satisfied with the way things were working out.

I got off the stool and he steered me through the foyer and into a small private elevator around the corner from the checkroom. I let him push the button and we went up one flight and along a narrow, heavily carpeted corridor with blue walls and past two or three doors to one at the end of the hall. My guide gave a pair of soft knocks on the panel and the lock began to click and he pushed open the door and we went in.

It wasn't a very large room but there was enough space for a kneehole desk in chrome with a blue composition top, and three leather chairs with bent metal tubing for legs. Heavy gold draperies with long fringing were drawn at the two windows and there was the feel of air conditioning.

The man behind the desk was someone I had never seen before. He was a good six feet four, two hundred and fifty pounds if an ounce, and about as much fat on him as you'd find on the handle of a cane. His shoulders were as broad as the jokes at a Legion stag and the head above them seemed too small to be his own. His hair was black and there wasn't much of it and what there was he wore long and combed across to hide the bald spot. He had small ears that lay close to his head and small black glittering eyes at the bottom of deep shadowy sockets. The hollows under his cheekbones were as deep as the pocket in a catcher's mitt.

When I was standing in front of the desk across from
him, he stared at me with a kind of brooding composure
like a department-store president about to bawl hell out
of an assistant buyer. You could tell right off that he
took himself seriously and expected you to take him the
same way.

His first words were to the guy who had brought me
there. "See if he is armed, Andrew." His voice was
deep but strangely flat, dry as an old bone.

Hands came from behind and patted over me, then fell
away. "He's clean, sir."

I got looked at some more before the man behind the
desk said, "My name is D'Allemand, sir. Who are you?"

I told him my name but it didn't seem to make much
of an impression. He picked up an ivory-handled letter
opener that matched the rest of the desk accessories and
moved it around in his broad heavy hands and continued
to stare at me. It would have been nice for him to ask
me to sit down but, clearly, the thought never crossed
his mind.

He said, "What is your business with Mr. Marlin?"

"I don't have any business with him," I said. "I don't
even know him."

"Yet you asked for him?"

"I asked *about* him," I corrected.

"Don't split hairs with me, Mr. Pine. I want to know
what your interest is in Marlin."

His feudal-baron air began to heat up the back of my
neck. I said, "What the hell do I care what you want,
Mac. I came up——"

Something hard came out of nowhere and exploded
against the side of my jaw. I spun sideways and slammed
against one of the tubular chairs and went over with it,
plowing the rough beige carpeting with my right cheek.
I tried to roll as I fell but a pointed shoe hammered into
my right side just below the ribs and the breath whooshed
out of me. The room began to swim in dim circles and
I went as limp as a sunburned candle. . . .

A hand twisted into my coat front and hauled me up on rubber legs. I blinked a few times and slowly the room came back into focus. The hand released me and I swayed and would have fallen if I hadn't reached out and caught hold of the desk across from D'Allemand.

He sat there toying with the letter opener, and if his expression had changed any I couldn't tell it. I straightened up gradually and looked around at foxy-faced Andrew. He was smiling a bitter little smile and running a thumb lightly over the knuckles of his right hand.

My voice sounded thick in my ears. "You kind of made a mistake there, friend. I'll talk to you about it sometime."

He could move quick, I'd say that for him. I started to jerk my head aside as his fist came up, but my reflexes weren't back to normal yet. The blow caught me high on one cheek and I sat down on the floor and leaned my head wearily against one of the cool metal desk legs. . . .

"Get me his wallet, Andrew."

A hand slid into my inner coat pocket. I didn't do anything about it. I couldn't do anything about it. It came out again with my billfold between the fingers and disappeared somewhere into the void above me.

"Get him to his feet, Andrew."

Up I came, with a jerk that made my teeth rattle. I leaned against the desk and put fingers gently against my cheek and said nothing at all.

D'Allemand was flipping idly through the transparent identification panels in my wallet. Presently he tossed it over in front of me and said, "You may put it away, Mr. Pine. I haven't kept anything."

I put it away.

"So you are a private detective." He nodded his head about a quarter of an inch and for some reason seemed faintly pleased. "I don't suppose you would care to tell me who has hired you to inquire after Mr. Marlin?"

I didn't say anything.

"Well, I won't press you, Mr. Pine. I will advise you

to forget your interest in Jerry, however. I don't like my employees to be bothered.''

He waited for me to say something to that but I failed him. The only thing I was capable of saying right then would have earned me another drop kick.

He shrugged. ''Very well, Mr. Pine. . . . Help him find his way out, Andrew.''

We went out and left him sitting there behind his desk. The man with the foxy face followed me down the corridor and into the elevator. He pushed the button and we dropped down a floor and stepped out into the foyer. And all the time neither of us so much as looked at the other.

I turned and walked through the door and left him standing there. . . .

· 5 ·

I parked a block north of Pratt Boulevard and walked around the corner to the apartment hotel where I kept my books and my other shirt. The tree-sheltered street was dark and quiet and I could hear, faintly, the traffic sounds from Sheridan Road two blocks to the east.

Most of the lights were out in the lobby of the Dinsmore Arms as I came in through the heavy screen door and crossed to the desk where Wilson, the night clerk, sat in his shirt sleeves behind the switchboard reading a pulp magazine.

I don't walk heavy and there was thick carpeting under my feet; but he heard me anyway. He jerked up his head and peered at me through the thick lenses bridging his shapeless nose.

I said, "Evening, Sam. Any mail?"

He got out of his chair and came over to the ledge, staring at me with his thick neck bent forward a little, like a dog that recognizes you but wants to take a sniff to be sure. His last shave had been a little careless and there was a patch of stubble on the underside of his second chin and another at one corner of his loose-lipped mouth. He smelled some of stale sweat and cigarette smoke. He always smelled that way.

"G'd evening, Mr. Pine," he said in his thin sharp voice. "No mail, no, sir. But this-here lady's been waiting for you."

I knew she was there before he was past the first three

words. There was a perfume—a scent so subtle you weren't really conscious of the odor; you knew only that a very lovely woman was somewhere near.

I turned around, not fast and not slow. It was Leona Sandmark.

She said, "You lied to me," in a small tight voice.

Behind me, Sam Wilson shifted his feet and began to breathe with his mouth open. He was probably thinking that my past had caught up with me and maybe she was going to pull a gun and make her illegitimate child half an orphan before it was born.

"You're pretty good," I said, staring at her. "My office address is the only one in the book."

For all I could tell she might not have heard me. She said, "You did see my father this afternoon, didn't you?" in the same small tight voice.

Sam's breathing was getting noisier. I said, "Shall we kick it around down here, or would you rather come upstairs for some privacy?"

She blinked and her head jerked back slightly as though I'd jabbed a finger at her eyes. Her glance shifted and went past me to the night clerk.

"Very well." She whirled around and marched stiffly across the lobby to the push-button elevator, and I trailed along. The cage was on one of the upper floors and I put an arm in front of her and pressed the button to bring it down. For all the attention she paid I might as well have been in Vancouver.

It seemed like a good time to look at her. She was wearing patent-leather pumps on narrow, well-bred feet below long slim ankles and beautiful calves in sheer hose that were not rayon. I couldn't see her knees but I remembered there was enough meat on them for dimples. Her two-piece suit was of very dark blue gabardine that fitted her slender lines as if it appreciated the opportunity. The blouse was white and simple, with a severe neckline, and probably had cost enough to pay my hotel bill for a week. She was still wearing her hair long and bare, but the swirl and the ribbon were gone, replaced by a ruler-straight part in the middle.

She was very beautiful and she was very angry. Anger, tightly controlled anger, showed in the pinched look around her nose and mouth, in the stiff set of her shoulders, in the way her long, ringless fingers dug into the surface of the shiny black leather bag she carried.

I opened the cage door and followed her in. Sam was still standing at the desk and staring, his mouth open. I had ruined the night for him.

Nothing was said on the way up. I couldn't think of anything to say and she was waiting to get me alone. We went along the corridor to 307 and I got out my keys and unlocked the door and flicked the wall switch, lighting the two end-table lamps that flanked the blue-and-beige-striped davenport against the far wall.

Leona Sandmark stalked in and stood in the middle of the room and looked around, although I don't think she saw anything. I closed the door and threw my hat on the lounge chair and said, "Won't you sit down, Miss Sandmark?"

Her eyes came around and clawed my face. "This isn't a social call," she said with a distant kind of coldness. "I came here to find out why you lied to me. And I want to know why you were calling on my father this afternoon."

"Is that going to keep you from sitting down?"

Some of the pinched tightness around her mouth smoothed out, leaving her with a curiously baffled expression that threatened to overshadow the anger. She said, "Thank you," in a vague kind of way and took two or three stiff steps over to the couch and sank down on the edge.

I took out my cigarettes, tapped a couple part way out and extended the pack. "Smoke?"

She took one and continued to hold it between the tips of her thumb and forefinger, her eyes never leaving my face. I gave all my attention to striking a match and

holding the flame out to her. She put the cigarette between her lips, bent her head and dragged smoke deep
into her lungs. Then she leaned back and crossed her
legs and exhaled the smoke in a thin blue line. . . .

When I looked up from lighting my own cigarette, she
was watching me again. It surprised me a little to see
that there was no expression at all on her face now, and
for the first time it really came to me that Leona Sandmark was very young in years.

I said, "Can I offer you a drink, Miss Sandmark?"

"You seem to insist on making this a social call."

"Is there any reason why it shouldn't be one?"

"Not if you decide to answer my questions."

"I might do that."

"Why were you calling on my father?"

"Will you have that drink?"

"No!"

"Okay," I said mildly. "You don't have to yell
at me."

Her lips twitched . . . and she was smiling. It was my
turn to stare. She wasn't an unspanked brat from the idle
rich any more. She was a nice firm round young woman,
with bowels and a complexion and a sense of humor.
There was a personality to her—a personality born of
fire and ice and tungsten steel. She could be a hell of a
lot of fun . . . and you could end up paying for your
fun, too.

"Damn you," she said, without rancor. "I'll have
that drink after all."

I said, "Excuse me," meekly and tottered into the
kitchen and got a bottle of Scotch and a couple of tall
glasses, some charged water and ice cubes. I brought the
stuff in and put it on the coffee table. She refused a
highball, took the Scotch bottle from me and poured
better than a jigger into one of the glasses and drank it
like water after an aspirin.

She made a face as she put down the glass. "I don't
think much of your choice of liquor, Mr. Pine."

"How would you know about my choice of liquor?" I said, nettled. "I'll bet that one never even touched your tongue."

She watched me sample my drink, her eyes thoughtful. Just when she was on the point of saying something, she bit her lip and stood up abruptly and began to wander aimlessly about the room. I sat where I was and watched the way her thighs moved under the blue gabardine skirt.

"At least you know how to furnish a room," she said, her back to me.

"Well, that's something," I said.

She had forgotten me. She was running her finger along the backs of the books in the corner shelf, while, in the other hand, her cigarette sent up a thin wavering line of smoke. The yellow light from the lamps picked out the red in her hair, forming a misty halo the color of a bloodstain.

"For a private detective," she said over her shoulder, "you certainly read some odd books. Wilkinson's *Flower Encyclopedia; Leave it to Psmith* by P. G. Wodehouse; and Marx's *Das Kapital*. What happened to your copy of *Five Little Peppers*?"

"I loaned it to another private detective," I said.

She drifted on, touching things, straightening the edge of a picture frame, smoothing the window draperies, fingering the material of the bridge lamp. She was trying to get across to me the impression of being perfectly at ease, but the tense lines in her face told a different story. . . .

I said: "Will you for Chrisakes light somewhere?"

She stopped in her tracks, her back to me, and it was half a minute before she turned around. The light gave a shine to her eyes that might have been tears. If it was, they weren't running down her cheeks. She put out her hands in a kind of futile gesture and said:

"I might as well leave. I can see I wasted my time coming here."

I continued to look at her without saying anything.

"All right." She crossed to the lounge chair and picked up my hat and put it on the coffee table and sat down, resting the black leather bag in her lap. "I've lit, Mr. Pine. Are you ready to talk to me?"

"Sure," I said. "Where did you get my address?"

She frowned impatiently. "What difference does it make?"

"None, probably. I'd just like to know."

"I took down your car's license number. A friend at the city hall got me the information on it."

"You go a long way to satisfy your curiosity, Miss Sandmark."

That put more color in her cheeks. "It wasn't just curiosity. I had to talk to you. I *must* know why you called on my father."

"Did your father say I called on him?"

"No. I . . . didn't ask him."

"Then how do you know?"

"Rose told me."

"Rose?"

"The maid."

"She must have told you my name. Then why all this hocus-pocus about my license number?"

"All she knew was that your name was Pine. . . . Will you answer one question, Mr. Pine?"

"That depends."

Her fingers tightened on the bag and she bent forward a little and stared into my eyes. "Did you call and ask my father to see you, or did he call you first for some reason of his own?"

I rotated the highball glass gently in my fingers and the tinkle of ice cubes against its sides was a cool sound against the silence. Leona Sandmark remained in her bent, strained position, her lips parted a trifle, her breasts rising and falling under shallow, uneven breathing. Her cigarette, forgotten, smoldered in the fingers of one hand.

I said, "Who's tightening the screws on you, Miss Sandmark?"

It made her jerk back as though I'd slapped her. The purse slid off her knees and hit the floor with a dull thud. I bent and scooped it up before she could move. It seemed heavier than necessary and my fingers felt out the shape of an object not usually carried in ladies' bags.

I unsnapped the catch, reached in and took out a gun. It was a blue steel Colt .32 Pocket Positive, the kind with the two-and-one-half-inch barrel and weighing around fifteen or sixteen ounces.

"Somebody," I said, glancing up at her, "should speak to you about your taste in compacts."

She was mad at me again. Her eyes flashed and the full lower lip had tightened up till her mouth was an uneven red line. "You—you snoop!" she spat at me. "You had no right to do that. Put it back where you found it and give me my bag."

I turned out the cylinder and spun it. There was a cartridge in every chamber. I clicked the cylinder back in place, took the handkerchief from the breast pocket of my coat, spread it over my right hand and laid the gun in its center. I wiped it carefully and let it slide from the handkerchief into the bag, closed the bag and laid it on the far end of the coffee table.

I tucked the handkerchief back in my pocket. "It's against the law to carry guns, Miss Sandmark," I said mildly. "Didn't you know?"

She shook her head impatiently. "Please. Whether or not I carry a gun is none of your business. I asked you whether your call on my father was his idea or yours."

"And I," I said, "asked who is blackmailing you."

Her eyes regarded me levelly. "I heard you. The question doesn't make sense. Why should anyone try to blackmail me? I've done nothing wrong."

"Everybody at one time or another has done something wrong, Miss Sandmark," I said soberly. "I make my

living at being a detective and I see things a certain way.
Look: this afternoon you get in a sweat because you find
me coming out of your house. I might have been the
maid's new boy friend, or reading the gas meter, or
selling can openers. But you got excited enough to take
my license number and find out who I was. You were
afraid to ask the old man what his business was with
me. Then you stick a gun in your purse and come tearing
out here to ask me if calling on John Sandmark was my
idea or his. Your nerves are jumping like a juke joint on
Saturday night.

"You know how that looks to me? It looks as if you
stubbed your toe on something and the wrong guy picked
you up. He wants dough to keep his mouth shut—lots
of it. Either you lay it in his mitt or your dad will be
asked to pay off. You've tried to stall him off, but you
can't be sure he'll wait.

"Then I show up. Maybe I'm working with the black-
mailer. You find out I'm a private dick. I could still be
working on the squeeze, or your old man has already
been contacted and is calling me in to work on it for
him. Either way, you've got to know."

There was a curious mixture of fear and relief and
rage in her face. Even with all that she managed to stay
beautiful. She stood up slowly and picked up her purse
from the table and put it under her arm.

"I want to know why you saw my father today, Mr.
Pine. How much will it cost me to find that out?"

I looked at her through the veil of smoke from my
cigarette. She was back on the idle-rich side of the tracks
again. Her eyes were hotly contemptuous, her mouth a
sneer that said every man had his price and how much
was mine?

I said, "How much have you got?"

She paid me the compliment of being surprised by the
question. That meant she hadn't really pegged me as a
guy who would sell out a client.

"Would—would four hundred do?"

"Nope."

"Well?"

"Shall I read you a sermon on human behavior, Miss Sandmark? When you want something from somebody, don't make him think he'd be a heel for giving it to you."

Her narrow nostrils flared. "I'll tell *you* something. Being superior and condescending won't get you anything, either."

"*I* don't want anything," I reminded her.

One more like that and I'd get that black leather purse against my jaw.

"Will you tell me why you called on my father, Mr. Pine?"

"Nope."

"Will you sell me the information?"

"Hunh-uh."

"Why not?"

"You wouldn't know why not if I told you."

"You're being superior again."

"Then stop making me feel superior."

"You . . . you're impossible!"

I grinned, stretched out my legs. "I am also a beast. May I offer you some more of my bad liquor, Miss Sandmark?"

For a moment her eyes blazed at me in a wildly futile way; then her teeth clicked shut and she turned abruptly and moved blindly toward the door. In the spirit of a true host, I got up to open it for her and say good night.

It was so much wasted effort. The door banged shut before I was halfway across the room. I went back to the davenport and took off my coat and shoes and made myself a fresh highball.

Evidently there were some angles to *l'affaire* Sandmark the old boy hadn't told me about. Maybe that was because he didn't know about them. Or maybe there was more in his mind than breaking up a romance. Maybe a lot of maybes.

It seemed my original idea for locating Marlin would be the best way after all. At least it would be the quickest—and the way things were shaping up, I'd better get in there quick, or be left out of it altogether.

· 6 ·

A baking west wind came down the canyon called Jackson Boulevard. I stood at the office window and watched the papers flutter on the newsstand under the el tracks at Wabash Avenue. Gusts whipped skirts under frantic fingers, but from eight floors up my interest was academic. The sun was gone behind the office buildings on LaSalle Street but had left plenty of heat to remember it by. Gray-blue dusk filled the streets, like fog in a valley. Display-window lights were already on and colored neon lights cut tunnels in the thin gloom. My cigarette tasted as if it had spent a week under a hair drier.

Chicago's Loop . . . in the hours between the time clock and the theater. The loneliest place on earth. The Sahara could be no lonelier.

Faintly through the wall of the neighboring office came the mosquito buzz of a dentist's drill. I opened the window wide in case a breeze developed, got out of my coat and hung it on the back of the customer's chair, turned on the desk lamp and unfolded the red-streak edition of the *Daily News* I had picked up on my way back from dinner at the Ontra, and sat down to catch up with the world.

I found a mildly interesting article on page three: a follow-up to the previous day's story of the funeral where twelve clergymen had taken turns smoothing a path to the hereafter for a man known only as John Doe.

John, it developed, had been a man in his early fifties,

around a hundred and fifty pounds, rather good-looking in a small-featured way, partially bald, and tanned almost to blackness. Despite the slightness of his build, the item said, Doe had been unusually muscular, and his hands were the callused hands of a laborer.

The killer had removed all labels from his victim's ready-made clothing, and not so much as a used razor blade had been found in the room. The clerk at the Laycroft told police that Doe had registered late one afternoon, paying a week in advance as he had no luggage. The following morning a chambermaid found Doe dead on the floor beside his untouched bed, the top of his head beaten in.

None of the hotel employees recalled seeing any mysterious strangers the previous evening, but the building stairs were just inside the hotel entrance, making it possible to reach the upper floors without passing the desk.

Lieutenant George Zarr of the Central Homicide Detail, said the article in conclusion, stated that in his belief the dead man had been some petty gangster from out of town. An enemy had tracked him down, killed him, then arranged the funeral as a weird kind of practical joke. It was evident, although the item didn't say as much, that Zarr was sick of the entire matter and would like it to be forgotten.

By the time I got past the sport page and Li'l Abner, my wrist watch showed a quarter to ten. I put the paper in the wastebasket, opened the bottom drawer of the desk and brought out a glass and the office bottle. The glass was smeared and there was a dead fly in it. Considering the kind of liquor I used, the fly should have known better.

I flushed the smoke from my throat with bourbon direct from the bottle, set fire to another cigarette and put the bottle and unused glass away. For another ten minutes I sat there and poisoned the air with smoke and listened to the Polish voices of the scrubwomen down the corridor. The building's musty wet-hay smell seeped into the room and outfought the odor of tobacco smoke. I would have liked to go home and take a shower and lie naked on the bed in front of the open window and leaf through the copy of an *Oahspe Bible* I had picked up a few days before. . . .

At ten o'clock I picked up the phone and dialed Information and asked for the number listed for Miss Leona Sandmark, 1317 Austin Boulevard.

There wasn't any. I put back the receiver and chewed my lip. If she had a telephone, it was unlisted. Okay, there was a way to get around that. I called another number. . . .

"Gregg?"

"Yeah."

"Pine."

"Paul? How they hanging, pal? We missed you."

"Like so much," I said. "Do something for me, Gregg?"

"Sure."

"I want a phone number. It isn't listed."

"All right. What's her name?"

"Maybe it's a man," I said. "It doesn't *have* to be a woman, does it? You State guys are all alike— always——"

"What's her name?"

I told him, including the address. He said, "It'll take a minute. Give me your number and I'll call you back."

Five minutes later the phone rang. "Austin 0017."

"Thanks, Gregg."

"Buss her for me."

"She's flat-chested," I said.

"I said buss. It means kiss. B-u-s-s, buss."

"I heard you," I said. "I was just admiring your education."

He grunted and hung up. I depressed the cut-off bar, released it and dialed the Austin number.

Two long buzzes. A click. A male voice, tenor, said, "Hello."

I was ready for that too. "Mr. Martin?" I said, slurring the name.

He didn't like it. He didn't like it even a little bit. His voice went down three octaves and got as cadgy as a virgin at a picnic.

"Who is this?"

I said, "This is Ed McGuire, Mr. Martin. I've thought it over and decided not to sell after all. I hope there's no hard feelings."

"What number do you want?" His voice was back to normal.

"Austin 0117," I said, getting short about it. "I want to speak to——"

"Wrong number." The phone went dead.

I took the receiver away from my ear, leered at it, said, "The hell you say, brother," and laid it gently back on the cradle. I put on my hat and coat, slipped an extra pack of cigarettes into a pocket, turned out the light, locked the inner office door and went out into the corridor.

The night man took me down in the elevator and I walked around the corner to the parking station and had one of the attendants bring out the car. He used a cloth on the windshield and came over to the window as I started the motor.

"She needs a wash job pretty bad, Mr. Pine."

"She always does," I said, reaching for the gearshift. "It's an indication of my character."

He was polite about it but he wasn't amused. I rolled out onto Wabash, dodged the el pillars south to Jackson, turned west and went on about my business.

Heavy clouds had piled up to the west, blotting out the stars. There were occasional flickers of heat lightning, and a weighted coolness in the air promised rain. Rain would be all right if I didn't have to get out into it. I figured I wouldn't have to get out into it.

At a quarter to eleven I turned north into Austin Boulevard. Beyond Lake Street the homes thinned out and high-grade apartment buildings took over. Trees lined the parkways between street and sidewalk, and while there were street lights, they couldn't do much because of all the leaves.

The 1300 block was just as dark and just as quiet as the others along there. A few cars, most of them beyond the popular-priced field, were parked parallel to both curbs, their outlines dim in the heavy tree shadows. The smell of rain was stronger now, the air cooler, and thunder grunted from far off.

There was plenty of room to park in front of where I judged 1317 to be. I pulled in at the curb, cut off my lights and the motor and stepped out onto the strip of grass.

It was a six-story yellow-brick apartment building, very new, with five entrances off a central court. The court was filled with bushes and flower beds laid out in neat lines by a gardener with no imagination, and bounded with the rectangle formed by the sidewalk leading to the entrances. A vine-covered arch of yellow brick straddled the walk in front of the court, with a massive iron lantern attached to each abutment. Yellow light from electric globes in the lanterns illuminated copper numerals directly below them. The number on the left was 1317; on the right, 1325.

I walked slowly through the arch and turned left where the walk divided. The sharp straight lines of the roof edge against the flickering sky gave me the illusion of standing at the bottom of a quarry.

Behind a few of the windows soft lights burned against the night, but most of them were dark. A very good radio let the muted strains of a dance orchestra drift down into the courtyard, and a woman laughed close by, full-throated yet subdued.

The first entrance showed 1317 in neat gold figures

painted in a slanted line across the door glass. I pushed open the door and came into a foyer with imitation marble walls and two-tone tessellated stone to walk on. It looked as clean as a hospital corridor; it probably always looked that clean.

Two rows of bell buttons and an intercom phone were set in a niche in the wall on my right. Six buttons to a row; that meant twelve apartments, two to a floor. The top button on the left was opposite a glassed-in card that read: *L. Sandmark 6A.*

As I remembered, the windows on the top floor had been dark. That could mean any one of several things. To learn exactly, I pressed the button next to *L. Sandmark 6A.*

Nothing happened. I shifted my feet to ruin the silence and put my thumb back on the button and left it there for maybe ten seconds.

It might as well have been ten years. Either they were afraid to answer, which hardly seemed likely, or they had gone out since I telephoned. And if they had gone out at that hour, it would probably be daylight before they thought of coming home.

All right. I would wait. I had the time. I had all the time in the world. I lighted a cigarette and threw the match stub on the nice clean tessellated floor, which put me in the same class as a guy who would wipe his feet on the "Mona Lisa," and went back out to the street and got in behind the wheel.

For a while I did nothing more exciting than sit there and blow smoke through my nose and listen to the cars whisper past and watch people walk by on their way home from the neighborhood movies or the corner tavern. What had been a slight breeze was now an uncertain wind that blew in brief angry gusts, like a fat man working up a rage. It had the clinging damp feel of rain close by, and the flicker of lightning was almost continuous.

Two or three times people turned in through the yellow-brick arch of the apartment building, but only once did anybody open the door to 1317, and that was an elderly couple.

Pedestrians got to be farther and farther apart and hardly any more cars went by. I struck a match and looked at my watch. Twelve-forty-five. I yawned and took off my hat, turned on the radio very soft, slumped down and put my feet on the dashboard and let the minutes drift. . . .

A box car going through a bass drum snapped me out of a light doze. Thunder. Lightning forked the sky bright enough to read by and another bucket of noise spilled over the car. And here came the rain.

I rolled up the side windows and switched off the radio and continued to sit, listening to the drumming drops against the roof. It was coming down very hard—too hard to last long. One of these summer rains you think is going to cool off the town for a few days but seldom does.

A car pulled in behind me, its headlights showing the big drops bouncing knee-high off the black pavement. A minute later the door slammed and a man and a woman in evening clothes dashed across the sidewalk. It wasn't my couple; I saw that right away. They disappeared quick and the car turned out and rolled past me and away. It was a Checker cab.

I took another look at my watch. Three-thirty-five. I began to wonder if Marlin and the Sandmark girl hadn't returned while I was pounding my ear. He could have taken her in and gone out again and all this was for nothing. Paul Pine, ace detective. Dependable for walking the dog and firing the cook.

Twenty more minutes went by like rolling a brick uphill. The rain had settled down to a steady cloudburst and the lightning and thunder were in there pitching. I smoked another cigarette and shivered a time or two and thought longingly of the Scotch I had had in John Sandmark's library the afternoon before.

Headlights cut a swath in the rain and a big black Packard convertible moved slowly past me and cut in to the curb not more than six feet in front of my radiator. Right then it seemed I caught the gleam of another set of headlights at my rear, but it was gone before I could be sure. The taillights of the convertible shone wetly red, like the bleary eyes of a drunk with a crying jag.

The car door opened and a man in a tan trench coat stepped out on the curb. He was an inch or two under six feet, slender, and the rain glistened on thick black hair with a wave in it. Lightning flashes let me see him clearly enough to be satisfied it was Jerry Marlin.

He put his hand in and helped out a girl in a red evening wrap over a long white dress. She was holding up a newspaper to protect the dark cloud of hair that fell to her shoulders. Marlin banged the door shut and they ran, side by side, toward the yellow arch. I sat there and watched them go.

Just as they reached the sidewalk, a man in a dark raincoat and a pulled-down felt hat came from behind my car and took four long fast strides that brought him up close behind Marlin. His right arm, bent at the elbow, was stiffly extended and something gleamed dully in that hand.

That much I saw during one flash of lightning. Then the light went out and thunder let loose like shooting a cannon in a cave. Right in the middle of it, there were three orange streaks of fire and three dim flat sounds.

By this time I could have been out of the car and on my way over there. I could have gone out and sailed twigs in the gutter, too. That would have made about as much sense and it would have been a lot safer. I was packing about as much heat as you'd find in an icicle, and without a gun I tackle no killers. Nor with a gun, if I can help it.

I sat very still and waited for the next flash of lightning. It came within a few seconds, just as a motor roared suddenly somewhere in back of me. Headlights flashed through my window in a sweeping arc and a small dark coupé slashed past me and faded into the night.

It seemed like a good time to be brave. I opened the door and went over to help gather up the pieces.

Jerry Marlin was flat on his face a yard or two short of the vine-covered arch. I bent over him and saw three small round holes in the material of the tan trench coat squarely between the shoulders. You could have covered all three with a silver dollar, if you had the kind of mind that ran to such experiments. Blood had not yet soaked through but there would be plenty underneath. He was dead. Even with practice he would never be any deader.

The girl stood there, swaying a little, hands locked together and pressed to her stomach, her mouth stupid with shock, small whimpering noises climbing over her teeth. She hadn't heard me, she didn't see me, there wasn't anything in the world but the limp length of life-lessness in front of her open-toed shoes.

I looked around but couldn't see anybody. I put my fingers around her arm and said, "You're getting wet, Miss Sandmark. We better go in, hunh?"

She heard me the way they heard me on Mars. I pulled a little on her arm to get her moving. That got results, but not the kind I could use. She opened her mouth a little wider and took a deep breath and started to yell. Before the first note was all the way out I slapped her across the face so hard that only my hold kept her from falling.

It stopped the yell. She put her free hand up to her cheek and her eyes came into focus. Very distinctly she said, "You didn't have to do that."

"Like hell I didn't," I said. "Now, do you move or do I carry you? Come on."

She came. She came as though she was walking in her sleep. I steered her into the imitation-marble hall and took the sequined bag out of her hand and fished out a key and unlocked the inner door. There was an automatic elevator but the cage was somewhere above. I pushed the button and the "in use" indicator glowed behind its small circle of amber glass.

She stood there, her shoulders slumped, her face a white oval of despair. Her eyes were half closed and saw nothing, nothing at all. Her chin and lips were trembling—little uneven movements that started strong and ran down slowly, then started over again.

She let me lead her in and we rode up to the sixth floor and got out there. It was a small square corridor, with two ivory-paneled doors facing each other. The one on the left was marked 6A. I unlocked it and found a wall switch just inside the door that lighted a drum lamp on a dark wood table in a small reception hall papered in pale yellow. Above the table hung a round mirror in a gold frame.

In the wall opposite the door was an arched opening to a darkened room. Leona Sandmark shucked off the red evening wrap, dropped it blindly on the table, and pressed another wall switch that lighted a pair of table lamps beyond the arch.

I followed her in there. It was a long, rather narrow room with five windows in a row overlooking the court. Beige carpeting extended to the ivory baseboards, and dark blue velvet window draperies pointed up the tapestried upholstery of the couch. The furniture was modern and there wasn't too much of it. An ivory grand piano blocked off most of the far wall.

I took a quick look around and said, "Where's your phone, Miss Sandmark?"

She stood there, blinking at me, and recognition came slowly into her eyes. For the first time I was something to her besides a voice. An expression I could not identify crossed her face, followed very quickly with good old-fashioned alarm.

"You!" she gasped. "You killed him!"

"Why, certainly," I said in disgust, "I kill everybody these days. Where's your phone?"

She put the back of one hand against her lips and took a couple of slow, cautious steps backward, like somebody trying to get out of a lion's cage without exciting the lion. The davenport stopped her and very carefully she let herself stiffly down on the edge, not once taking her eyes off my face.

"Look," I said, "tomorrow we'll play *East Lynne* and I'll let you carry the baby. But right now you've got to follow orders or you'll get your neck in a sling. First thing: where's your phone? And don't make me ask you again."

She took the hand away from her mouth and looked at it vaguely, then pointed it at one of the two ivory doors leading off the room. "In th-there."

"Fine," I said. I gave her a smile that was meant to make her realize I was actually a very nice guy—a guy to be trusted. "I didn't kill him, Miss Sandmark. But maybe I can find out who did."

I crossed over and went through the door she had indicated, closing it behind me. It was a bedroom with mirrors and crystal doodads and a Hollywood bed the size of a truck garden. The rose-satin spread was mussed some, with a couple of depressions sideways across it as though two people had been lying there. I clicked my tongue a time or two when I saw those marks, and looked around until I spotted an ivory telephone on a night stand near the bed. An ivory index pad lay beside the instrument; I opened it at the letter S, found what I wanted, dialed the operator and gave an Oak Park number.

A middle-aged voice, female, answered without too much delay, considering the hour. It sounded sleepy and cautiously indignant. I said, "Get Mr. Sandmark to the phone and do it quick. This is Paul Pine."

The woman was outraged. "Mr. Sandmark is sleeping and I——"

I said, "Get him, God damn it, and stop horsing around."

The receiver went down as though she had thrown it on the floor. I stood there and waited, my free ear listening for the wail of police sirens. Beads of sweat felt cool against my forehead. . . .

"Hello." The woman was back again.

"What's the matter with you? I want Mr. Sandmark."

"He isn't in, sir." She was too worried to be resentful. "I don't know what to make of it, I don't. After four in the morning, it is, and he——"

I hung up and went back into the living room. Leona Sandmark was still sitting stiff, hands lying limp in her lap. Against the white of her gown, her skin seemed much too colorless. Faint red streaks marked the cheek where my hand had landed. I said:

"Listen to me and don't miss a word. Go in there and dial Police 1313. Tell what's happened. Get a little hysterical; they'll expect it. You've got some acting to do, sister, and don't you forget it."

She was only half listening. I went over to her and put my hand under her chin and tilted back her head until our eyes met. She made no effort to pull away. The shock was wearing off, leaving her free to think in something like a straight line. She said:

"What if he wasn't dead? We shouldn't have just let him lie there in the r-rain like a——"

"Quit it," I said sharply. "He was dead before he bounced. You're the one who is wide open, and you're going to get clipped by a craphouse—pardon me—full of law if you don't get on that telephone and get your licks in first. The time and the rain have probably covered you this far, but your luck can't last forever. Somebody's going to see Marlin's body and call the cops. Cops are very smart people, Miss Sandmark; before you can blow your nose they'll find out he was your boy friend. Eventually they'll find out you were with him when he got it, and they'll be angry and suspicious because you didn't let them know right away what happened. You can afford their anger; but by God you can't afford their suspicion.''

She took her chin out of my hand by standing up. She swayed a little and put a hand on my arm to steady herself. We faced each other across hardly any distance at all. Her head was tilted back a trifle to look me in the eyes. Perfume came up to me from her body—a perfume so faint I could have been mistaken about its being perfume. Maybe she just naturally smelled that way.

There was no more alarm in her face. No more fear. If anything, she was calmer than I was right then.

''If you didn't shoot Jerry,'' she said softly, ''what was your reason for being out there?''

''Okay,'' I said. ''You're entitled to know that, now. Your stepfather hired me yesterday to keep an eye on you. He's been worried about you, Miss Sandmark; he didn't say why.''

''No other reason?''

''No other reason.''

''Did you see who—who did it?''

''Yes,'' I said.

Her voice went down to a whisper. ''Was it my . . . stepfather?''

''I doubt it, Miss Sandmark. There'd be no sense to that.''

''But it could have been?''

I stepped back out of range of all that charm and said, ''Shall we dance? Of course, there's a corpse down on the sidewalk but the police wouldn't want their pinochle game busted up over a little thing like that.''

She let out her breath and her lips tightened. ''All right. I'll call the police.''

I went into the bedroom with her. She reached for the receiver, but I put my hand on it ahead of her, holding it against the cradle. ''Tell them exactly what happened. Only leave me out of it. Don't forget, Miss Sandmark;

leave me out of it. That's important, and when we have more time I'll tell you why it's important. Okay?''

"I think so." There was still the drowsy, heavy-lidded look about her that means strain and shock. "Perhaps you'd better tell me what I'm to say."

"He brought you home from wherever you were. The two of you got out of the car and ran, because of the rain, for the building entrance. You heard three shots and Marlin fell down and you saw a tall slender man in a gray raincoat and a pull-down hat run to the street and drive away in a car—a coupé, maybe; you can't be sure. He drove north. You don't remember much after that. The next thing you knew for sure, you were sitting in a chair in your apartment, trying to get control of yourself. It might have been two minutes; it might have been ten. Then was when you realized the police must be notified.

"And that's all you say, Miss Sandmark. Nothing about your stepfather not liking Marlin; nothing on why you left the house in Oak Park to take this apartment. Now go ahead and make the call."

Her eyes narrowed into a frown and anger deepened her voice. "Did John—my stepfather—tell you he didn't like Jerry?"

I shook my head. "Can't you understand we've no time for that now?" I picked up the receiver and dialed Central Station, then shoved it into her hand. "Go ahead. You're on your own."

She put the instrument against her ear, her eyes never leaving my face. ". . . Hello. I want to report a—a shooting. . . . Yes. My escort was shot by somebody as we got out of my car in front of my apartment. . . . Miss Leona Sandmark, 1317 North Austin Boulevard." She spelled the name and repeated the address. ". . . I'm afraid so, but I—I can't be sure. . . . No, he's probably still there. . . . This number? Austin 0017. It's my own. . . . Thank you."

She put back the receiver like a soap bubble she didn't

want to break. "They're sending someone. . . . Poor Jerry." She dropped down on her knees and put her head against the night table and began to cry with a sort of subdued intensity.

I let her go at it for two minutes by my watch, although I hated to spare the time. Finally I put my hand on her bare white shoulder and shook it a little. "That's enough for now. Don't use any make-up until after the law sees you. They'll feel better if your eyes are reddened up some."

She jerked up her head and looked at me, through tears, as though I had crawled out of the woodwork. "How can you *talk* that way! Do you think I'm doing this to satisfy the police? We were going to be m-married, and now he's—he's——"

"Dead," I said. "That's bad and I'm sorry. But it can be worse and maybe it will be. Temporarily I'm throwing you to the wolves. As long as you stick to what I've told you to say, you'll get by. I'm pretty sure the police won't hold you, although don't ever think they'll just tip their hats and walk out. But you've got looks and your stepfather has a lot of money: a combination that will make the boys walk on eggs unless they get something mighty strong on you. . . .

"One other thing. Don't bring John Sandmark into this before you have to. If it gets too tough, call him. But make it at the last possible minute."

She was alarmed again, and worried. "Why?"

"Not what you're thinking. Just do it my way. Okay?"

"Yes."

"You know I'm on your side, Miss Sandmark?"

"Yes . . . yes."

I gave her a big grin. "Let's keep it that way. Good morning, Miss Sandmark."

I walked out of the apartment, leaving her still kneeling by the night table in the bedroom. I got into the elevator and rode down to the first floor and went out into the court. The rain was still coming down as though it hated the earth, but the thunder and lightning had slacked off.

The body still lay where it had fallen after the bullets went into it. I went around it, walking neither fast nor slow, and got into the Plymouth. The engine turned over quick enough, but it backfired twice and I could have chewed my heart like a stick of gum.

Just before I reached North Avenue a twenty-eighth-district prowl car passed me from the opposite direction, going very fast. The boys weren't using the siren, and that was fine. My nerves wouldn't have liked the noise.

·7·

After a hot shower had taken the chill out of my bones, I got into pajamas and went into the living room. I drew the lounge chair over to the big window, put my bare feet up on the sill and lighted a cigarette with fingers that shook hardly at all.

The rain had stopped shortly before dawn, but the sky was still heavily overcast and it promised to be a cool day after all. I sat there and thought my way through two cigarettes, glancing from time to time at my wrist watch.

At seven-thirty I went into the kitchen and put together a glass of bourbon, water and ice, brought it back to the lounge chair and put the telephone in my lap. At seven-forty-five I dialed the operator and gave her John Sandmark's number.

A young voice, female, answered. I gave her my name and told her to put Sandmark on.

"I'm very much afraid Mr. Sandmark isn't up yet, Mr. Pine." Her voice hinted a half-witted cretin from the highest of the Alps would have known that. "Won't you call back later?"

"I will not," I said. "Try tickling his feet."

Her gasp was half giggle. "But . . . are you certain it's important enough for me to wake him?"

"Yeah."

" . . . Hold the wire, please."

I put my feet on the sill and sipped from my glass and

waited. Presently an extension receiver went up and Sandmark's deep voice said:

"Pine? What's so important?"

I said, "Just a moment, Mr. Sandmark." About five seconds later I caught the small click of a receiver being replaced. I said, "Did you get my message?"

"What message?"

"I called you a little after four this morning. Didn't they tell you?"

"No."

"They said you were out."

"Yes."

"Were you?"

"Yes. But I don't see——"

"Where?"

"Where what?"

"Where were you at four o'clock?"

"You're overdoing things a little, aren't you, Mr. Pine?" Enough chill came over the wire to make me wonder if I should rub my ear with snow to ward off frostbite.

"I've had plenty of practice," I said. "And I'm not asking questions just for the hell of it."

"If you've got something to say, say it."

"Sure," I said. "At four this morning Jerry Marlin was shot to death in front of 1317 Austin Boulevard. With him, at the time, was a young woman. If you want her name I can furnish that too. She——"

"Leona!" It wasn't much more than a whisper, but I've heard screams that had less horror in them. "I can't believe . . . Listen to me, Pine."

"Yes, sir?"

"She . . . Leona . . . she didn't—I mean to say, it wasn't Leona who——"

"I know what you mean," I said soothingly. "She didn't fog him; no. Matter of fact, she called the buttons herself."

"Buttons?"

"Police."

"Who did kill him?"

"I couldn't say, Mr. Sandmark."

"You didn't kill him, did you?"

"Nope."

"What are the police doing about it?"

"What they always do when there's a killing," I said.

"Ask questions and dig into the lives of the people involved and look for motives and hunt up witnesses and pick up whoever was standing around when it happened."

"What kind of gun did the killer use?"

I couldn't figure the reason for that question. I said, "I don't know, Mr. Sandmark. Why do you ask?"

"Well—well, my stepdaughter often carries one. She carries quite a bit of money at times, particularly when she gambles." He hated saying those last four words. "She owns a pair of Colt revolvers and she knows how to shoot. A friend of hers who works for the City obtained a license for her."

I thought of the .32 Pocket Positive she had brought to my apartment. Maybe it hadn't been in her purse for my benefit after all. I said, "She could have had one of them with her when Marlin was erased. But I know she didn't use it."

"All right." He sounded relieved, but doubtful. "Have the police arrested her?"

"I don't think so. They probably took her down to Central Headquarters to make a statement. But I doubt very much that they'll hold her."

The wire hummed. Sandmark was thinking. I wiggled my toes and got outside some more of my highball.

He said slowly, "It seems strange that neither Leona nor the police have got in touch with me by this time. I'm her father."

"Not so strange," I said. "She strikes me as an ankle who doesn't yell easy. The cops will get around to you before long, but it won't be because she gave them the idea.''

"How do you know all these things, Pine?"

I set the empty glass on the floor, put a cigarette between my lips and lighted the bobbing end of it while I answered that one. Actually it wasn't an answer. I said, "Let's leave that part of it go for a while, Mr. Sandmark. Look, there's a pretty fair chance the homicide boys are going to find out how you felt about Marlin. On top of that there's a possibility they'll learn you weren't at home when he was ironed out. So if you have a nice tight alibi for 4:00 A.M., well and good; if not, it would be intelligent of you to arrange one. Because if the law gets hold of those facts, you can bet your drawers you're going to be asked questions. Lots of questions . . . under lights, and a guy with a notebook taking down the answers.''

He said, "Are you accusing me of murder, sir?" in a voice as tight as a fat woman's shoe.

I looked at my fingers. "No. I doubt if you did it, Mr. Sandmark. It's not reasonable to think you'd hire me to get something on Marlin, then bump him yourself the same night. Unless—no.''

"Just what do you advise, Pine?" he said quietly. "You seem to know about matters such as this. And you are working for me, you know.''

That last one got a grin out of me. "Not any more, Mr. Sandmark. You hired me to get something on Marlin to prevent him from becoming your son-in-law. I've found out he's a corpse. That ought to be good enough.''

He sighed. Atlas must have sounded like that when they put the world on his shoulders. "I don't know what to do, Mr. Pine. I just don't know. . . . And I'm worried about Leona. She's so . . . You'd think she would call me. I can't stand by and let the police subject her to any—well—ordeal.''

"You'll have to watch that," I told him. "Since she hasn't called you, and since the papers aren't out yet with the story, there's no way you could have learned about this. Wait until you find out officially before starting anything. The police can understand that.''

I took a few drags on my cigarette while he chewed his nails, or whatever. Presently he said, ''I must have time to think about this. Meanwhile, I'll follow your advice and do nothing. There's always the chance the police will find the real killer.''

''Right,'' I said. There was no harm in cheering him up a little. ''Police make a business of solving murders, Mr. Sandmark, and they're good at it too.''

He sighed again. If he had cheered up any, I couldn't tell it. ''All right. All right. Thank you for calling me about . . . If I need you I'll——''

People talk like that sometimes. I said, ''Do that, Mr. Sandmark,'' and put back the receiver.

Seven-fifty-five. I blew some lopsided smoke rings and wiggled my bare toes some more and decided against going to bed. It appeared I didn't have a client any more, so it might be a good idea to get down to the office and wait for the phone to ring and give me one.

I put a pot of fresh coffee on to boil while I shaved and got into clean underwear and a fresh white shirt and the brown suit that was just back from the cleaner. While I knotted the best of my three Sulka ties, I saw that the red mark on my face where D'Allemand's foxy Andrew had belted me was mostly gone. Remembering that meeting gave me no pleasure. I went back into the kitchen and drank two cups of coffee black as the devil's reputation and strong as Tarzan of the Apes.

Afterward, I stood by the window while I buttoned my raincoat and stared at the gun-metal sky and the rain-sodden branches of the trees in the strip of grass between sidewalk and street.

I found myself thinking of Leona Sandmark. First I thought of her as a girl who started out by making a high-school romance go a long way, following that with left-handed honeymoons with somebody else's husband and a pedigreed crook.

That kind of canoodling, plus the old man's money and a taste for roulette, should have shaped her into a cocktail-lounge cutie, one of these smooth-surfaced sisters who never look anything but bored and have a wisecrack for everything from muscle dancing to murder.

I couldn't fit Leona Sandmark in there. It was tough fitting her in anywhere. During the three times we had been together she was either haughty, angry or scared. When you cover character with emotions like those, it's hard to get at the real thing.

But the physical side of her kept pushing out the rest. I thought of the slender, highbred lines of her figure; of the narrow eyes that sometimes were green and sometimes gray-blue; of the full underlip that would be fun to gnaw on; of the way she smelled.

And I thought of the twin depressions in the rose-satin spread of her bed. . . .

I went out into a morning that was like the steam room of a Turkish bath. It wasn't going to be a cool day after all. The Plymouth started as though I was kicking it out of a sound sleep. I drove east to Sheridan and turned south to the Loop.

I left the car with one of the day attendants at the parking station, crossed over Jackson and went into the Clawson Building. At exactly nine o'clock I opened the door of my reception room.

A tall man with beefy shoulders and his hat on was sitting on the couch and reading a paper as I walked in. It was Lieutenant George Zarr of the Homicide and Sex Detail. He lowered the paper and said, "I want to see you, Pine," in a tight cold voice that matched his eyes.

Being more or less involved in a killing one night and finding a homicide dick on the doorstep the next morning can make a man a little nervous. I was a little nervous. I said, "Sure. What about—homicide or sex?"

It didn't amuse him. Nothing I would ever say would amuse him. He stood up and folded his newspaper with deliberate motions of his stubby fingers and stuck it in the pocket of his suit coat and waited for me to unlock the inner office door.

He followed me in and sat down in the visitor's chair alongside the desk and broke the cellophane on a cigar while I drew the Venetian blind all the way up and opened the window. Traffic sounds floated in and settled over the furniture. A faint faraway buzzing was the drill in the dentist's office next door.

I yawned and got out of the raincoat and went over and picked four envelopes off the carpet under the letter drop. Zarr struck a kitchen match against his thumbnail and it cracked into flame with a noise like a cap pistol. He lighted his cigar, turning it slowly to get it burning evenly, his expressionless eyes on me while I went back around the desk and sat down and tucked the envelopes into a corner of the desk blotter pad. The room smelled a little of stale cigarette smoke and damp plaster.

Zarr took the cigar from his mouth and looked approvingly at the glowing end. He said, "You been reading the papers lately?" in a too-casual voice.

I eased up inside. It was too early for any mention of Marlin's murder to be in the news sheets. "Not any more than usual. Why?"

"Your friend's been hogging a lot of space."

Put it down to my lack of sleep, but I didn't get it right away. I wrinkled my forehead at him and said, "Who's that?"

He squeezed out a smile that was meant to tell me if I wanted to play it dumb he'd humor me along—within reason. "The one they planted day before yesterday. Remember?"

I said, "Stop acting so goddam coy. He wasn't my friend; I pointed that out to you then. I also told you how I happened to get into that procession. Maybe my friends *don't* live in penthouses, but they don't hang out in Madison Street flea-traps, either.''

His breath made a sudden rustling sound in his nostrils and his heavy eyebrows pulled sharply together. "I don't recall saying anything about a flophouse, shamus. Let's kind of hear about that part of it."

I curled my lip at him. "Nuts. You can comb the rubber hose out of your eyebrows, Lieutenant. I read about that angle in the *News*." I found my cigarettes and shook one out and lighted it. "Let's you and me get straightened out on this business, Zarr. All I know about that screwy funeral is what I saw out there and what the *News* had to say. I'll go along with you to the extent of admitting I'm curious why it should take twelve harp polishers to bury an unidentified bum. But I exercise my curiosity for nobody but clients. If Homicide wants to put me to work on the thing, okay; it'll cost the taxpayers thirty bucks a day. If not, then the hell with it and stop bothering me."

I opened the middle drawer of the desk and took out a copper letter knife with a blue enamel medallion on the handle—a gift my automobile-insurance company sent me one Christmas—picked up the first of the four envelopes and slit open the top edge. It was white and the size business houses use. There was no return address, front or back, and there was a three-cent stamp where it should have been.

Zarr's broad stubby-fingered hand reached out before I was aware of what he was doing. He grabbed the opener and the letter out of my fingers and slammed them down on the desk so hard it sounded like a gunshot.

I stared at him with my mouth open. His eyes weren't cold any more. They were hotter than a two-dollar pistol, and his face was red and his lips were twitching a little. He said thickly:

"Who the hell do you think you're brushing off, gum-shoe? I came here to talk to you, and by God you'll ters! You're not pushing around some crummy client to show him what a hotshot you are. I'm the law, Jack; when I ask a question I want an answer quick and respectful, get it?''

I grinned—the last thing in the world he expected. ''You want to watch yourself, George. Guys bust blood vessels that way. I wasn't giving you a brush; I told you what I knew. Shall I make up some details to keep you happy?''

The extra color began to seep out of his cheeks and his eyes cooled down some and his lips stopped twitching. He put his cigar back in his mouth and moved it around to one corner and stared at my necktie. When he spoke again his voice was clear.

''I'm a homicide man, Pine. My job is to find people who kill other people—find them and give enough information to the State's Attorney to put them in the chair—if it can be made to go that far.

''If whoever gets killed is prominent, then somebody's got to pay for it. The papers play it up and the mayor starts getting ants about the third day and lights a fire under the commissioner. Then it's a case of find the killer—or a reasonable facsimile—or the department gets a shake-up . . . and some honest, hard-working cop gets shoved out in the sticks and has to start all over again getting back what took him years, probably, to get in the first place.''

None of this was news to me. A private detective learns about life in the big city before his license makes a clean spot on his office wall. But Zarr had the ball and wanted to run with it and he was in the mood to step on anybody trying to take it away from him.

He crossed his legs the other way and jiggled his toe lightly up and down and kept on talking. ''Usually, though, the guy that gets rubbed is some nobody. The killing starts on page three and falls out of the paper the next day. That don't mean we don't try to get whoever done it; you know damn well we do, Pine. But if the answer comes hard—which ain't often—then the whole works sort of slides into the unsolved files and the hell with it. Nobody cares much except maybe the relatives, and by that time they're sick of cops and questions, so they don't beef.''

Very casually I picked up the slit envelope and fiddled it around in my fingers. He watched me with brooding eyes and kept on talking. Cops don't usually talk so much.

"Once in a long while one of those unsolved cases blows up again long after it should've been forgotten. The papers get hold of some nutty angle and first thing you know everybody's talking about it and the department's got to get to work. And there's nothing tougher to dig into than a murder that's had time to cool off.

"Which is what's happened in this John Doe thing. It was bad enough when some screwball laid out the dough to bury him. But when he hires *twelve* preachers to say the last words—well, there's your dynamite. One of the evening rags lighted the fuse; now both morning sheets have written it up. I happen to know that Malone of the *Tribune* has orders to stay with the thing until he gets the complete story. If he breaks it ahead of the department, I'll be lucky not to get transferred farther than Roseland.''

He puffed a time or two at his cigar, took it out of his mouth and stared at it and ran the nails of his left hand lightly along the back of his other thumb. Outside, the clouds were beginning to lift and a strained yellow light came in at the window.

"I've been a cop ever since I came to this town over twenty years ago, Pine. I started little but I got big . . . and I'm going to get a lot bigger if I don't get put behind the eight ball on some such lousy pitch as this one. That's why I got to bust this before it gets out of hand, and I don't give a greased goddam who gets hurt while I'm busting it, either.''

"Well, don't get mad at me," I said.

He eyed me bleakly. "You're in it, ain't you? You say it was by accident. I don't believe in accidents like that, friend. I think maybe you were sent out there by somebody for some reason. That means you know something I don't, and that's why I'm up here now, talking to you a lot more than I get any fun out of."

"All right," I said. "I heard you; now it's my turn. Nobody sent me to that funeral; I've told you so until my tonsils are sore. Check up with the cycle cop on duty at that intersection and he'll tell you how I got into the line. But instead of doing any checking, you come busting in here and shoot off your bazoo at me and tell me if I don't like it I can go to hell. Well, I don't like it, brother. If you want to make something out of that, go ahead and see where it gets you. I know my——"

The telephone rang.

I jumped a little, and Zarr allowed himself a sardonic smile. I picked up the receiver, scowling, and barked: "Hello."

"Mr. Pine?" It was a man's voice, steady, pleasant, not young and not old. A handshaking voice, rich, smooth, self-confident in a modest sort of way. The voice of a radio announcer or a con man.

"That's right," I said.

"My name is Baird, Mr. Pine. C. L. Baird. You have my letter?"

"Not that I know of," I said.

"I mailed it yesterday afternoon." He sounded a little worried. "Perhaps you haven't had a delivery yet."

My eyes went to the four envelopes on the blotter. "I haven't got around to the morning mail, that's all."

"Yes. Well, I wrote to you asking for an appointment at eleven this morning. Would that be convenient for you?"

"It can be arranged," I said. I shifted my glance to where Zarr was sitting. He was being obvious about not paying any attention to the conversation. "Do you want to come to the office or would you like me to call on you?"

"It would be better," the voice said crisply, "if I came there."

"Okay," I said. "I'll expect you."

He said good-by and hung up. I put back the receiver and fished a cigarette from the pack on the desk top and reached for a match. "I'm going to be busy, Lieutenant. Is there anything else I can tell you before you go?"

Zarr grunted and rose to his feet and drew down the brim of his hat. "What does that mean—anything *else*?" he said heavily. He went over and put a hand on the knob, then he turned around slowly and gave me a long, thoughtful look.

"All right, Pine. Maybe it did work out the way you say. Anyhow, just remember I'm working on this thing; and if you fall into it again . . . well, I can get awful sick of coincidence."

He went out, banging the door behind him.

It seemed suddenly very quiet in the room. I picked up the slit envelope and drew out the single sheet of white bond paper, unfolded it and read the few neatly typewritten lines.

My Dear Mr. Pine:

I should like to call on you at your office tomorrow, Wednesday, morning at eleven. I wish to engage your services in a highly confidential matter of extreme importance.

> *Respectfully,*

> > *C. L. Baird.*

It sounded like one of the notes Sherlock Holmes used to get. I refolded the sheet, slid it back into the envelope and dropped it back in the drawer. Then I put on my hat and went downstairs for a sandwich.

·8·

He said, "Good morning. Are you Mr. Pine?"

I told him I was. He came all the way into the office and turned around and very softly closed the door. Then he turned around again and smiled winningly and said, "I hope you don't mind my closing the door, Mr. Pine. I shouldn't want anyone overhearing what I have to say."

There wasn't anyone in the reception room to overhear him, but I let it pass. I nodded without getting up and pointed to the customer's chair. He sat down gracefully and laid his woven-under-water panama on a corner of the desk and crossed the legs of a reddish-brown tropical-worsted suit that had been put together by a tailor who loved his work, and adjusted the cuffs of his fifteen-dollar brown madras shirt. The brown-and-red figured handkerchief with hand-rolled edges in his breast pocket matched his foulard tie, and the brown-and-white oxfords on his slender high-arched feet probably cost more than my best suit.

It was a treat just to look at him. He turned on his white-toothed smile again and leaned back in the chair and said:

"My name is Baird, Mr. Pine." He spoke softly, in an almost purring voice. "You did receive my letter?"

"Uh-hunh."

"You're free to do a job for me?"

"That," I said, "will depend on what the job is."

He nodded his head approvingly. He liked me. He

thought I was wonderful. I didn't know why. "Naturally, you'd want to know that first."

He was a year or two past thirty and an inch or two under six feet, with long slender legs, not enough belly to mention and a pair of football shoulders. He wore his crisp black hair parted on the left side, with sideburns that came down to the tragi. He had a rounded chin, thin smart lips, rather a pointed nose with a high bridge, brown eyes set wide apart, thick black eyebrows and a high smooth forehead with a widow's peak. The skin of his hands was a little too white, but his face showed a tan—the kind of tan that comes either from Florida or a sun lamp.

If I had been a girl I would have loved to let him take me dancing.

He worked a cigarette case out of a pocket and got one of the contents burning. It was a cheap plastic case that clashed with the rest of his getup. I refused a cigarette and he put the case away. He leaned back again and looked at me and gave me the benefit of his insurance-salesman's smile.

"Shall we get right down to it, Mr. Pine? My partner and I own a small manufacturing plant out on Belmont Avenue. We're engaged in making gambling equipment: dice tables, roulette layouts, chuck-a-luck cages, and so on.

"Two mornings ago my partner failed to show up to keep a golfing date with me. I called a few places where he might be, but without success. I wasn't especially alarmed; any one of several reasons might have explained his absence. Then, yesterday afternoon, I found this note in my apartment mailbox."

He thrust a hand into the inner pocket of his jacket and brought out a folded sheet of sulphite bond and handed it to me. I unfolded it, smoothed out the wrinkles. Words were printed on it with a hard lead pencil. They read:

Baird:

We've got Taggart. You can have him back for twenty-five grand. Bring it, in small used bills, to the dirt road that runs behind the Glenhaven Cemetery. The road turns off Addison, just west of Harlem. Drive along it for a hundred feet, then park. We'll contact you. One o'clock Thursday morning. You only get one chance. We don't have to tell you to keep away from the cops.

There was no signature. There didn't have to be. I slid the paper back to him across the blotter and he refolded it and returned it to his pocket. I said, "What do you want me to do, Mr. Baird?"

He put the tips of his thumbs together and looked at them. His mouth was without the salesman's smile right then and it was a lot harder around the edges than I had noticed before.

"I should like you to handle the matter for me," he said, keeping his eyes on his thumbs. Between the first and second fingers of his right hand, his cigarette sent up a wavering gray line. "I'll turn the money over to you, and you go out there and make the contact."

I pushed the letter knife around with the tip of a forefinger. "Why not handle it yourself, Mr. Baird?"

He left off fooling with his thumbs and took a long drag from his cigarette. He said, "I'm fairly new in the gambling-supply business, Mr. Pine, and I'm not used to associating with the type of people who buy our merchandise. They talk hard and they act hard, and frankly they—well—they frighten me a little." He laughed briefly and his face colored. "Taggart was the victim of a snatch once before. He tells me it's a sort of occupational hazard for anyone in our line of business."

It added up okay. It was just that he didn't look much like a coward. But then you never know. I said, "What do you figure the job's worth to you, Mr. Baird?"

The wide shoulders under the tropical-weave jacket

rose and fell. "Three C's ought to be fair enough. I could pay that."

"The price is right," I said. "Where's the money I'm to pay out?"

"I'll get it to you this afternoon."

"How?"

He looked faintly astonished. "Does that make a difference?"

"You bet it does," I said. "A lot of difference. I wouldn't want some kid walking in and handing me a package and walking out. When I opened the package I might find some cut-up newspapers, and then you'd be mad at me for stealing your money."

He shook his head and smiled. "I trust you, Pine."

"That's fine," I said. "I like to be trusted. But maybe I don't trust you."

His nice soft brown eyes turned hard as paving stones. "Perhaps you had better explain that."

I nodded carelessly. "It's fairly obvious. You come in here and see me for the first time in your life and offer me twenty-five grand to carry around like a bag of margarined popcorn. You'd do that, maybe, if somebody you trusted a lot had recommended me. In that case you'd have mentioned his name right away. But you haven't mentioned anybody's name."

Back came the smile. "That's clear enough. I'll bring the money to you myself."

"What time? I'll want to be here."

"Around five o'clock."

"That will be all right. You said three hundred. You can pay me half now and the rest when the job is done. Okay?"

He took a brown alligator billfold from the same pocket the note had come from and slid out three one-hundred-dollar bills. He fanned them out so I could see the figures in the corners and put them gently down in front of me. "In advance," he said lightly. "All of it. I said I trusted you, Mr. Pine."

I opened the middle drawer and brushed the bills into it with a careless motion as though there were hundreds more like them in there. Baird stood up and ground out his cigarette in the glass ash tray, straightened, put on his panama, tilting it a little over the right eye, and stuck out his hand. I got out of my chair and shook his hand for him and walked with him as far as the corridor door.

He said: "About five, then, Mr. Pine," and opened the door and went down the hall without a backward glance. I closed the door and went back to my desk and took out the three bills.

There didn't seem to be any marks on them that didn't belong there. I got out my wallet and tucked them in with the fifties John Sandmark had given me two days before. Four hundred and fifty dollars in slightly under forty-eight hours. The landlord was going to start being respectful to me again.

The alarm bell went off at eleven-forty-five, but I didn't need it. I hadn't dozed off after all. I stretched, reached over and cut the alarm, put a marker between the pages of my copy of *Modern Criminal Investigation*, and got off the bed. I went into the kitchen and lighted the gas under the pot, then went back to the bedroom, took a quick shower and put on a tan sport shirt and dark trousers.

I drank coffee laced with black molasses rum, returned to the living room and took a gun—a .38 Colt Detective Special, a black leather shoulder holster, and a brown-paper parcel from the drawer of one of the end tables flanking the couch.

After adjusting the holster under my left arm, I put the gun into it and slipped on my jacket.

The parcel had twenty-five thousand dollars in it—in one-hundred-dollar bills. I knew that because I had opened it in front of C. L. Baird at a quarter to five that same afternoon and counted them. I didn't figure I'd need the gun, but in calling on people who have so little regard for the law that they put the sneeze on a fairly respectable businessman, it doesn't hurt to have something under your coat besides muscle.

I put out the lights and walked down the corridor, past the self-service elevator and through the door to the building stairs. I went down two flights and came out into the lobby across from the desk.

Wilson, the night man, was sitting behind the switchboard reading a pulp magazine. He tipped a hand at me, gave the brown-paper bundle under my arm a glittering stare and said, "Going out, Mr. Pine?" in his reedy voice.

"Nice deduction, Sam," I said.

He was the most literal-minded guy I knew . . . and the most inquisitive. His eyes stayed on the package. "I'm afraid all the laundries are closed by now, Mr. Pine."

"You mean this?" I indicated the parcel. I made a show of looking around to see if the lobby was deserted. "Keep it to yourself, Sam, but there's twenty-five grand in there."

He said, "Ha, ha," sourly and went back to his detective story. I walked on out through the screen door and stood on the sidewalk and looked at the sky.

The stars were out, also half a moon. That was a relief; I'd have hated to use a dirt road on a dark and rainy night. It was hot and sticky out and there wasn't enough breeze to break a smoke ring. I blew out my breath and turned left and walked slowly around the corner to where my heap drooped at the curb.

I unlocked the door and slid in behind the wheel. The air was hot and lifeless the way it is when the sun beats down on the roof of a closed car. I rolled down the windows, started the motor and drove east. There were a couple of cars behind me by the time traffic thinned out on Sheridan enough for me to swing south.

At Irving Park I turned into Marine Drive and followed the inner lane to Addison Boulevard. Another car swung

in behind me as I made the turn there, and for a moment
I wondered if maybe I didn't have a tail. But traffic was
heavy enough to make it hard to be sure. I could have
circled around a few side streets to make sure but there
would be time enough for that later on.

The moving car stirred the air enough to give an illusion of coolness. I lighted a cigarette with the dashboard lighter and slipped out of my jacket. I unshipped
the .38 and laid it beside the parcel on the seat next
to me.

The car radio gave me "Whispering," very softly,
with a lot of strings, a growling doghouse and a sobbing
trumpet. The wet half-moons under my arms began to
dry out. Way off somewhere a train whistle mourned for
the miles ground under iron wheels. Now and then a car
whished past my open windows, the headlights laying
an unsteady carpet in its path. A huge cross-country
Greyhound bus hissed its air brakes briefly at me and
went by with its nose in the air.

When Harlem Avenue was fifty yards up ahead, I
figured it was time to start being clever. The traffic signal
at the intersection was green for me; but instead of taking
advantage of it, I cut my speed and inched toward the
right-hand curb to give the cars behind me a chance to
get through.

There were two: one very close, the other pretty well
back. The guy on my tail seemed confused; instead of
swerving past me to beat the light, he slowed too, and
kept his position. The second car came up fast but had
been too far back to cross before the signal changed, so
it drew up alongside me at the crosswalk.

It was a big dark-blue LaSalle, with a lot of chrome
and a minor gouge in the right front fender. There were
two men in the front seat, but not enough light to make
out the faces under the snap-brim felt hats. I kept my
left hand on the wheel and put the other down slowly
and felt around for the gun and put it to rest on the seat
between my legs. . . .

The amber showed and the sedan leaped ahead with
a drumming roar and became a dwindling taillight. I sat
there and watched it fade until the horn blasts from the
other car sounded impatient instead of polite.

I let out my breath and gave the car just enough gas
to turn the wheels. By the time I was halfway across the
intersection, the guy behind me was fit to be tied. He
slammed his horn button a time or two more, then swung
out and went by on my left. A fat man with his coat off
was driving a Ford Tudor that couldn't have been as old
as it looked; and next to him, holding a baby, was a
skinny woman in a house dress. The woman stuck her
head out and yelled something as they went by, but all
I got of it was a couple of words I don't ordinarily use
myself.

I grinned to show that Paul Pine had nerves of steel
and put the gun back on the seat and got up to about
fifteen miles an hour. The Glenhaven Cemetery was on
my left now, behind an ornamental iron fence, and my
headlights picked out an occasional white stone among
the trees. It occurred to me that there seemed to be a lot
of cemeteries in my life lately.

I lighted a cigarette with the dashboard lighter, meanwhile keeping my eyes open for the entrance to the dirt
road mentioned in the letter to Baird.

It appeared finally, a good two city blocks past Harlem
Avenue. An eight-foot red-brick wall flanked it on the
left; that would be the western end of the cemetery. On
the right side of the road were trees and bushes and grass,
and enough weeds to hide the Taj Mahal.

I waited until there were no headlights in either direction, then cut my own lights, turned off Addison and
rolled along the dirt road until I figured I was a hundred
feet into it.

I let the motor die with a lonesome cough, and sat
there with my hands resting lightly on the wheel and
turned my head in little jerks from side to side. I could
see a little but not enough. Not nearly enough. There

were two very large cottonwoods just ahead, their upper branches tangled with those of a giant elm on the other side of the cemetery wall. Together they formed a tunnel that was like being inside a length of old stovepipe. It would have been a good spot to bring a blanket and a blonde.

I sat there and dragged on my cigarette and listened to the little ticking noises the engine made as it cooled. After a minute or two a pair of crickets started up, trying to make things cheerful for me. They could have saved their strength. Even Spike Jones and his boys wouldn't have done me much good right then.

A tree frog right over my head went *ee-ee* suddenly and I jumped and cracked my knee on the steering post. I said, "The hell with it," out loud, and reached around and took my coat off the back of the seat and got into it. I put the .38 under my arm and released the door catch and got out into the road, leaving the brown-paper parcel where it was.

The road was packed pretty hard considering the previous night's rain. I stretched my arms and took off my hat and scratched my head where it didn't itch, just to be doing something, and put the hat back on my head. I walked ten feet up the road and turned around and walked back again to prove I wasn't nervous. I proved it to everybody except me.

My wrist watch showed ten minutes short of one o'clock. I walked some more; fifteen feet this time. At that rate I'd be able to spit in a tiger's eye by the time the ten minutes were up.

I went back to the car and leaned on the fender and practiced getting used to seeing in the dark. Bit by bit I was able to make out the shapes of bushes and assorted undergrowth, none of it worth the trouble. It was a little cooler now, not enough to help much, and there was a sort of tired breeze to make rustling noises among the weeds, like feet sneaking around. I would have made a hell of a pioneer.

Something made a noise behind me. It wasn't much of a noise. About as loud as a cigarette ash falling on a snowdrift. I started to turn around.

I should have turned faster. Something came down on the back of my head. It couldn't have been the *Queen Mary*'s anchor; there wasn't enough water around.

I dived into a shoreless sea of black ink, pulled folds of black velvet over my head and burrowed into a coal pile.

I was out.

· 9 ·

Dim sounds . . . a sort of uneven chant, coming across a black universe of dull pain. Little specks of fire appeared, light-years away, danced crazily and disappeared. Then nothing. . . .

The chant came back. It became loud, very loud. The void was still there but this time it was filled with a greenish-yellow light impossible to look at. . . .

" . . . other guy says, 'Naw, I don't care if she has one.' So the first guy says, 'Then let's take them damn things off!' Haw, haw, haw!"

"Ha, ha! That's a good one, all right. That's a good one."

"Yeah, I kind of like that one myself. 'Let's take the damn things off!' he says. Haw, haw, haw!"

I opened my eyes. I was in a room. It was a very nice room, too, although it took a while before I could see well enough to know that. It had oak paneling and a beamed ceiling and magenta carpeting. A heavy walnut desk with an inlaid top of blue leather stood in front of a square casement window of leaded glass squares. There were a few square-backed leather chairs scattered around, and a blue leather couch against one wall. I didn't know about the couch right away because I was stretched out on it.

There were two men up near the desk, just standing there. The chant I had heard while getting past that sock on the head had been their voices.

From what I could make out, they were just a couple of guys. The one in the shapeless gray suit was fairly tall, with thick bowed shoulders, a lumpy face the color of fish bait, and coarse black hair that needed combing. The other man was slightly below medium height and his plump body was covered with a neatly pressed brown suit that should have been an inch larger all around. He had hips like a woman and a round, pink, patient face with features a shade too delicate for a man.

The big guy started another smoking-car story. It wasn't as old as the one I'd heard the tag line on, but it wasn't as funny either.

I moved a couple of fingers; not much, just enough to make sure orders from the head office could get through to them all right. I let my feet down to the floor and sat up. Immediately the room hit an air pocket and the light from the overhead fixture began to get fuzzy. I put both hands around one arm of the couch and closed my eyes. But the groan got out before I could do anything about it.

The bathroom ballad pulled up short, which kept my groan from being a total loss, and feet came across the carpet and stopped in front of me. I didn't look up. I didn't even open my eyes.

"You look a little rocky, pal." A voice like that would have vocal cords made of sandpaper.

I didn't say anything. I hardly even thought anything.

"You don't feel like talking, hunh?"

I got my eyelids apart again. It wasn't easy either. There were two muddy spots on the knees of my dark trousers. For some blurred reason those two spots made me almost as angry as the belt I had taken on the head. I said, "Which one of you bastards sapped me?" My voice sounded as if it was coming out of a well.

"You hadn't ought to talk that way, pal. We your friends. We don't hit you around none."

Thin legs in gray pants. That would make it the pasty-faced one. I got my eyes up past his knees, his crotch, his belt, his green necktie. . . . It was the pasty-faced guy all right. The one with the hips was there too, off to one side a little.

I said, "Okay. You didn't sap me. Somebody did. I think I'll kind of go home."

"Sure, pal." I was being humored. "Only not right now. You ain't no shape to get around."

"Don't tell me what kind of shape I'm in," I said. I stood up. It took some doing, but I stood up. The guy with the fish-food face put a spatulate forefinger against my chest and gave it a little-bitty push and I sat down again, hard. The room moved around like a fat woman on a hard mattress and the light dimmed.

"You believe me now, hunh?" Pasty Face said, showing me his big chalk-white teeth. "You ain't in good shape, honest. Maybe we talk a little while, you feel better, hunh?"

I don't think he liked the way I looked at him. He pushed out the tip of his tongue and dislodged his cigarette butt. It fell on the rug but he ignored it. He tightened the slack line of his lips and grinned with cold menace. His hands opened and closed slowly at his sides. He said:

"It don't look like you got nice manners, pal. Seems as if you should talk when I ask you something, hunh?"

I said two words. They were words that hardly anybody likes having said to them.

He brought around a hand that seemed mostly bones and laid it alongside my jaw so hard I fell off the couch. There had been nothing in his face to warn me so I could set myself for the blow. I tried to get up but there was too much rubber in my arms and legs. Then a couple of fingers hooked under the back of my collar, lifted me up and dumped me into a sitting position on the couch.

The fog lifted an inch at a time. That pasty face was looking down at me. It was the kind of face that peeps into bedroom windows. I gave my leg a jerk and slammed the toe of my oxford into his shin.

It hurt him. There was only one place I could have

hurt him worse but I couldn't get my foot quite that high. He let out a yell and staggered back and clawed a black leather sap from his hip pocket and swung it at my head like a tennis player making a flat drive.

But this time I had a chance to see it coming. I ducked under the blow and came off the couch, low, and put my shoulder into his gut. His breath whistled between his teeth and he fell on the floor, taking with him one of the leather chairs that happened to be in the vicinity.

He didn't get up right away. For that matter, I didn't either. My head felt like a discarded polo ball and somebody had been fooling with the lights again. . . .

"Pick him up, Cleve," a voice said. I had heard that voice before—a hundred years before. It was a deep voice, a flat voice, a voice as dry as talcum powder.

A pair of not very strong hands slid under my armpits and hoisted me onto the leather couch once more. By this time I was willing to stay there.

There were three of them lined up in front of me: the little guy with the hips; Pasty Face (he was holding onto the back of a chair and bent over a little, his face even pastier than before and his eyes as mean as a slapped Sicilian); and the man I had met the night before behind a desk upstairs at the Peacock Club. Two hundred fifty pounds, six feet four. D'Allemand.

He said, "We meet again, Mr. Pine."

I waggled my jaw experimentally and was pleasantly surprised when it didn't fall in my lap. My head still ached, but dully now, like a last summer's love affair.

D'Allemand tried again. "How are you feeling, sir?"

"What the hell do you care?" I said. It wasn't very original. I was too used up to be original.

He reached out and swung a chair into position in front of me and lowered himself slowly onto it. With that bulk he would always lower himself slowly onto chairs. He took a loose cigarette from a pocket and gave it to me and struck a match. I filled my lungs with smoke and let it trickle slowly out and looked down into the caves where he kept his eyes.

He said, "There seem to be people who do not like you, Mr. Pine."

I said, "I've got an ache in my head to tell me that. From the way your pasty-faced punk handles a blackjack I figure he put the ache there. Given the chance I'll make him eat his sap without opening his mouth."

Pasty Face growled something and took a step toward me. Without turning his head D'Allemand said, "Ownie," softly and it froze my playmate where he stood.

To me, D'Allemand said, "I had you brought here, Mr. Pine, to get answers to a few questions that have been bothering me."

"I don't know any answers," I said. "A man named Baird hired me to hand twenty-five grand to you for the release of a guy named Taggart. Right now I'd say the entire deal was rigged so you could get your hands on me. All that keeps me from being sure is that Baird actually gave me the twenty-five, and there are a lot of simpler ways for you to nab me if you wanted to."

D'Allemand stared at me levelly. "Take my word for it: I haven't the slightest idea what you're talking about."

It might have been the truth. I shrugged. "All right. What do you want to talk about?"

"I want to talk about a man. A man named Jerry Marlin."

It got very quiet in the room. Nobody seemed to be breathing. D'Allemand's deep-set eyes had sparks in them—small hot sparks that were probably reflections from the overhead light fixture. His two muscle boys stood there and stared at me too.

"You seem surprised, Mr. Pine," D'Allemand said softly.

"Why not?" I said. "I can be surprised. What about Marlin?"

"You were looking for him last night."

"We've been over that."

"Do you know where he is now?"

"No."

"Don't lie to me, you son of a bitch."

There was no heat in his words. That way it sounded worse.

"Flattery won't get you anywhere," I said.

He crossed his knees and looked at the nails of his left hand. His lips moved a little as if he was counting up to ten. Smoke spiraled gracefully up from the cigarette lost between the first and second fingers of his right hand.

"Perhaps the boys should work you over a little, Mr. Pine."

I felt that one in my belly but I didn't say anything.

Ownie, the lad with the toadstool complexion, folded the fingers of one hand and rubbed the knuckles lightly along a leg of his gray pants. He said: "It wouldn't hurt none to try, boss."

D'Allemand appeared to have made up his mind. He said, "Keep your hands off him," and got off the chair and went over to a door in the opposite wall and went out.

Ownie and Cleve, the one with the hips, stood there and watched me. I watched them and twirled my thumbs and wondered what had happened to Baird's bundle of C notes. Ownie made pawing motions at his shirt pocket and brought out a crumpled pack of cigarettes, lighted one and put back the pack without offering it to Cleve. I gathered that Cleve didn't have any vices that would look good in public. Ownie threw the used match in my lap and said, "I don't forget that kick in the shins, peeper."

"Then don't earn yourself another one."

He thought about that and nodded his head. "I can wait. I'm good at waiting. You better get used to going without teeth, pal."

I dropped my cigarette stub on the carpet and stepped on it. Five minutes went by, then the door opened again and D'Allemand came in carrying a folded newspaper.

He tossed it to me and said, "You will find it under the cartoon on page one, Mr. Pine."

I knew what it was going to be while I unfolded the paper. The item carried a one-column head.

GIRL'S ESCORT VICTIM OF
MYSTERY SLAYING

Shortly before dawn yesterday, Gerald Marlin, 34, 1291 Dearborn Parkway, was shot and instantly killed in front of an apartment building at 1317 North Austin Boulevard.

Marlin was accompanied by a Miss Leona Sandmark, who lives at the Austin Boulevard address, and had just driven the woman home from a round of night clubs. The couple was hurrying across the sidewalk to avoid an early morning shower when three bullets struck Marlin in the back, felling him instantly.

Terror-stricken, Miss Sandmark fled to her apartment and summoned the police, who found Marlin's lifeless body where it lay in the rain.

Miss Sandmark, almost completely unnerved by the shock of her experience, told police she did not see the killer. Captain Locke of the Homicide Detail reports little is known about Marlin, but that an investigation is under way.

There was more, but that was all I needed just then. I folded the sheet back into its original creases and put it down on the couch and said:

"All right. I read it. Marlin was one of your boys and somebody shot him and you don't like it. Where do I fit?"

He sat down on the chair across from me and took a

small penknife with a platinum handle and six diamonds set in a circle on one side, and set about cleaning his nails. If I had had a knife like that, I would have pawned it and bought myself a Cadillac.

He finished his left thumb before he looked up and met my eyes. Very quietly he said, "Did you kill Marlin, Mr. Pine?"

I blinked. "Certainly not."

"Who did?"

"I don't know. How could I know?"

"You were there, Mr. Pine."

"Who says I was there?"

He seemed a bit disappointed in me. He took his eyes off me and put them back on his left hand and started work on the nail of his forefinger. Behind him, Ownie and Cleve shifted their feet a little, as if they wanted to sit down but didn't dare without an okay from the boss.

"I am going to be frank with you, Mr. Pine," D'Allemand said, talking to his nails. "I own several gaming locations in and around Chicago. Not many people know that I own them.

"Jerry Marlin was employed by me. His was a highly specialized vocation. He mingled with unattached women who came to my places, became friendly with them, acted as their escorts. When they wanted to gamble, he would bring them where it would be profitable to me. Will you have a highball?"

I said that I would. He motioned to Cleve, who went out swinging his hips.

"Jerry was dependable," D'Allemand continued, "and we got along very well together. He was handsome and had all the social graces, and he was very popular with the ladies. Then one night this Sandmark girl came, unescorted, into my place on Rush Street—the Peacock Club."

"Sure," I said. "Where we had our first interview."

"Yes. Well, Jerry became acquainted with Miss Sandmark. She was fond of gambling and she usually put down more than she picked up. Quite a bit more. Jerry was always with her, and they were at one or another of my places several nights a week.

"It went on that way until perhaps a month ago. Then they stopped coming in so often. When it got to the point where it was two weeks between visits, I began to wonder a bit."

Cleve came in with two highball glasses, pulled a large copper ash stand, made to resemble a ship's binnacle, over where we could reach it, and set the glasses on the edge. D'Allemand ignored his, but I took some of mine. It was all right.

D'Allemand went on: "Jerry was always one to be close-mouthed. But he had a very good friend. I called in this friend and put down some money and asked him a few questions. I did not get a great deal in the way of answers. The friend said Jerry had dropped a hint or two that he was on the edge of something important; that he knew where the body was buried, and when it was dug up there would a million dollars with his name on it in the coffin. At times Jerry was given to rather grandiose talk."

"It would seem so," I said.

He picked up his glass, glanced at it absent-mindedly and put it down again without tasting the contents. I punched out my cigarette in the ash stand, lighted one of my own and glanced at the dial of my wrist watch. Two-twenty-three. All the grocery clerks and necktie salesmen were home in bed. But I had to be a private detective.

"I became curious about all that, Mr. Pine," D'Allemand continued. "So I had one of my boys follow Jerry around. It turned out to be pretty much a waste of time. Jerry saw the girl almost every night. Sometimes they would go out to the nice places, at times they would just drive around in her car, on occasions they were content to stay in her apartment. He stayed over for breakfast now and then, but that was his business . . . and hers.''

I thought of twin depressions in a rose bedspread, but I didn't say anything. It did seem a little strange to me, though, that right then I was content to know that Jerry Marlin was dead. . . .

D'Allemand closed one of his huge hands around his glass and this time he drank some of the highball. He set it down and licked his lips and drilled me with those deep-set eyes. "All this leads up to one important point, Mr. Pine. One of my boys was following Jerry the morning he was shot.''

I said, "What am I supposed to do—jump out of my skin?"

He made a noise deep in his throat but his expression did not change. "Let me tell you about it, Mr. Pine," he said. "My boy was a trifle careless that morning. He had watched Jerry and the girl all evening, and when he saw they were on their way to her apartment, he let down a bit. He stopped in at a tavern for some cigarettes and a beer, then drove on over to the Austin address to make sure Jerry and Miss Sandmark were through for the day.

"He saw a body on the walk and recognized it as Jerry's. He parked at the opposite curbing and ran over in the rain and made sure. Just as he returned to his own car, you came out of the building, Mr. Pine. Your unconcern at seeing the body was enough. My boy followed you to your hotel, got your name from the night clerk and telephoned me.''

He tested the point of the penknife blade with a careful forefinger and let out his breath with a little whistling sigh. "Now I think you had better do some talking, Mr. Pine. I'm afraid I can't take no for an answer.''

"Some of it I can give you," I said; "some of it I can't. The first thing you can make book on is that I didn't plug your gigolo. I have a client—you'd better change that to 'had'—who was interested in Marlin. Don't ask me his name, because he didn't have anything to do with the killing, and I wouldn't give it to you anyway. I was parked in front of the apartment house when the shooting came off.''

I gave him the rest of it, holding back only my reason for being interested in Marlin. He listened without interrupting, concentrating all the while on his nail-cleaning job.

After I finished, he sat there without moving and thought it over. Presently he looked up at me and said, ''You didn't get much of a look at the killer?''

''No.''

''How do you know it wasn't your client?''

''Reason, mostly. What the books call deduction. He isn't the kind who would make a good torpedo. There were three holes in Marlin's back—holes so close together you could cover them with a milk-bottle top. It takes experience to shoot that good, D'Allemand. A professional k'lled your boy. That's my guess.''

''Maybe he was working for your client.''

''Then there wouldn't have been any point in hiring me.''

He nodded slowly. ''Very well. . . . I might not take your word so easily, Mr. Pine, except that I asked a friend of mine at police headquarters about you. As nearly as I can recall his exact words, he said Pine was a flip-lipped bastard who should have had his ears pinned back long ago.'' He raised his thin brows at me and smiled like a department-store president who had forgiven an assistant buyer. ''He went on to say you were reasonably honest and would fight harder for a client than for yourself. He mentioned that you are about half as smart as you like to think, and less than ten percent as tough.''

I said, ''You ought to see me when my hair is marcelled.''

He took another pull at his glass, draining it this time,

and placed it carefully on the binnacle. He patted his lips with a ten-dollar white handkerchief from the breast pocket of his dark blue coat, tucked it away and leaned back and toyed with the penknife while he said:

"You owe me something, Mr. Pine. But for my interest in you, you would be wearing your brains on your coat collar."

I put a hand gingerly to the back of my head. "Your boys came pretty near putting them there tonight."

"I'll get to that part of it in a moment. You see, because I considered the possibility that you may have been responsible for Jerry's death, I had the boys follow you when you left your office shortly after five yesterday afternoon. They followed you home; and when you left your car around the corner from the hotel, they concluded you might be going out again later, so they stayed on the job, after telephoning me for instructions.

"Shortly before midnight, you came out, carrying the same brown-paper parcel you had taken home from the office. They trailed after you until your driving indicated you were becoming suspicious; then they drove past you at Harlem Avenue and turned off at the next intersection and stopped, planning to follow you again when you went by."

"You ought to have the fender on that blue LaSalle fixed," I said.

"Yes." He ducked his head about a quarter-inch in tribute to my perspicacity or something. "As it was, they drove back, surmising you might have turned off at the roadway flanking the cemetery rear. It seemed the only place you could have turned off.

"They parked the car and Cleve, here, went in on foot. He is a native of northern Michigan and is accustomed to moving around among bushes and trees without making a great deal of noise."

"I'll back him up on that," I said. "I didn't know anybody was within miles of me until half a second before he wrapped that sap around my ears."

He ran his thumb lightly along the blade of the pen-knife. "No, Mr. Pine. Cleve was not the one who struck you."

"Then who the hell did?"

"I do not know, sir. According to Cleve he arrived on the scene just as a man stepped from behind a bush and struck you down with a blackjack. It was evident that he meant to continue striking you until you were dead. Cleve, believing I would not want that to happen, considering my interest in you, shouted at the man, who immediately turned and ran away. Ownie, hearing the shout, came in; and between the two of them they got you into your car, and Cleve drove you here.

"Make no mistake about it, Mr. Pine. But for Cleve's intervention, you would be quite dead at this moment."

"Seems as if," I said. I thought about it for a moment. "What did this guy with the sap look like?"

"It was much too dark to tell, Cleve tells me. Fairly tall and not too bulky, he believes. Although that is not much more than a guess."

Something else occurred to me then. I said, "There was twenty-five thousand dollars in bills in that brown-paper package. I would like to know about it."

His eyes chilled and the hollows under his cheekbones grew more pronounced. "What do you want to know about it?"

"It belongs to a client. Since my errand didn't work out, he'll want his money back."

"How do you know there was the amount you stated in the parcel?"

"Don't give me that," I said. "I counted it myself. There were two hundred and fifty bills—in bundles of twenty-five. Each bill was a C note."

"Numbered consecutively?"

"I didn't notice. It wasn't my business to notice. My interest only went far enough to check the total. I'm responsible for that money, D'Allemand. Do I get it back or are you figuring to charge me that amount for the pretty story about keeping my brains off my coat collar?''

He clicked shut the blade of his penknife and put it back in his vest pocket. He stood up and crossed the rug and went around behind the desk. He opened the center drawer and took out the brown-paper package and slapped it down on the leather top. One corner of the paper was torn away and greenbacks showed through the rent.

I got off the couch and walked slowly over to the desk and picked up the parcel and ripped away the paper. There were ten bundles of bills, each with its paper band that said First National Bank in neat printed capitals.

D'Allemand watched me, his death's-head face washed of all expression, while I counted every bill in each bundle. There were two hundred and fifty, exactly as there should have been. I shaped the bundles into a neat pile, squared up the edges and said:

"Not that I meant to embarrass you, Mr. D'Allemand, but I had to be sure. You have a piece of paper handy?''

He continued to stare at me, a sort of puzzled uncertainty shadowing his deep-set eyes. "You are satisfied, Mr. Pine?''

"Just about. I'm taking it for granted that you're going to allow me to walk out of here with this. Or am I being optimistic?''

"Not at all, sir. Although I must confess I'm a little disappointed in you.''

I tapped the stack of bills gently against the desk top. "The hell with this kittens-and-mice stuff, Mac. What's the angle?''

For an answer, he reached into the drawer again and brought out a small reading glass on a black rubber handle and slid it across the desk to me. He said, "I suggest you examine a few of those bills, Mr. Pine.''

All of it put together was enough to tell me what I would see through the glass. I looked anyway . . . just to satisfy myself.

By the time I finished going over the fifth bill, I had

had enough. I put down the reading glass gently and lighted a cigarette, leaned a hip against a corner of the desk and stared moodily at the neat pile of counterfeit money.

"Well?" D'Allemand said softly.

"It's wallpaper all right," I said. "And very good, too. It would have to be good. The sourdough boys don't usually shoot so high. People have a habit of looking sharp at C notes."

"You should have acquired that habit, Mr. Pine," D'Allemand said dryly.

I couldn't reach that one, so I let it go by. I flicked ashes on the magenta carpeting and talked to the glowing end of my cigarette. I said: "So it was a frame. A nice fancy frame, with scrollwork around the edges. 'Take these pretty pictures of Mr. Franklin around behind the cemetery wall,' he says, 'and give them to the man in the green hat.' Only he forgot to tell me that the man intended to beat my head off."

I reached into my coat for my wallet, never doubting it would be there. It was. I took out the three bills Baird had paid me and put them under the glass. They were okay, of course; Baird would have figured I might try to pass them before running his errand for him. I returned the bills to the wallet and put it away and said:

"It seems I owe you something all right. How do you want it paid?"

He pointed to a chair beside the desk. "Be seated, sir. This may take a little time."

I sat down and he got into the wide-bottomed swivel chair. He folded his hands, one on top of the other, on the desk and bent forward slightly and said:

"I want to engage your services, Mr. Pine. I want you to learn who killed Jerry Marlin. Of course, that might not be to the best interests of your other client." He gave me another of his sword-point glances.

"I told you he's not my client any more."

"Then you will take the job?"

"Yeah. I think so. With the understanding that anything I find out goes to the bulls. I'm not putting the finger on somebody for you to wrap concrete around his toes and drop him into the drainage canal."

There was a flicker at the bottom of the caverns where he kept his eyes—a flicker like heat lightning on a cloudy night. "I don't object to having the State of Illinois take care of my executions for me, Mr. Pine. I prefer it that way. Only . . . I want the story first. *All* the story."

He turned up his right hand and stared fixedly at the palm and his voice went down a few notches. "You owe me something, sir. I will settle for that."

I can see across the street when the wind is right. The erudite Mr. D'Allemand didn't give a cracked roulette chip whether Marlin's killer was caught. What he wanted was information—information about the million dollars Marlin had expected to pick up when the body was found . . . whatever that meant. Mr. D'Allemand figured maybe he could get his hand in that coffin first.

I punched out the cigarette and got off the chair. I said, "I'll do what I can. How do I get in touch with you?"

He stood up with an effort and came around to my side of the desk. "Leave a message with Larson at the Peacock Club. You will hear from me." He slid a hand into a trouser pocket and brought out a sheaf of bills and took one out of the middle and gave it to me.

Five hundred bucks, all in one oblong piece of paper. "Let us call that a retainer, Mr. Pine."

"Let's," I said.

At a word from D'Allemand, Cleve found me a hunk of paper and I wrapped up the bad money and shoved it into one of my coat pockets. While I was doing that, D'Allemand took a gun from a desk drawer and held it out to me, butt first. He said:

"I took the liberty of holding this for you, sir."

It was my .38. I took it from him. He was watching me without particular expression on his gaunt face. Instead of putting the gun under my arm, I lifted the short barrel and sniffed at the muzzle. It reeked of fresh powder fumes. I pushed out the cylinder. One of the shells was empty. I looked at D'Allemand. His expression had changed about as much as the *Tribune's* opinion of Roosevelt.

I said, "It must have gone off, hunh?"

"Accidentally," he murmured.

"Sure," I said. "Accidentally. Only Colt makes these guns so they don't go off accidentally. You have to pull the trigger, brother."

D'Allemand said patiently, "No one has been shot with your revolver, Mr. Pine."

"You're not telling me anything," I said. "You fired a test bullet, intending to have your friend at police headquarters match it with the ones taken out of Marlin. You don't overlook much."

He smiled slightly. "I have learned not to overlook anything, sir. That is why I put your money under a glass."

I shoved the gun into the holster and buttoned my coat. I said, "I'd better go now. Before you decide to examine the lint in my belly button."

He nodded distantly. "Show him where you left his car, Cleve."

I followed Cleve's swaying hips through the door, along a narrow hall and out the front door. It was pretty dark, but I could make out some lilac bushes in front of the porch and there were three or four big trees between the house and the highway. We went down the three steps and around the corner of the English-type red brick bungalow. After a few yards, I felt a cinder driveway underfoot, and there was the Plymouth.

When I was behind the wheel, Cleve closed the car door and stood by the open window, his face a pale blob in the darkness. "You're out a ways from town, peeper. Turn right on the highway and keep going till you hit Peterson Road. You ought to know the way after that."

He moved back and I started the motor and rolled carefully along the cinders to the highway. It had four lanes, and at that hour of the morning there was no traffic to speak of.

Three hundred yards after I was on the pavement, I passed a roadhouse. It had a glass-brick front alongside a circular driveway, and a blue and red neon sign on the roof said: LEON'S. The parking lot to one side was nearly filled with upper-bracket cars and I caught the beat of a dance orchestra above the sound of my motor.

I knew about Leon's. Dine and dance and drink . . . and if you had a card with Tony Leonardi's initials in one corner you could go in the back room and make like you were Nick the Greek—if you had the money.

Maybe it took Tony's initials to let you gamble at Leon's. But from where I sat, it looked like the take went to a man named D'Allemand.

· 10 ·

There are a lot of hotels like the Northcrest along Dearborn Parkway and North State and as far west as LaSalle.
Some go up fifteen or twenty floors and some never get
past the third, but they are all the same really. They cater
to people who call themselves Bohemians, and the hotel
help acquires a permanent leer from long familiarity with
the psychopathic antics of some of the guests.

I leaned on the black-glass counter in the Northcrest
and showed three prongs of a 1928 deputy sheriff's star
to a small middle-aged clerk with ninety-year-old eyes
and rouge on his lips. I could have shown him a suspender
button and had the same reaction. He sneered at the
buzzer and he sneered at me and waited for me to say
something bright.

"It's about this Marlin murder," I said. "I'd like to
kind of take a look at his apartment."

He wasn't impressed. Nothing had impressed him since
his fifteenth birthday. "You would have to see the manager about that, mister."

"Where do I find the manager?"

A burly guy in coveralls and cap came into the lobby
carrying a pair of new telephone directories under each
arm. He stacked them on the counter next to me and
said, "Them are the four you was short," to the clerk.

The clerk sneered at him too . . . but not quite as
openly as he had at me. "What about the old ones?"

"They'll be picked up."

"When? They been stacked up here for two days and they take up room."

"They'll get picked up, mister," the man said. He sounded as though he had been saying the same thing for days. "I just bring 'em in. That's all I do."

He turned and went out into the morning sunlight. The clerk twitched his pointed nose and bit his lower lip and came within a shade of stamping his foot. While he was getting over it, I stood there and looked around. A couple of high-backed chairs in dark wood, with dark-red frieze seats, flanked the arched cream-colored stone entrance to the lounge. The blinds were drawn in there, cloaking the room with a dusty dusk that gave to the overstuffed couches and chairs an atmosphere of unnatural lusts.

By the time I got back to him, the middle-aged clerk had dug out an ink pad and a number stamp and was checking a list to learn what numbers should go on the new directories. I said: "Where can I find him?"

He put the stamp down like a girl returning your engagement ring, and gave me the frigid eye. "Find *whom*?"

That was all right. There are times to get tough and there are times when being tough doesn't get you anything. A cop with the city behind him would have thrown his weight right in that pansy's lap and got what he wanted. I didn't have a city behind me; I was just a private guy.

"The manager," I said. "I wanted to see him. About getting a look at Marlin's apartment."

He said, "The manager is out," and picked up the stamp. That should finish me. I was supposed to say, "Thank you," and crawl out the front door.

I reached in my pocket and took out a five-dollar bill and began twisting it around in my fingers. I did it idly, unobtrusively; it was just something to play with.

"Go on with you," I said politely. "I'll bet you're the manager. I can tell an executive when I see one."

He put down the stamp again but kept his hand on it.

He managed to look at me and the bill at the same time. He said, "The police have been through Mr. Marlin's effects."

"I know," I said. "There are just a couple of points I want to check on."

"I'd have to send somebody up with you."

"Sure." I pushed the bill toward him. "Would this pay for his time?"

I never saw that bill again. He went over to the switchboard and plugged in a line and fiddled the key. He jerked out the cord and came back to the counter, said, "Just a minute," and went back to stamping numbers on the phone books.

A boy of about eighteen came into the lobby from the inner corridor. His face was older than mine and he was wearing a maroon bell jacket and gray slacks. There were spots on one of the jacket sleeves and two of the buttons were missing. He came up to the desk and said, "Yes, sir," to the clerk. He made it sound like a swearword.

The clerk took a key from one of the pigeonholes behind him and handed it to the boy. "This gentleman is from the police, Fred. He wants to look through Mr. Marlin's apartment. You can wait until he's through."

I said, "Nothing's been taken from the apartment?"

"No. Other than some personal things, like letters. The police took them. We're awaiting word from our attorneys before disposing of the rest."

I said, "Okay," and let Fred lead me over to the automatic elevator across the lobby. He followed me into the cage and closed the outer door and pushed the top button. The inner door slid shut and we started up, slowly, with a purring sound.

Fred folded his arms and leaned against one of the panels with his back to me. I looked at my reflection in the chipped mirror on the back wall and decided I could use a haircut.

At the top floor, five, the cage shuddered to a stop.

Fred opened the doors for me and I trailed after him down a narrow corridor that smelled of tobacco and cologne and depravities.

We stopped in front of a walnut-stained door with 532 in bronze numerals on it. Fred used the key and let me go in first.

There were two rooms and a bath. The living room proved to be better than I might have expected. It was fairly large, furnished with cherry-red mahogany pieces, and a light and dark striped green tapestry on the couch and lounge chair. The rug was sand-colored broadloom, and figured russet drapes and a valance framed the three windows overlooking the parkway.

The bedroom was small and masculine, with two small Chinese rugs on the polished floor. A heavy walnut chifforobe stood along one wall, with a pair of German silver military brushes placed at an angle on the top. The bed was low and narrow, with a square headboard and an orange batik spread that was too gaudy for the rest of the room. The bathroom was just a bathroom.

I made like a detective. I dug into everything. I found out a few things, too. I learned that the late Mr. Marlin bought his shirts at Field's, his ties at Sulka's, his underwear and pajamas at Finchley's, his suits at Rothschild's and Carson's. Only his socks baffled me. I learned he shaved with an electric razor. I found out what kind of soap and deodorant he used, and I discovered he liked lavender dusting powder. Paul Pine, the supersleuth.

I pushed past Freddie and went back to the living room. I took the place to pieces and put it back together again. Nothing. Not a thing. The cops had taken everything that could tell about Jerry Marlin. There wasn't even a matchbook cover to tell where he bought his cigarettes or did his off-duty drinking.

I stood in the middle of the rug and mangled a cigarette and looked for some angle I might have missed. The telephone. I walked over to the niche in the wall where it stood and examined the wood around it, hunting for phone numbers. There weren't any.

I took the phone book from the shelf underneath and glanced at the inside cover to see if any numbers were written in the spaces provided. It was as clean as a monk's mind. It would be; the book was brand-new.

Brand-new. I turned back to the outside cover and saw the neat black numbers 532 in one corner. I thought of something. I got excited thinking about it. I said, "Freddie."

He straightened up from where he was leaning against the wall watching me. "Yes, sir?"

"These phone books were just changed?"

"Yes, sir."

"The old ones have room numbers on them too? Like these?"

"Yeah. Yes, sir. We do that on all the books soon's we get them. That keeps——"

"Never mind what it keeps," I said. "The clerk downstairs said the old books hadn't been picked up yet. Where are they?"

"Why, in some boxes down on the first floor next the service elevator. The phone people——"

"Show me."

He took me down in the service elevator and we stepped out into a big square room with whitewashed walls just off the alleyway. There was a lot of miscellaneous junk scattered around, but all I was interested in were four or five big pasteboard cartons filled with telephone directories with pale green covers.

Freddie stood there with his mouth open while I dug into them. I didn't hit pay dirt until near the bottom of the second box. The numbers 532 jumped out at me and I sat down on a pile of the books and flipped back the cover.

Four names, with telephone numbers behind them. No

addresses. I got out my notebook and a pencil and copied them down.

Millie	*GRA 9165*
Liquor store	*DEL 3311*
Ken	*ROG 0473*
Leona	*AUS 0017*

The first three were written with pencil, the last with ink. That meant Leona's name had been put down some time after the others. They had met and got around to being friends . . . such good friends, in fact, that he had her phone number listed along with the place he bought his liquor. Pythias never rated any higher with Damon.

The notebook and pencil went into my pocket. "Back to the desk, Freddie," I said cheerfully. "I aim to ask your boss something."

"He ain't no boss of mine," Freddie growled, but he took me through a door and along a corridor and into the lobby.

The clerk was sorting mail. I rapped on the counter and he turned around and gave me one of his sneers. It seemed I had used up my five dollars' worth of co-operation. I said, "You keep a record of outgoing calls. Let me have those on 532 for as far back as you've got them."

He bristled a little at my tone. "It seems you don't know much about the police for a man who claims to be one. They took those records yesterday. I have a receipt."

It didn't surprise me any. The homicide boys weren't always so thorough. Once in a while you could pick up something they'd missed:

I tried to think of something else. "What about incoming calls?"

"There is no record of them. Naturally." His tone said I was a fool.

"There's a record kept of incoming long-distance calls," I said.

I had him there. He bit his lip and twitched his nose before he got around to saying, "Mr. Marlin received no long-distance calls."

Freddie kicked a hole in that one for him. He said, "Yes, he did too, Mr. Simack. Maybe a week back, he did. I was on the board, Mr. Simack. From San' Anita, I think. I remember."

Mr. Simack gave Freddie a glare you could have boiled water with. He bent down and dug around under the ledge and finally came up with a clipboard holding some ruled sheets with writing on them. He slapped it down in front of me without a word and went back to sorting mail at the far end of the counter.

There had been two long-distance calls for Jerry Marlin during the two months or so he had lived at the North-crest. Both came in within the past two weeks—one on June 14, the other three days later—and both were from San Diego. Freddie's mention of Santa Anita was the natural error of a man who thinks a nose is the part of a horse where you put two dollars.

It wouldn't be any trick to find out who had placed those calls, provided they hadn't been made from a pay station. But that could come later. First there were the numbers I'd found in Marlin's phone book to dig into. Actually there were only two; Leona Sandmark I already knew about, and I didn't think the liquor store was going to be much help.

I gave Freddie a dollar, since he would never see any of the five in Mr. Simack's pocket, and drifted out onto Dearborn Parkway.

It was half an hour short of noon. The sun was hot against the pavement and the humidity made my clothes a lump of sodden cloth. Five minutes under a shower right then would have been like two weeks in the mountains.

But I was a workingman. I crawled into the Plymouth and drove slowly downtown.

· 11 ·

Instead of going directly to the office, I had a light lunch where there was air conditioning, then dropped in at the bank and deposited most of the money that had been pushed at me during the past two days. That made it well after one o'clock by the time I crossed the empty reception room and unlocked the inner office door and went in.

I opened the window and put my hat on one of the file cabinets and got out of my coat. There was mail under the slot: an ad on men's suits, a letter from a girl I used to know who was now private secretary to a big shot in a New York advertising agency, and a short note on a fancy letterhead from Cliff Morrison out in Los Angeles, asking when I was going to get tired of being my own boss and go to work for his detective agency.

The ad went into the wastebasket and the letters into the middle drawer. I mopped my face with my handkerchief and lighted a cigarette and got out my notebook with the phone numbers in it.

Millie was on top. Okay . . . Millie. I dialed the number and hooked a leg over the chair arm and swung my foot and waited.

"Hel-lo."

She had a blonde voice with a kittenish drawl, and I could feel her yawn all the way over here.

"Millie?"

"Uh-hunh."

"This is Paul."

"Oh? Hiyoo, honey?"

Hell, I didn't need television. She was in the middle of a crumpled bed in a one-room kitchenette apartment. There were hairpins and spilled face powder on the dresser and pieces of Kleenex stained with lip rouge on the carpet and stockings and rayon panties drying in the bathroom. She was sprawled out with her head on a pillow and the receiver against her ear and her free hand fluffing her blonde mop which could stand a new permanent and a fresh rinse.

I said, "Millie, Jerry Marlin is dead."

"Oh?" She yawned, a delicious, intimate little yawn. Turkey had signed an agreement with Bulgaria on importing manganese ore, Kansas City had beat Milwaukee 5 to 4 in the tenth, Jerry Marlin was dead, Labrador was having a heat wave. "Gee, I'm sure sorry to hear that. When'd it happen?"

"Night before last. Don't you read the papers?"

"I guess I must of missed it. What *you* been doing, honey? You haven't been around lately."

I put back the receiver and looked at my fingernails. She probably knew Jerry . . . and fifty others like him. Every man has that kind of phone number stuck around somewhere.

I made a decision. I picked up the receiver again and called long distance and said: "I want someone at the telephone company in San Diego, California."

"Did you want to make a station-to-station call?"

"That's the ticket."

"What's your number, please?"

I gave it to her and waited. There followed some chitchat between various operators that was none of my business. Pretty soon someone far off said, "This is the telephone company," and my operator said "Chicago is calling. Go ahead, party."

I said, "Hello. I want some information on a long-distance call from San Diego to Chicago that was made on June 14.''

"One moment, please.''

A few seconds later another female came on the wire and I said, "My name is Jerry Marlin, in Chicago, Illinois. On June 14 I received a call from San Diego. It could have been placed by one of several people and I neglected to get the name. Can you tell me the name of the party and from where the call was placed?''

"It will take a little time, Mr. Marlin. Do you want to hold the wire?''

"All right. Remembering, of course, that this is a long-distance call.''

I blew smoke at the ceiling and doodled on a scratch pad and waited. . . .

"Hello, Mr. Marlin.''

"Yeah?''

"That call was placed by a Mr. Kenneth Clyne, from room 628, Hotel San Diego.''

I wrote the name and address on the scratch pad and hung up. Kenneth Clyne. And on the list of numbers copied from those in Jerry Marlin's phone book was one that read: *Ken . . . ROG 0473.* Things were looking up.

I did some thinking around. San Diego. Somewhere during the past few days I had run into something else that had to do with California. It wasn't until I went carefully back over the events of the past three days that I found what it was.

A picture. A snapshot of a girl in shorts and a sweater against a background of bougainvillaea and pepper trees. You find bougainvillaea and pepper trees in California. San Diego is in California. Pretty thin, so far, but it could get thicker.

I used the phone again, calling a Central exchange number, and asked for a Mr. Ingram, the attorney who had recommended me to John Sandmark. I had found some jewelry his wife lost in a stick-up, one time, and he thought I was pretty hot stuff.

Ingram was a big, bluff, hearty guy and he came on the wire booming, "Hello, Paul. Glad to hear from you. What's on your mind?"

"Nothing special," I said. "I just wanted to thank you for throwing some business my way."

"John Sandmark? Glad to do it, Paul." His voice went down. "Speaking of the Sandmarks, what's this about the daughter being mixed up in some killing?"

"All I know is what I see in the papers," I told him. "My job has nothing to do with it. Far as I know, she isn't involved. Just an unfortunate choice in escorts."

"I suppose that's it." He sounded doubtful. "They're nice people. How did you get along with John?"

"Fine. Incidentally, is he a native of Chicago?"

"Native? Why, I guess you could call it that. He was born here, but after college he went out to California. Married out there; his father-in-law owned the Gannett Armored Express Company, with branches in several West Coast cities. When the old man died, the business went to John. He sold out shortly afterward and came back to Chicago with his wife and daughter. That's been— oh, a good fifteen years ago, I'd say."

I had what I wanted. I thanked him and hung up and leaned back and swung my foot while I tried on a few facts for size.

Jerry Marlin had been running around with a cute little society number named Leona Sandmark. Leona's stepfather had hired me to get something on Jerry Marlin. The Sandmark family once lived in San Diego. A close friend of Marlin's had been in San Diego recently and had telephoned Marlin twice from there. Marlin had been talking around about knowing where the body was buried . . . a common way of saying he had something hot on somebody—something so hot that he expected to get a lot of money out of it. That meant blackmail.

The facts fitted. And this is how they fitted: Marlin meets Leona Sandmark. From some remark she may have dropped, or from some lead that came to his hands through knowing her, he gets started on something the family is trying to hide. The roots of the secret are in San Diego. Marlin can't get out there himself to investigate, so he sends his best friend, a guy named Ken Clyne. Clyne gets the dope and comes back and gives it to Marlin. So Marlin starts putting the squeeze on one of the Sandmarks.

Which one? Well, it can't be Leona; she was just a kid when she left San Diego. That makes it the old man. But the old man decides to hit back. He hires a private dick to get something on Marlin. Then he goes out and shoots Marlin in the back. If facts come out that make him a suspect, he can say he offered that private dick a nice bonus to keep Marlin from bothering his charming daughter. "Naturally I didn't mean murder, gentlemen; I merely wanted Mr. Pine to get something so damning on Mr. Marlin that my daughter would be relieved of his attentions."

I began to wonder about Mr. Sandmark.

There was another angle. This guy Ken Clyne may have decided there was no reason why he shouldn't get rid of Marlin and put the squeeze on Sandmark by himself. No sense splitting all that dough two ways.

I kind of liked that one.

The time had come to see a man . . . a man named Ken Clyne.

The phone again. I called a special office at the Rogers Park exchange and asked for the listing on Rogers Park 0473. The girl gave it to me and I wrote it down on the scratch pad and cradled the receiver.

The Lakefield Apartments, 5312 Lakewood. Out on the North Side, a block north of Foster Avenue, a few blocks in from the lake shore. Not a neighborhood for the wealthy, but not a slum district either.

I took out the .38 and moved it around thoughtfully in my hands . . . and slid it back in my underarm holster. Since I was going to call on a guy that could have bumped Jerry Marlin, it might be smart to take some heat with me.

I put on my hat and coat and went out into the summer sun.

The Lakefield Apartments was an oblong gray stone building of seven floors. It needed sandblasting and a fresh paint job on the woodwork around the windows. There was a dark green canvas canopy with the words LAKEFIELD APARTMENTS in white letters on the sides and the number 5312 on the section facing the street.

I opened one of a pair of copper screen doors with diagonal brass rods across them for handles, and walked into a good-sized lobby with light gray stippled-plaster walls and a Caenstone trim. On one side was a sunken lounge that looked a lot more cheerful than most apartment lounges, and there was a semicircular polished red-sandstone ledge across from it where the office and switchboard were kept.

An elderly man with glasses and a shiny bald head said, "Good afternoon," in a gentle voice from behind the ledge. He had a thin body and a knifeblade face, and the skin of his neck seemed mostly wrinkles under a stiff detachable white collar and a black four-in-hand tie.

I said, "Mr. Clyne is expecting me. What's his apartment number?"

"3H, sir. But I'm afraid he isn't in."

I appeared to be as surprised as he thought I should be. "I don't get it," I said. "I was supposed to meet him here today at two-thirty. Isn't he back from San Diego?"

"Oh, yes, sir. Over a week now. He went out just a few minutes ago. Would you care to wait? Possibly he just step——"

He looked past my shoulder and raised his voice. "Oh, Mr. Clyne. This gentleman is waiting for you."

I turned around and there was a tall square-shouldered lad about my own age standing there looking at me. He had the high rounded forehead of a bank examiner, with regular features to match. His suit was of gray twill and not particularly well tailored. He held a panama hat with a narrow blue band in one hand and a cigarette hung between the fingers of the other. There was a folded copy of an afternoon edition of the *Daily News* shoved into one of his jacket pockets. His sharp blue eyes went over me carefully and without recognition. That was to be expected since, to my knowledge, he had never seen me before.

I said, "Hello, Ken. Where can we talk?"

He studied me warily, suspicious as an orchestra leader's wife. "I don't recall knowing you."

"I'm an old friend of Jerry's."

His eyes widened slightly but not with relief. He said, "What do you want?"

"What I want won't sound good in public."

That didn't seem to bother him especially. He said, "Who are you?" still chilly, still tough.

"All right," I said. "If you want to talk in front of people, let's go down to Eleventh and State where a police sergeant can take it down in shorthand."

"Come up to my apartment."

He turned around stiffly and stalked over to the elevator a few feet past the desk, and I tagged along behind him.

We got out at the third floor and went along a pleasant corridor to a door marked 3H. He produced a key chain and opened up and I followed him into a wide dim cool-looking living room, With a bedroom off it visible through an open door. He shut the hall door, spun around and glared at me.

"All right," he snarled. "Spit it out. Who are you and what do you want?"

I lifted my eyebrows at him. "Just like that?"

He gave me a thin smile. He now had charge of the situation. "Exactly like that."

"Okay," I said. "It keeps from wasting time. My

name is Pine and I'm a detective and where were you at
four o'clock yesterday morning?''

I would hate to be as stupid as his eyes said I was.
He gave a sharp snort that could have been a laugh and
turned his back on me to go over and sit down on a
padded ledge in front of the room's three windows. I
stood where he had left me, my hat pushed back on my
head and my arms dangling. He eyed me with cool con-
tempt and gave an airy wave of his cigarette and said,
''Is this a pinch?''

''It can grow to be one.''

''You're wasting your time.''

''I've got the time to waste.''

''You didn't have, a minute ago.''

''Be cute tomorrow,'' I said. ''I asked you a question.''

''I was in bed.''

''Here?''

''Yes.''

''Alone?''

''Certainly.''

''I didn't mean to insult you,'' I said.

He colored up and his fingers worked but he didn't
say anything.

''How was the trip to San Diego?'' I asked.

Wariness veiled his eyes. ''Who said I was in San
Diego?''

''*I* said you were in San Diego.'' I put an edge on my
voice. ''I know when you were there and I know why
you were there. That makes two of the reasons I'm asking
where you were at four yesterday morning. Now start
using that tongue before I wipe your nose with it.''

His hands balled and he hopped off the ledge with his
not very strong jaw shoved out. ''Don't talk that way to
me!'' he sputtered. ''John or no John, I don't take that
kind of stuff.''

I walked up to him and put a palm where his lapels
crossed and slammed him back onto the window seat.

''You'll take it, sweetheart. I'm talking about a murder

and you know whose murder. Tell me you don't know whose murder and I'll feed you knuckles until you puke."

A white ring formed around his mouth and his eyes rolled a little. "I read the papers," he mumbled. "I know Jerry was killed around that time, but I had nothing to do with it."

"You had a reason to plug him," I said. "You had a hell of a good reason. There isn't a better reason than money. After you picked up that information out on the West Coast, you knew as much as Marlin. Get him out of the way, you figured, and the dough would go to you. All of it. So you put some bullets in him. Get your toothbrush and a clean handkerchief, lover. You and me are going downtown."

"No!" The courage was leaking out of him like sweat from a steel puddler. "I didn't kill Jerry. I didn't know what angles he was working. He was too closemouthed to spill anything."

"What did you find out at the San Diego end?"

"Nothing that was any good to him."

"Cut it, Clyne. I won't take that kind of answer."

"But it's true! Jerry told me the information I brought back was worthless to him. It didn't seem to bother him, though; he said what he already had would get him five thousand down and five hundred a month until the big pay-off worked out."

"What big pay-off?"

"That's what he wouldn't tell me."

"Give me the details on what you were digging into out on the Coast."

He wet his lips while his eyes slid nervously about the room. "I . . . can't go into that. It would tie me up with something else. I'm not going to get involved in—in anything."

"That's a laugh," I said. "You're in over your hat-band right now and you know it. Don't make us pound it out of you, Clyne."

His jaw set. "It don't go, copper. I didn't shoot Jerry and you can't make saying I did it stick. So go ahead and take me in and the hell with it."

Rats can get as stubborn as people. I swung a chair around and sat down facing him with the chair's back between us. I lighted a cigarette and rested my arms across the back of the chair and blew smoke through my nose and gave him the gimlet eye. I said:

"Maybe we can kind of make a deal. You say you didn't do in your pal, so I'll play it along that way for a while. My interest is in finding out who did kill him, and you can help me find out.

"I'm not one of the City boys. I'm a private eye and I've got a customer who wants to know who kissed off Marlin . . . and why. Far as I know the homicide lads don't have you linked up with Marlin. They don't necessarily have to either, if you feel like playing catch with me."

Relief piled back into his face and he began to get cocky again. "A snooper, hunh? I should of caught on when you didn't flash a buzzer on me."

"All I carry is a sheriff's star," I said. "But I can get the boys at Central to show you the real thing."

His lips stopped curling. "What do you want to know?" he muttered.

"The works. Some of it I know already. But don't let that handicap you. Just start at the beginning and get it all in."

He fumbled for a cigarette and I tossed him my matches. He sucked in smoke and let it trickle out and stared at the rug. "Jerry looked me up about three weeks ago," he began. "He told me he was running around with a hot little mouse named Leona Sandmark, whose old man had a bankful. Jerry said he'd stumbled onto something that could turn into a lot of money if it was handled right, but that it would take a while to really clean up unless he could uncover more information. He said he had a lead that might get him what he needed, but someone would have to help him run it down, as he couldn't afford to let things cool off by going out of town.

"It seems the Sandmarks came here from San Diego about fifteen years ago. About eight or ten years before that, Sandmark, who was just a working stiff, fell into a sweet spot with his boss's daughter and married her. Her old man was Michael Gannett, who owned an express company out there.

"Before that, the Gannett doll had married one of the company officials, a guy named Raoul Fleming . . . a fast-stepping lad, from all reports. Well, it seems Fleming tried to knock off the contents of the company safe one night, but something went wrong and a watchman got killed. Fleming scooped up fifty grand and took it on the lam.

"This was back in the early twenties, before outfits like Gannett's were careful to fingerprint the help, so all they had on Fleming was his description. They got readers out on him and there was quite a hunt, but he never showed. Meanwhile, Sandmark sucked around Fleming's wife and talked her into divorcing her husband and marrying him. This Leona Sandmark was Fleming's kid, and just a baby when all this took place."

He looked up at me to see how I was taking it. "And that," he said, "is all there was to it. Gannett died about five or six years later, leaving everything to Sandmark's wife, which is how Sandmark came to get it. He sold out the company and moved his family to Chicago. His wife died right after that."

I sorted it over in my mind. "Did Marlin know any of this before he sent you out there?"

"No. All he seemed to know was that there had been some trouble in the family back in San Diego that involved the girl's real father."

"And what you've told me is all you were able to dig up out there?"

"You've got the works, Pine."

"Nuts!" I said. "Marlin could have got all that out of the back files of a newspaper. He'd have been better off letting a private dick do his snooping—if he could find one who didn't mind dabbling in a little polite blackmail."

I thought some more, then said, "This Fleming. The case against him was tight?"

"Tight as a ten-day drunk. He left prints all over the place; the gun used was his; fifty G's was gone and so was he. What more would you need?"

It looked like enough, all right. I fingered through what Clyne had told me, looking for some angle I might have missed.

"Any loose ends that could have meant something?"

He stopped in the middle of shaking his head, and a couple of wrinkles developed in the smooth rounded surface of his forehead.

"Come to think of it," he said slowly, "the same morning they found the dead watchman and the empty safe, one of the Gannett guards didn't report for duty. Man named Engle . . . Engle—no, Ederle. Jeff Ederle. For a while there the law thought he might have figured in the caper with Fleming; but it turned out later he'd been cozying with the wife of a San Diego gambler and had probably taken a powder to keep his health. Those Coast boys play pretty rough, I hear."

"What did Marlin hope to get from all this?"

"I told you that," Clyne said impatiently. "He had an idea maybe there were angles that didn't get into the papers. Sandmark could have had a hand in that robbery somehow. You must admit it was sure as hell nice the way things worked out so he could marry all that money. Gannett left better than a million."

"I suppose the papers out there really played up the killing?"

"Yeah. Pictures of the principals, diagrams, life histories—it chased everything else off the first three pages for a week.''

"But none of it could do Marlin any good?"

"So he told me. He said he guessed he could get along on what he already had—at least until the big dough was untied. And he did say he didn't think it would be too long until then."

"Meaning what?"

He scowled. "We've been over that, Pine," he complained. "I don't know what he meant. My personal belief is that he was putting the bite on Sandmark on some other matter. It's possible, you know, that Sandmark put those slugs into Jerry—either by himself or by hiring somebody to do it for him."

I sighed. "Could be." I got off the chair, and Clyne went with me to the door. In the hall, I turned to where he was standing in the open door, and said:

"Keep thinking about it, Clyne. You may remember something I can use. If you do, call me. There could be dough in it for you."

"Where do I reach you?"

I got out a business card and wrote my hotel phone number on the back and gave it to him. "If I'm not at the office, leave a message with the hotel operator."

"Okay."

I rode down to the first floor and got into my heap and drove back to the office.

· 12 ·

There weren't any customers. I sat down behind the desk and put my heels on the blotter and unfolded the *Daily News* I had picked up after parking the car. The heavy blue line along the right side of page one still smelled strongly of printers' ink.

I found two items on page three that were worth reading all the way through. One told about the inquest, that same morning, on the Marlin murder. Leona Sandmark, being related to a million dollars, came in for a lot of favorable and sympathetic mention. The rest was just words about no one knowing anything about anything, and at the request of the police, proceedings were postponed a few weeks.

On the other side of the same page was a two-column follow-up of the story about the unidentified corpse twelve preachers had buried. There was a small cut of the dead man's face—the kind of picture taken after death for police files. It was the face of a man who could have been almost any age past forty; a thin, hard-bitten face without much chin; a face that once might have been on the handsome side in a sort of dashing, to-hell-with-you way. The article itself wasn't much: a few stickfuls of type about "the unusual turn taken by what seemed nothing more than an obscure murder, has the police digging frantically for new information."

I grunted and turned the page. While I was in the middle of O'Brien's column, the phone rang sharply. Or maybe it just seemed to ring that way.

I picked up the receiver and said, "Hello."

"Mr. Pine?" It was a man's voice, deep and brisk and dry.

"Yeah. Who's this?"

"I would rather not mention names over the phone. At least, not my name. Let's say, instead, that I'm the man who paid you five hundred dollars very early this morning."

That made it D'Allemand. "Okay," I said. "What can I do for you?"

"How is your head?"

"It's a little lopsided but I'm still wearing it."

The receiver made a dry sound that might have been a chuckle. "Are you making any progress, sir?"

"On what?"

"On what I hired you to do."

"I've been looking around here and there," I said.

"Was Clyne able to tell you anything of value?"

Anger began to turn over in me. I said, "You wouldn't still have a tail on me by any chance?"

His voice sounded stiff, probably because of my tone. "As you yourself pointed out, Mr. Pine, I do not overlook much. I like to keep informed on matters of importance to me. Does that answer your question?"

My fingers tightened on the receiver until the knuckles shone. I said, "Get that tail off me, you hear? I don't like tails; they make me nervous and interfere with my work. You paid me to do a job and I'm doing it my way and I don't want any sidewalk superintendents. Is that clear?"

"I called to tell you, sir, that Clyne won't be able to do much for you. He is the friend of Marlin's I mentioned . . . the man I called in and paid money to. I am a bit curious as to how you learned about him."

I gritted my teeth into the mouthpiece. "Look. If you want my professional secrets, it'll cost you extra. Either unpin that goddam tail or send around to pick up your five hundred bucks and get yourself another investigator.''

I slammed up the receiver and put my feet on the floor, talking to myself, and got out the office bottle. While I was pouring a drink, the corridor door opened and closed and feet came lightly across the reception hall.

It was Leona Sandmark. She was wearing an expensively simple silvery green linen dress with a virginal V at the throat and a patch pocket over her left breast, and there was a white envelope bag with a green jeweled initial L, under her left arm. A circular white hat the size of a bicycle wheel slanted on her shining hair. She looked cool and competent and impossibly beautiful, and there was a humorous quirk to her lips and the corners of her gray-blue eyes.

She leaned a white-gloved hand against the frame of the door and said, ''Hello there.''

''And very nice, too,'' I said, getting up because I had been raised right when I was a kid. ''Won't you come in and sit down, Miss Sandmark?''

She came slowly over to the customer's chair and sat down gracefully, crossed her legs and laid the bag on a corner of the desk. Her shoes were brown and white, open-toed. Her legs were just as lovely as I remembered them.

She sighed a little. ''Goodness, it's warm in here.''

''Take off your hat,'' I said, ''and let whatever air there is find you.''

She fumbled out a hatpin and took off the wheel and put it on the desk too. That didn't leave much surface showing but I wasn't using it anyway.

I watched her look around the office. The Varga calendar seemed to fascinate her. It was that kind of calendar. She said, ''I hope you don't mind my dropping in on you this way. Are you very busy?''

''I just this minute finished my midafternoon drinking,'' I said. ''Sorry I can't offer you one, but all I have is bad bourbon and a glass that needs washing.''

Her nose wrinkled a little and she laughed. "No, thank you. . . . I've been to a movie. It seemed much too warm to go back to the apartment."

"For that matter," I said, making light conversation, "it's too warm to be downtown at all."

"I had to come down. I was at the—the inquest this morning." She shuddered abruptly and her lips twitched. "It was rather horrible. I thought perhaps you'd like to hear about it."

"Not especially," I said. "Is there any reason I should hear about it?"

"Well . . ." She looked at me from the corners of her eyes. "You were there when Jerry . . . when it happened."

"So I was," I said. "Did that come out at the inquest?"

"Oh, no!" She seemed shocked at the question, as though I had accused her of a breach of faith or something. "You asked me not to tell anybody. . . . What did my stepfather hire you to do, Mr. Pine?"

"If you're being subtle," I said, "you need more practice."

I was given the benefit of a wide, uncomprehending stare. "That sounds like one of those 'fraught-with-meaning' statements, Mr. Pine. Would you mind making it a little clearer?"

I stared into her eyes, letting her see my poker face. "Not at all, Miss Sandmark. It goes something like this: You have a secret of mine—a secret the police might like to be let in on. But you wouldn't dream of telling them, because after all you and I are friends, and telling a friend's secret is simply not done. Of course, friends shouldn't have secrets from each other; otherwise they couldn't stay friends. So you would like me to tell you what my business was with John Sandmark."

She was young enough to get red in the face, but her eyes never wavered. "Well . . . what was your business with John?"

I leaned back in my chair and laced my fingers and smiled at her. "The real reason is going to disappoint you, Miss Sandmark. Your stepfather hired me to throw hooks into Jerry Marlin."

She gasped, and the color drained from her cheeks. "You mean . . . he hired you to . . . to . . . kill——" Her voice started as a whisper and got weaker with each word, dying out completely on the last one.

I said patiently, "Not to kill him, no. I don't get hired to kill people. I was hired to dig into Marlin's past and get something on him that would keep him away from you. You see, your stepfather didn't regard Marlin highly as a future in-law."

She looked away from me then, and her eyes turned soft and misty with a faraway expression. "That's like John," she murmured. "He has always insisted on protecting me, even when I didn't want, or need, protection. It's no wonder I'd do anything for him."

"Maybe he figures a girl like you could stand some protecting."

It took three seconds for that to sink in to where she could feel it. Then her eyes stopped being tender; they were blazing when she hit me with them. "What is that supposed to mean?" she demanded.

I said, "My God, you're touchy. I didn't mean anything in particular. Did I step on one of your corns?"

The heat faded from her eyes and the long dark lashes swept down, veiling them. She drew off her white gloves and laid them on the brim of the hat, took her purse in her lap and dug out a cigarette and a gold lighter. I had a match burning for her before she could use the lighter.

She exhaled a thin blue line of smoke, dropped the lighter back in the bag and snapped it shut. She was her old self again. She said, "I'll bet it would be fun to take you apart." She smiled when I looked startled. "I mean in an analytical sense, of course."

"Go as far as you like," I said.

"You've got a hard finish," she said slowly, not smiling now. "But I don't believe you are quite so hard underneath it. Perhaps that finish is there because you've seen too much of the wrong side of people. You go in for crisp speech and a complete lack of emotion. In a way you're playing a part . . . and it's not always an attractive part. Yet there's plenty of strength to you, and a kind of hard-bitten code of ethics. A woman could find a lot of things in you that no other man could give her." She flashed a sudden smile at me. "Besides, you're rather good-looking in the lean, battered sort of way that all sensible women find so attractive in a man."

"How you do go on!" I said. I lighted a cigarette and threw the match out the open window. "What shall we talk about next?"

"Are all detectives like you, Mr. Pine? I never knew one before."

"That makes us even," I said. "I never knew an heiress before."

"We should investigate each other."

Her eyes were daring me, provoking me. I sat there and smiled a meaningless smile and let funny notions roll around inside my skull. I thought of a high-school girl alone with a boy in a Wisconsin cabin; of a seven-kinds-of-crook who had messed around with that high-school girl when she was a little older; of a married man whose wife had named that same girl as corespondent in a divorce suit. And abruptly my notions no longer seemed funny. I said:

"I'm good at investigations. In this case, I would suggest dinner and a show and a ride by moonlight. I'm an open book when the moon hits me right. Come to think of it, there's that kind of moon tonight—or there will be."

This time she laughed—a full-throated laugh that was good to hear. "Are you trying to date me, Mr. Pine?"

"Not if you keep on calling me Mr. Pine."

"Paul? Paul. . . . That shouldn't be hard."

"You could make it 'darling' with a little practice."

The smile went off her face like a chalk mark under a damp cloth. I had gone a little too fast for her. I said, "Just clowning, Miss Sandmark. Anything unexpected develop at the inquest?"

She stared at me. "I thought you weren't interested in the inquest."

"I'm not. But I figured you wanted the subject changed."

To that I got an oblique answer. "I should be getting home. I took a taxi down; parking is such a problem in the Loop."

"I'll be glad to drive you home, Miss Sandmark."

"Oh, I wasn't hinting."

"I'll still take you home—if you like."

"That would be sweet of you . . . Paul."

My blood stirred. I have blood and it can be stirred. "Not at all . . . Leona."

That earned me another smile to tuck away. She stood up and anchored her hat, put on her gloves and picked up her purse. She tamped her cigarette out in the ash tray and went with me to the door. I was reaching around to close it when the phone rang.

"One minute," I said and went back and picked up the receiver and said, "Hello," into the mouthpiece.

"Pine?" A man's voice I didn't recognize, and I would hate to get as excited as it sounded.

"Yeah," I said. "This is Pine. Who——"

"I've got it, shamus! I had it right in my pocket all the time you were here and never knew it! No wonder——"

"Who is this?" I said mechanically. Actually I knew by now.

"Clyne. What the hell do you use for a memory? I tell you I've got the answer to everything!"

"Give."

He went cagy on me. "You said something about dough, Pine. I want to see some green in front of my eyes. Get over here and we'll do some haggling."

I glanced over to where Leona Sandmark was standing in the doorway watching me. Into the mouthpiece I said, "Are you doing a little high-powered guessing or do you really know something?"

"This is no guesswork. I leave that to private dicks. You want this, you come after it . . . with your hands full of money."

The click against my ear told me he had hung up. I replaced the receiver thoughtfully and went out into the reception room and locked the office door.

Leona Sandmark was watching me, a puzzled frown ruining her lovely brow. "Is something wrong, Paul?"

I said, "When were you in San Diego last?"

Her shoulders jerked and she stared at me, completely bewildered. "What in the world . . ."

I didn't say anything. I was waiting for an answer.

"If it makes any difference," she said shortly, "I was there last year for a month or two."

"It doesn't mean a thing," I said. "I just like to appear mysterious. It's an old detective custom. Incidentally, it looks like I'm going to have to renig on that lift home. Something's come up."

"Of course. Some other time, then."

"This isn't going to take all night," I said. "We could still get in that dinner and a show."

"You could call me," she said gravely. "The number is Austin 0017."

Just as gravely I wrote it down.

I left her at the corner of Jackson and Wabash, after getting her a cab, and went on to the lot to get my own car. I wasn't too excited about Clyne's call. He probably had remembered some minor detail and got all hot over it after tying some guesses on it. Either way, I couldn't let it go by without checking. In my business you never know. Nor in any other, I suppose.

Twenty-five minutes was long enough to get me there by way of the Outer Drive. I parked around the corner on Berwyn Avenue, got out of the car and walked along the quiet sun-filled street to the Lakefield Apartments.

The same bald-pated old gentleman was behind the desk. I nodded to him and went into the elevator and rode to the third floor.

There was an imitation pearl button set in the wood-work outside 3H. I pressed it and a buzzer sounded inside. Nothing happened and there was no sound of feet coming to answer the buzzer. I jabbed the button again but it didn't mean any more than the first time. I rattled the knob and the door swung back . . . and there he was.

I went in and closed the door and bent over him. He was lying on his belly and he looked all right except there was no back to his head. In the form of a neat circular stain in the blue-and-black patterned rug was a great deal of blood, with gray patches of stuff in it and a couple of hunks of white bone. He was still warm; he couldn't have been anything else after talking to me about half an hour earlier.

The rest of the room looked just as it had when I last was there. The bedroom door was still open and every-thing was neat and clean and in order. I took out my .38 and walked into the bedroom and snooped around. Nothing. The black-and-white bathroom didn't have any bloody towels in the bowl or red fingerprints on the walls. There were clothes in the closets but nobody was wearing them.

I hummed a little tune and went back into the living room and picked up the phone. It looked as though I wasn't going to have dinner with Miss Sandmark tonight.

"Office," a girlish voice said in my ear.

I was aware that the fingers of my right hand were beginning to ache a little. I looked down and saw I was still gripping the checked walnut handle of the .38. My face felt a trifle stiff as I smiled about it. I put the gun back under my arm.

"Office," the girlish voice said again, a little on the waspish side this time.

I let my breath out slowly. "Let's have some police, lady."

· 13 ·

I sat on the blue-and-gold rayon bedspread in the bedroom of the late Kenneth Clyne, and smoked a cigarette and waited for Lieutenant George Zarr to satisfy himself that the spindly-legged bedroom chair would hold his weight. Ike Crandall, an investigator from the State's Attorney's office, leaned against the closed bedroom door and tapped his lips lightly over and over with the stem of a gnarled black pipe.

Crandall was a new one to me—a slender, stoop-shouldered man in his early forties, with bushy graying hair and a long intelligent face and hooded eyes. His complexion had the faintly yellow cast that goes with a faulty liver.

Through the closed door came vague sounds as the homicide boys did the things the city paid them to do. A fly buzzed now and then against the screen of the open window in back of me, and street noises filtered in and died on the floor.

Zarr was finally ready. He put away the blue-bordered handkerchief he had used to mop the sweat from the gray slopes of his prominent jaw, blew out his breath and looked at me without pleasure. He said, "Let's have it, Pine. All of it."

"Sure," I said. "It begins with this Marlin killing a couple of days ago. I have a client who's interested in knowing who murdered him. I dug up a lead on this Kenneth Clyne; seems he was pretty thick with Marlin.

Anyway, I came out to see him earlier this P.M. and we had a talk. He wasn't able to give me much I could use, but said if anything occurred to him he'd let me know.

"Along about four o'clock he called me at the office and said to get out here quick, that he knew the answer to everything. At the time, I figured maybe he was being a little too optimistic. Now I'm not so sure. Anyway, I walked in and found him on the floor the way you saw him. I called you right away, just as any other public-spirited citizen would have done."

Lieutenant Zarr looked over at the placid expression on Crandall's face. Crandall shrugged slightly and went back to his lip tapping. I flicked ashes on the rug and just sat.

"Who," Zarr asked me, "is this party that's so interested in Marlin's murder?"

"Hunh-uh," I said. "I don't have to tell you that, Lieutenant. Not that I wouldn't like to, understand. My client wants to know who shot Marlin only because Marlin was a friend of his and he wants the killer to pay the hard way. Not that he thinks Homicide will gum up the job; it's simply that he wants it wound up quick. But he doesn't want to appear in the picture . . . and he won't. Not on my account he won't."

Zarr said with controlled savagery, "Why, you goddam piddling little bastard! Where do you get off—shoving the department around this way? You've been under my feet too much lately; I think I'll do something about it."

I rubbed a palm along one of my thighs and looked at the opposite wall. Crandall dug a transparent tobacco pouch out of a pocket and drew back the zipper and put some of the contents in the bowl of his pipe. He said, "There's no point in going off half-cocked, Lieutenant," in mild protest. "After all, Mr. Pine is working on our side of the fence." He gave me a friendly smile that was as empty as a bride's nightgown.

I said, "Yeah."

He struck a match against his thumbnail and took his time lighting his pipe. Zarr's bushy eyebrows came together in a scowl and he opened his mouth to say something, closed it instead and gave a meaningless grunt.

Crandall said, "You can understand our position, Pine. Anyone who has worked for the State's Attorney knows what we're up against."

He waited for an answer from me but didn't get one. He hadn't said anything yet.

"There's no reason why we shouldn't pool our information," Crandall continued, reasoning with me. "If we succeed in learning who killed Marlin and Clyne—they're tied together, of course—there's no reason why we can't let you have the information before it's made public. That way you can get your fee and nobody's the wiser." His hooded eyes shifted to Zarr. "That can be arranged, can't it, Lieutenant?"

Zarr said, "Why not?" and looked at me, no expression on his gray face.

"That will be dandy," I said. "Just as soon as I find out anything I'll run right over and tell you all about it."

The blood poured into Zarr's cheeks and he snarled, "Why, you——" But Crandall cut him off with a small motion of one hand. "Right now," he said mildly, "we'd like to know how you happened to learn that Clyne was mixed up with Marlin."

"I'm a detective," I said. "I went over where Marlin lived and I asked questions."

"You mean the Northcrest?"

"Yeah."

"We went through things pretty thoroughly there, Pine, but drew only a blank."

I grinned at him. "I'm pretty smart, hunh?"

Silence. I looked around for an ash tray, saw none, and compromised by grinding the butt into the rug with my heel.

Crandall said, "We want to be reasonable about this, fellow, but you're not helping any. Sandmark hired you to find out who killed Marlin, didn't he?"

"Why should he be interested?" I said. "I understand his daughter is in the clear."

"Who told you that?"

"Nobody. I'm going by the newspaper accounts."

"You ought to know better than that."

I shrugged. "That's all I had to go on."

Crandall bounced the tobacco pouch gently on his palm, studied me gravely for a moment, dropped the pouch back into his pocket, turned around and went out of the bedroom, closing the door softly behind him.

The room was quiet again. Zarr put his open hands on his knees and moved his fingers carefully up and down while he stared at them as though they belonged to someone else. A patch of sunlight made a sharp square on one of the side walls. The same fly droned fitfully against the screen.

Zarr stood up suddenly, said, "I told you I don't like coincidences, damn you," and hit me hard in the mouth with his right fist. I went over backward and fell to the floor on the opposite side of the bed. By the time I was back on my feet I was alone in the room.

My legs were shaking a little as I walked over and looked into the full-length mirror set into the closet door. My eyes stared back at me, hot, fever-bright, ashamed. A muscle in my left cheek began to twitch. There was blood at one corner of my mouth; as I watched, it trickled down to my chin, leaving a crooked red path. There was a tiny cut there and the underlip was beginning to swell. I stood there, waiting for that muscle to stop jumping and my legs to stop shaking. . . .

I went over and opened the door and walked into the living room. The body was gone, but there were chalk marks on the rug, and the puddle of blood and brains stuck out sharp and clear, as that kind of mess always does. A photographer with horn-rimmed glasses was putting plates in a black bag, and a little guy in a baggy blue suit was making a sketch in a notebook.

Over by the window seat Crandall and Zarr had their heads together. Crandall was holding a triangular piece of newspaper in the fingers of one hand. He thrust the paper out at me as I came over.

"This was found under the body, Pine. Know anything about it?"

It wasn't much larger than his hand. There was red on one corner . . . a sticky red that was beginning to turn dark brown. Along one side was a straight blue line of printers' ink.

"It's a piece of newspaper," I said.

"Hell, I can see that."

"Well, you asked me." I took off my hat and laid it on the window ledge and ran my hands through my hair and lighted a cigarette.

Crandall was staring at my face, his expression one of sudden concern. "Hey," he said, "there's blood on your mouth."

"So there is," I said coldly.

"What happened?"

There was a faint curl to Zarr's lips. I said, "I tripped over something. . . . Did you find the newspaper this hunk came from?"

"No." He was still staring at me. "Too bad about your mouth, Pine. What did you trip on?"

"Make it Mount Everest," I said wearily, "and the hell with it. I've been thinking things over, Crandall. Maybe I can put you onto something after all."

Crandall's smile was faintly sardonic as his eyes met Zarr's. "Funny how tripping over something can change a guy's way of thinking, eh, George?"

"Don't squeeze it too hard, Crandall," I growled. "It might break on you."

"Oh, don't think for a minute we don't appreciate

your help, Pine. Let's go back in the other room and you can have your say.''

"I'll say it right here,'' I told him. "It won't take too long.'' I leaned against the window frame and thought a minute. Crandall was watching me from under the hooded lids of his eyes, while Zarr still wore traces of his sneer.

"A lot of this,'' I began, "comes from putting two and two together. I can be wrong on some points but not on many. It all started around twenty-five years ago out in San Diego, California. A couple of guys were working for an armored-express company out there. One, the owner's son-in-law, was named Raoul Fleming; the other was John Sandmark.

"One night, Fleming, a pretty wild sort from what I hear, knocked off a watchman at the company and lit out with fifty grand. He made a clean getaway and nobody ever heard from him again. Meanwhile, John Sandmark held the wife's hand and sympathized her into getting a divorce and marrying him. When his father-in-law died, Sandmark was the boy who took over the business. Eventually he sold out and moved to Chicago with his wife and stepdaughter.''

I shifted my position and took a long drag on my cigarette. "Before I go any farther,'' I said, "I'd like to point out that something stinks about this job Fleming was supposed to have pulled. There he was—sitting on top of the heap, swell job, married to the boss's daughter, in a spot to take over a big company and his father-in-law's fortune when the time came. Still he tosses all that away on a crazy attempt to heist fifty G's. Maybe you two will buy it but I won't. I'll admit there was plenty of evidence to fasten the job on Fleming: fingerprints, his gun, all that. But for my money it still smells.

"All right. Now we come up to this year. Around a month ago a middle-aged man was found in a Madison Street hotel with his skull bashed in. No identification, no nothing—not even a toothbrush. Yet that Madison

Street killing ties right in with Sandmark and San Diego. In a minute or two I'll show you how it ties in.''

Zarr had stiffened the moment I mentioned the Madison Street killing. He muttered something under his breath that I didn't catch. It probably wasn't important anyway.

''About two-three months ago,'' I went on, ''Leona Sandmark, Fleming's daughter and now John Sandmark's stepdaughter, started to run around with Jerry Marlin—nightclub pickup from what I hear. Marlin was the kind of character that would take a fast dollar and not worry how clean it was. In some way he got hold of some dirt on Sandmark. It was pretty hot stuff the way he had it but he figured he could make it still better. With that in mind, he sent Ken Clyne out to San Diego to dig into that old robbery and killing. But Clyne came back with nothing to add to what Marlin already knew.

''Then Marlin gets knocked off. It could have been done by a lot of people we never heard of, or it could be by one of two people we have heard of. One of those two is Sandmark; the other was Clyne. Sandmark, because Marlin was blackmailing him; Clyne, because he wanted to take over the job himself.''

Crandall was pulling at his chin. ''You've left a couple of angles wide open, Pine. What did Marlin have on Sandmark, and how do you tie in this Madison Street killing?''

''Okay,'' I said. ''Those are good questions and I think I can give you a fair answer to at least the last one.

''When I saw Clyne here earlier this afternoon he told me he didn't know what Marlin had on Sandmark. He said he'd gone over the back-newspaper files in San Diego, read about the case, looked at the pictures, and so on, without having any luck. Yet around an hour after I left him, he was on my phone yelling he had the answer to everything and I should run over with my hands full of lettuce and buy it from him.''

I stopped and snicked cigarette ash onto the rug. ''Right

here," I said, grinning, "is where my knack of observing details pays off. By putting together a couple of what seemed to be only minor——"

"Skim it down!" Zarr interrupted angrily. "Let's have the rest of it."

"Well," I said, "when I came here the first time, I met Clyne down in the lobby. He had just come in from the street and there was a blue-streak edition of today's *News* in his coat pocket. I didn't think anything of it at the time; but on my way back to the office it happened I bought a copy of the same edition.

"On page three were two items of interest. One was on the Marlin inquest; the other was a follow-up to earlier stories about the stiff it took twelve preachers to bury. Along with this story was a picture of the guy. It wasn't a very good picture, but anybody who knew the guy would have recognized it.

"Now here's what I say happened. Clyne, reading his paper, turns to page three and sees the face of the unknown corpse. *He recognizes it as that of one of the principals in the San Diego caper*. Remember, he'd been studying those pictures out there."

Crandall and Zarr stared at each other in silence for a long moment. I sat down on the window seat, feeling suddenly very old and very tired, as though I'd run a hundred miles only to learn I must run all the way back again.

"No." Lieutenant Zarr was shaking his head. "You can't tell me Clyne could look at two pictures taken twenty-five years apart and identify them as being of the same man. That would be hard to do even for somebody who had known the guy personally. And Clyne didn't. The people in that Gannett case don't look today like they did when those pictures were taken in San Diego."

"He's got something there, Pine," Ike Crandall said.

"And you guys calls yourselves cops," I said. It was my turn to curl a lip, and I made the most of it. "This man the preachers buried was one of these lean-faced men who change very little between the ages of, say, thirty and fifty-five. A man who fattens up around the time he reaches middle age can be hard to make from an old picture, sure. But this one was skinny and he stayed skinny.''

Crandall nodded, impressed. ''That makes sense, George,'' he said to Zarr. ''A guy without much weight on him keeps on looking pretty much the same through the years.'' He eyed me thoughtfully. ''If you're right about this, Pine, that would make the Laycroft Hotel victim almost sure to be Raoul Fleming, Leona Sandmark's missing father.''

''Either him,'' I said, ''or a guy named Ederle—Jeff Ederle.''

They stared at me some more. ''And just who the hell,'' Zarr rasped, ''is Jeff Ederle?''

''He was a guard,'' I said, ''at the Gannett Express Company. He disappeared the day after Fleming was supposed to have rubbed out the watchman and gone south with the swag.'' I took a deep breath. ''I don't think much of it, though. The dead guy being Ederle, I mean. My guess is that he was Fleming all right. Ederle had a very good reason for getting out of San Diego when he did. Married-woman trouble. And if he did have something on Sandmark, why wait twenty-five years to put on the pressure?''

''It holds together, by God!'' Crandall was beginning to get excited. ''The way you tell it, it looks as if Fleming waited long enough for the heat to die out on the express job, then set about hunting up Sandmark. Maybe he figured Sandmark had framed that rap on him; maybe he was sore because Sandmark got his wife. Either way, Sandmark didn't want the best part of him, so he killed him or had somebody else do it. Then Jerry Marlin found out about it some way and started twisting the screws. So Sandmark gets rid of Marlin. . . .''

His voice trailed off and he did some lip chewing while he shaped things up in his mind. To me, he said, "But why would Sandmark want Clyne out of the way? And it has to follow: if he killed Marlin, he must have killed Clyne."

I shrugged. "That will have to be a guess, Crandall. Mine is that Clyne tried to bluff through a little blackmail of his own after Marlin was killed . . . and that was all for Clyne."

There was still plenty of skepticism on Zarr's thin face. He said, "The way you paint it, shamus, this Sandmark must be a dilly. Three murders in a month is better than par—even for this town."

"The hell of it is," I said, "nobody'd ever take him for a killer. He's big and he's no pansy, but he's more the bank-president type . . . the kind who'd use a mortgage instead of a blackjack."

Crandall rubbed his palms briskly together. "It looks like we'd better have a talk with this John Sandmark, George. Where does he live?"

"Oak Park," Zarr said slowly. "We better not go at this with our chins out, Ike. This Sandmark's liable to be potent stuff, what with all his money. You don't walk up to a million bucks and spit in its eye. Or do I have to tell you?"

"That doesn't buy him immunity from the law." Crandall's eyes took on a fanatical shine: a crusader after the wealthy infidel. "Sandmark's got some explaining to do. I don't say we should barge in and slap bracelets on him. It can be a matter of a polite call, a smooth approach, a few questions . . . then give him both barrels!"

But Zarr was shaking his head. "There's another angle, Ike. The Marlin killing is all Captain Locke's. When the stepdaughter's call came in early Wednesday morning, I sent the squad out and called Locke at home and told him about it. You know how he likes his name in the headlines. I knew damn well the papers would play up a killing involving a rich man's daughter. Locke has handled it all the way, and if we go shoving in our nickel's worth, he's going to get sore. He's the head of the department and he's my boss. I don't want him sore at me.''

Office politics. There may be a police department somewhere without it, but I never heard of it.

Crandall said hotly, ''Well, he's not *my* boss. You can pull in your neck if you want to, but I'm going out to Sandmark's and do some digging.'' He swung his eyes back to me. ''You seem to know a lot about Sandmark, Pine. How come? He a client of yours?''

''He came pretty near being one,'' I said. ''But it kind of fell through.''

''He didn't want you to rub out somebody, did he?''

''Go ahead, be funny,'' I said wearily. ''Just leave my name out of this when you talk to him, is all. I don't want it noised around that I do the cops' work for them. It could hurt my business.''

Zarr gave me a leer. ''Then you want to be careful about tripping over things. It seems as though you leak a lot of information when that happens.''

I put up a hand and touched my lips gingerly. ''Yeah. I'll admit I bruise easy. I don't always heal quick though. My memory won't let me.''

The lieutenant's leer became a thin smile. ''Don't stretch that memory of yours too far, sport. It might snap back and tear your head off.''

I stood up and took my hat off the ledge and put it back on my head. ''If you boys are through sticking pins in me, I'd like to go. I think maybe I got a date.''

Crandall said absently, ''It's up to Lieutenant Zarr, Pine. Personally I'd say you've been of great help to us and I appreciate it.''

Zarr jerked his head toward the door. ''All right, shamus, blow.''

I went out and walked slowly along the corridor to the

elevator and rode down to the first floor. The bald old gentleman behind the desk gave me an icy glare as though I was the one who had bled all over the upstairs rug. A dark-haired girl with a sallow skin peered around the switchboard at me with mingled loathing and fascination. I went out into the sun-yellowed street and dragged around the corner to where I had left the Plymouth.

It was still there. I climbed in behind the wheel and sat there for a minute or two, looking at nothing at all, fingering my swelling lip and thinking bitter thoughts.

I couldn't find anything admirable in throwing a man to the wolves, particularly since I was more than reasonably sure he had killed neither Marlin nor Clyne. But the real killer had to be smoked out and I was hard pressed for fuel. John Sandmark would have to serve that purpose. Let the cops think they'd bluffed me into talking. A hell of a lot I cared what they thought.

I started the motor, turned north at the corner and went home.

·14·

"It's probably too late for dinner and a show," I said. "But that's no reason why we shouldn't take in a couple of night spots, is it?"

Even on the telephone, her laugh was musical. "I'd just about given you up," she said. "Where are you?"

"At home. I just this minute got in. I'm weary and I smell of policemen but it's nothing a hot shower won't fix up."

"Policemen? Don't tell me you got yourself arrested!"

"I didn't miss it by far," I said. "I called on a man who wanted to see me, but somebody emptied the life out of him before I got there. The boys with the hard hats always ask a lot of questions about such goings-on."

"Heavens! Murder makes a habit of happening around you, it seems. I wonder if I dare go out with you."

"I've used up my quota for the month. You'll be as safe as a babe in arms. Which isn't a bad idea, come to think of it."

"I think I'll ignore that," she said severely. Anyway she tried to sound severe but it didn't work out too well. "About the night spots. I think I'd like that. Would you call for me around ten? And . . . detectives have dinner clothes, don't they?"

"I should hope to tell you," I said. "You don't think I go around eating in my underwear, do you?"

She laughed again, said, "See you at ten, Paul," and broke the connection.

I put back the receiver, said, "Dinner clothes yet!" and went into the bedroom and dug through the closet and hauled out the tuxedo I bought two years before to attend the dinner of the American Private Detectives' convention at the Hotel Sherman. That was the night I shook Ray Schindler's hand and drank twenty-seven Old-Fashioneds and woke up the next afternoon in a room with a northern exposure and a southern blonde.

There were no liquor stains on the suit and only two or three wrinkles. I figured no one would notice the wrinkles. The dress shirt in the bottom dresser drawer was still in the tissue paper the laundry had returned it in. I discovered they had managed to get the lipstick off the bosom.

I took my time over showering, shaving and dressing; and it was fifteen minutes past nine before I was ready to leave the apartment. I stopped for a last look in the mirror and it slapped me on the back and told me feminine hearts would go pitty-pat this night. I wondered about taking along a gun, decided it would spoil the coat's faultless drape and locked it away in a drawer. If Miss Sandmark made improper advances I could always appeal to her better nature.

Neither of my two hats went well with the monkey suit, so I wore my hair and let it go at that. I rode down in the elevator to keep from bending my knees more than necessary. Sam Wilson was behind the switchboard with his nose in another pulp magazine. Or maybe it was the same one.

He looked up as I came out of the elevator, said, "Evening, Mr. Pine," and waggled his eyebrows at the tuxedo.

I said, "How they going, Sam?"

He said, "Stepping out tonight, hunh?"

I said, "You've been reading my mail, damn you."

He was cut to the quick. It hadn't been sharp enough to cut to core. "I wouldn't do nothing like that, Mr.

Pine. Honest. I meant you being all dressed up and every-thing, you must be stepping out." His muddy brown eyes grew wistful. "A big society case, I bet. You sure lead yourself a tough life, Mr. Pine."

"Someday," I said, "I'll trade you and sit behind a switchboard that never buzzes and read detective stories."

He slid off the stool and came over to the counter and looked around the lobby with a secretive air, like a spy in an E. Phillips Oppenheim novel, and whispered: "Honest, Mr. Pine, was there really all that money in the package you had last night?"

Last night. It seemed a hundred years ago.

I matched his look at the lobby and put my lips near his ear and said, "Straight goods, Sam. Twenty-five grand. You know what I did with it?"

He was so excited he began to sweat. "No, sir. I can keep my mouth shut, Mr. Pine. You can tell *me*."

"Okay," I said. "I burned it and flushed the ashes down the can."

He straightened like somebody had used a thumb on him, said, "Aw, for Pete's sake!" in an offended tone and went back to his magazine.

They'll believe anything but the truth.

There was a thick hunk of moon out and you could see the stars if you tried hard enough. A hint of coolness in the air came from the first lake breeze in nearly a week. It would keep my collar from wilting. I got into the Plymouth, rolled down the windows and drove off into the night.

It lacked a few minutes of being ten o'clock by the time I pulled in at the curb in front of the Austin Boule-vard address. There were other cars moving along the street and I waited a minute or two to find out if I might have a tail. Nothing showed, however; it seemed D'Al-lemand had taken me at my word.

I got out and went past the spot where Jerry Marlin died with three holes in his back and his mouth full of blood, and on into the foyer of 1317, its imitation marble walls and tessellated flooring as antiseptic as I remembered them. I jabbed the button beside 6A and almost immediately the lock on the inner door began to click. I went through and rode the chrome-and-mirror cage to the sixth floor . . . and there she was waiting for me, with an uneven smile on her lips and fear in her eyes.

She said, "Come in, Paul. How nice you look," without any bounce to her voice. We went into the living room and she sat me in one of the two lounge chairs and put a glass in my right hand. She moved slowly over to the couch and sat down where the light from a table lamp wouldn't show her face clearly to me.

I drank some of my drink and put the glass on the corner of the coffee table and stared with approval at what I could see of her. I could see considerable. She was wearing a hunk of soft yellow stuff that narrowly missed being white. There wasn't enough above the waist to make Sunday dinner for a moth, but downstairs there were yards of it. Her shining reddish-brown hair was swept up on top of her head, with a pair of gold diamond-set clips above her ears to keep it off her face.

"You," I said, "are as lovely as the fourth queen in a poker hand. Also something is eating on you— something that wasn't there when I talked to you on the phone. Give it to me, beautiful."

She sat there and watched me out of a shadow, her breathing ragged, her lower lip twisted as if it was being punished for quivering. She said, "Paul . . ." stopped, swallowed, tried again.

"Paul, tell me what you know about Jerry Marlin's murder."

I shook my head. "I don't think I can do that."

"Why can't you?"

"Maybe because I don't know much about it."

"That's not an answer."

"It's the only answer you're going to get, Miss Sandmark."

Her hands came slowly together, the long, carefully groomed fingers curling about themselves. "Must you be disagreeable?"

"Tell me how to say 'no' agreeably."

"I'm sorry, Paul."

"That's all right," I said.

I sat there and watched her take deep unsteady breaths that forced her breasts against the tight-fitting bodice of the evening gown. Her hands were locked together in her lap but that didn't keep them from trembling.

"About a minute," I said mildly, "and you're going to throw a wing-ding they'll hear in Detroit. You're wound up tighter than a dollar watch, and the more questions you ask the tighter you get. Why don't you try giving some information instead of demanding it?"

She tried to knock off a light little laugh but it broke on her. "You run true to form, don't you, Mr. Pine? Detectives are all alike, aren't they? Even private detectives. Even private detectives with broad shoulders and bony faces and eyes that fool you into thinking they're honest eyes." Her voice was climbing. "All they really want is information—the kind of information they can use to hound and torture innocent people you l-love . . ."

I said, "Relax, Tallulah. We've run out of film."

That made her mad. She came off the couch like a cat off a stove and took a couple of steps toward me, her face white and twisted until it was hardly beautiful any more.

"Get out!" she said, her voice hardly more than a whisper. "Get out, you sneaking, filthy little—little——"

"—detective," I said. "And I'm not little, so watch your step." I picked up my glass and leaned back and grinned at her. "Sit down, Miss Sandmark, and try to be as nice as you look. I'm sure you didn't ask me to put on a boiled shirt and come over just to point out what a dirty name I am."

She backed up and let herself slowly down on the couch without taking her eyes off me. She was still angry, but it was an uncertain, groping kind of anger that was chiefly fear—fear that had nothing at all to do with me.

"They are after him, Paul." Her voice was still a whisper. "They say he killed him. He didn't kill him, Paul. I know he didn't. He couldn't kill anyone. . . ."

"If you say so," I said. I lighted a cigarette to give her time to steady down some. "I'm a little hazy on identities, Miss Sandmark. Who says who killed who? Or is it whom?"

"There was a man out to see my stepfather." She was getting past the whispering stage. "He was some kind of policeman from the State's Attorney's office."

That would be Crandall, I thought. "He accuse your stepfather of killing somebody, Miss Sandmark?"

"Yes. That is—not right out. But he seemed to know a lot of things and . . . Well, the way he asked questions was really an accusation."

"How do you know about it?" I asked. "Were you present when he talked to your stepfather?"

"No. John called me a few minutes before you arrived."

"Why did he do that? I mean, you'd sort of expect him not to upset you with something that actually hadn't come to a head so far."

"He had to, Paul. This man wants to talk to my stepfather again tomorrow and he wants to ask me some questions, too."

I nodded. "They do things like that. They hand out just enough heat to worry you so that you'll talk things over with the other suspects and get a story worked out to fit all the points mentioned. Then they call in everyone concerned and ask questions until they get the story you've prepared. Everything checks. Then, wham! they throw in a few high trumps you didn't know they were holding, and your nice little story blows up and you get rattled and start contradicting one another. The beginning of the end, as somebody so aptly put it."

She spread her hands in a helpless gesture. "What can John and I do?"

"Tell the truth, if you can stand it. Otherwise, get a lawyer and make the best deal possible."

"He didn't kill him," she said stubbornly.

"Then what are you worried about?"

She wet her lips. "They might make it seem that he did. It—it's kind of a mix-up, Paul. I—can't explain it."

"Maybe I can," I said. "Who is it your stepfather is supposed to have killed?"

She began to shiver uncontrollably and her face went behind her hands. "He didn't do it! He didn't do it!"

I put some smoke in my lungs and let it out slowly and waited. A few minutes went by with stones in their shoes. I could hear a piano in one of the neighboring apartments. Somebody was playing the "Largo" from Dvořák's *Fifth Symphony*, playing it with too heavy a touch.

Presently the girl on the sofa stopped shaking enough to get up and take a handkerchief from a bag lying on one of the end tables. She wiped her eyes and dug up a smile that looked like a scream sounds.

"I'm sorry, Paul. It's just that I don't believe—don't know . . . I just don't *know!*"

"Let's try it again," I said. "Who do they think your stepfather murdered?"

"My real father."

I said, "This is important: Did the investigator *say* it was your real father?"

"No. No, this man from the State's Attorney's office wouldn't say anything definite. He wanted to know about a man who was found murdered in a hotel on Madison Street about a month ago."

"But *you* knew this man was your real father?"

"Yes."

"How did you know?"

"I was there. At the hotel."

"When?"

"The night he was—was killed."

Well, brother! I got up and walked the rug a time or two before I stopped in front of her. I said, "It looks like you better start at the beginning and let me have it all, Miss Sandmark."

She looked away from me, and for a moment there I thought she was going to refuse to say any more. Finally she sighed the deepest sigh in the world and said, "I think I'd like a drink, Paul."

"Okay. Where do you keep the stuff?"

She pointed out a portable bar in a walnut cabinet with a built-in freezing unit for ice cubes. I made her a highball and freshened up my own and sat down on the couch next to her.

A lusty pull at the highball put some color back in her cheeks. She leaned back against the sofa as though her head was something she'd been carrying too long and too far.

"It began one evening about five weeks ago. Jerry had been here and he left quite early—around ten, I think. As he reached the street, a man called to him from a car parked in front of the apartment.

"He asked Jerry all about me. When Jerry wanted to know what his interest was, the man explained he'd been watching me at a distance for more than a week, trying to get up the courage to approach me himself. He said he'd noticed that Jerry was with me a lot and he would like to know if Jerry was in love with me. Jerry told him yes, that we were to be married. It wasn't exactly the truth; he said it to find out what the man wanted.

"The man then said his name was Raoul Fleming— my real father's name—and wanted to know if the name meant anything to Jerry. When Jerry said it didn't, Mr. Fleming told him that I was his daughter and that circumstances had kept him from seeing me for many years. He said there had been a shadow over his name all that time, but now he was in a position to reopen the case and that he would spend a fortune, if necessary, to clear himself and regain the love of his only child; that, while it was too late to redeem himself in the eyes of the woman he loved, he could bring retribution to the man who had taken her from him.''

"Sounds like a very old, very bad movie," I said. "But then the truth often sounds that way."

"Jerry wanted him to come up right then and there and talk to me," Leona continued, as though I hadn't spoken. "But he wouldn't. Said I had probably been taught to hate him, and it would be too much of a shock for me to face him without warning. He asked Jerry to tell me of their conversation, to beg me not to tell anyone, especially John Sandmark, and that he would get in touch with me in a day or two. Then he drove away.

"Of course, Jerry came back up and told me about it. I was too astonished and confused to know exactly what to do. The man seemed to know too much about me and my family to be an impostor; and it was true that I had been taught to hate him. Not taught, exactly; it was just that his name was never mentioned, there were no pictures of him, nothing that ever belonged to him. It was as though he had never existed. My mother wanted it that way, I suppose. . . .

"We finally decided, Jerry and I, to do nothing until Mr. Fleming came directly to me. I worried a little about not telling my stepfather, because of what the man had said about revenge.

"The next night, Jerry and I went out and didn't get in until very late. The following morning my stepfather stopped by to see me; he often does so on his way downtown. While he was here, the postman rang and John went down to get the mail for me. He came back up and gave me some bills or something, and said that was all there was. He seemed strangely disturbed about something and left almost at once.

"Around one o'clock that same afternoon," she went on, "my phone rang. It was my real father. He said Jerry had given him my number, and that he was calling to learn if I would come to see him that night, as he had requested in his note. When I told him I knew nothing of any note, he said he left one in my mailbox the evening before. I asked him to hold the wire while I went down and looked for it. There was no note in the box. I realized that John must have taken it, although I didn't tell Mr. Fleming that.

"He wanted me to come to the Laycroft Hotel on Madison and Hermitage at ten o'clock that evening. I asked him why he couldn't come to my apartment. He was afraid my stepfather might stop by unexpectedly, he said, and he wasn't ready for that . . . yet. He talked a little wildly about having come five thousand miles to cover me with diamonds, about living far from civilized people for years with only the thought of someday seeing me to keep him from going mad—things like that.

"I finally agreed to meet him. He told me his room number and said to come directly to the room without stopping at the desk."

She stopped talking and sat there with her head back, her eyes closed, her face empty of emotion. When she showed no sign of saying anything more, I tried prodding her a little.

"Did you keep the appointment, Miss Sandmark?"

"Yes." She sounded tired. She had talked enough to be tired.

"What did he have to say?"

Her head turned slowly toward me and the long-lashed eyes slowly opened. "That's the odd part of it," she said musingly. "He hardly said a word. He seemed almost anxious to get rid of me, in fact."

" 'Hardly a word' means some words. What did he say?"

"Oh, that he would like to have a long talk with me,

but since he was leaving town in a few hours, he would need time to pack. He said I would hear from him again but not to worry if it wasn't for a long time. Before I knew it I was out in the corridor and the door was shut. Actually, Paul, I think he was expecting another visitor.''

"Did you wait around to make sure?''

"Certainly not. It was none of my business.''

"If the visitor was John Sandmark, it would have been your business.''

That hurt her, but she tried hard not to show how much it hurt her. "I know,'' she whispered. "And that could mean John——'' She couldn't get out the rest of it.

"All right.'' I got up to do some more pacing. "You went right home after that?''

"Yes.''

"You mention any of this to John Sandmark?''

"No. I . . . no.''

"Why not?''

"It wouldn't have done any good.''

"Was it because you were afraid he would admit to you that he murdered Fleming?''

"John didn't kill him,'' she said stubbornly, without conviction.

"Why didn't you let the cops know who he was?''

"And get mixed up in a murder?'' she blazed.

"Too damn bad. He was your father, wasn't he?''

"That means nothing to me! Not a thing! How could it, after what he did to my mother? John Sandmark is the only true father I——''

"Okay,'' I said resignedly. "Don't get yourself all worked up again. In my own awkward way I'm trying to straighten things out for you.''

"I know, Paul. But John didn't kill him.''

"So you've said.'' I punched out my cigarette, lighted another and drank the rest of my highball. I stood there, looking down at her, thinking over what she had told me. . . .

"What about Jerry Marlin?" I said at last.

She stared at me woodenly. "What about him?"

"He have a date with you that night?"

"Oh." Somehow she seemed relieved. "He was to call for me at eight. I got rid of him immediately."

"Then you went out to keep the appointment with Fleming?"

"Yes."

"How did you learn your father had been killed?"

"It . . . was in the paper. The hotel and room number were given."

"All right," I said. "Let's go back a ways. You say Fleming eased you out of his room by saying he had to pack because he was leaving town right away?"

"That's right."

"It was a stall, then," I said. "Because when the cops were called, after the body was discovered, there wasn't a thing in the room *to* pack. Not so much as another shirt."

Her eyes widened into a blank stare. "That *is* odd."

"You're damn right it's odd," I said. "Unless maybe he had a room someplace else and used this one at the Laycroft to meet you in, like an office. . . . You see any personal stuff lying around while you were there? Stuff like a suitcase, or clothing, or shaving tools?"

"No-o. Although his suitcase might have been in the closet, and his clothing and things in the dresser drawers."

I rubbed the back of my neck and scowled and thought some more. This thing was making me old before my time. . . .

"Just what gave you the idea that he might be expecting another visitor?"

She thought about that while inspecting a manicured forefinger. "I don't really know," she said to the finger. "It was just that he kept looking toward the door as though listening for somebody. Then he'd turn back to me and say a few words, stop in the middle of a sentence and look at the door again. He would set his long jaw in hard lines and his thin nostrils would flare a little and his eyes would get like blue steel. He would sort of draw up his big shoulders as though he were going to hit somebody."

My mouth was open by this time. I said, "Someone's lying. I think it's you." It sounded harsh, even to my own ears.

She jerked her eyes off that finger and put them on me. If she wasn't astonished, they've been giving Oscars to the wrong people. "Are you crazy?"

"No," I said. "I'm not crazy. I'm not a fool, either. Your father didn't have big shoulders or a long jaw or steel in his eyes. Your father was a little guy, with a thin face and a weak sort of handsomeness that has nothing to do with your description."

She did nothing but sit there and look dazed at me.

I reached in my pocket and took out my wallet, opened it, pulled out a newspaper clipping and shoved it into one of her hands. "Look at it."

She looked at it.

"Did you ever see that face before?"

Her expression gave me her answer before she said, "Who is it supposed to be?"

I said, "Are you telling me that is not your father?"

"My *father?* It certainly is not!"

I was licked. I was finished. I was a hell of a detective. I went over and poured some Scotch in my empty glass and drank it like distilled water.

Leona Sandmark got off the sofa and came over and put a hand on my arm. Something was beginning to come into her faces and eyes . . . a kind of wild unbelieving hope. She shook my arm impatiently, holding the clipping out to me with her other hand.

"Paul! Listen to me, Paul! Why did you think this was a picture of my father?"

"That picture," I said, "is of the man who was found dead in your father's room at the Laycroft."

"But I—but how——"

"I cut it out of the paper less than an hour ago," I said dully. "I was going to send it out to a detective friend of mine on the West Coast and ask him to compare it with the pictures of the people who were mixed up in an old murder case out there, just to make sure I was on the right road."

She wasn't listening. She stood there, holding onto my arm, her shining green eyes looking at me, through me, beyond me. She was beginning to understand something . . . something I had realized ten seconds after learning the picture was not of Raoul Fleming.

"Paul! Listen to me, Paul! Don't you see what this means? It *has* to mean that!"

"Sure," I said. "I'm glad for you that it's worked out this way. If I sounded a little sore, it was only me being sore at me. I was so sure I knew all the answers. And all the time I didn't even know the questions. . . .

"Here's what it means, Leona. It means John Sandmark didn't kill your father. It was your father who did the killing; and the dead man was the visitor your father was expecting while you were there. That means tomorrow you and John Sandmark can tell the State's Attorney's man to go see a ball game, or something. It means——"

Suddenly she threw her arms around my neck and buried her face against my shoulder and began a wild mixture of laughs and sobs that would have brought in the neighbors if my coat hadn't muffled her. I stood there and patted the soft smooth skin of her bare shoulder and waited for the storm to pass.

Finally she drew away a little and looked up at me, her face streaked with tears and blotches of caked powder but still too lovely to feed to the hogs.

"Oh, darling, I'm so happy," she said, her words hardly more than a spent whimper. "You've no idea what a horrible weight I've carried this past month. If it hadn't been for you . . ."

She was so close to me I could smell her. It was that same smell, a good smell, an exciting smell that walked over my skin and made it tingle.

Her eyes were more green than blue, heavy with the dreamy look that comes from emotion. Her hands came up and fluttered against the lapels of my coat. Her face was inches from mine, tilted up, her lips full and soft and glistening a little, as though they were wet.

My arms were getting to be a problem, so I put them around her. I couldn't have picked a nicer place to put them. That didn't leave much room for her hands on my lapels, so she slid her arms up and put them around my neck.

Her lips were warm, but they got warmer. . . .

She drew her head away and gave a small unsteady laugh and put her hands back on my lapels and pressed her cheek against my shirt front.

"I can hear your heart beating, darling."

"Pretty noisy, I guess."

"I was so afraid I would never find . . . this."

There was nothing I could think of to say to that.

When she spoke again, the words were so low I could barely hear them. "Kiss me again, dearest. . . ."

I kissed her again. I even nibbled a little on her lower lip. She shivered suddenly and tightened her hold on my neck and her breathing came quick and shallow, almost rasping. Asthma, probably. Her knees began to shake against my legs and she drew her face away from mine and hid it against me.

I thought once more of the high-school boy and the ex-convict and the married man, of Jerry Marlin and twin hollows in a rose-satin bedspread. None of those bothered me. I was never cut out to be a trail blazer anyway.

Sure. I knew what to do. My body was telling me what to do. But part of my mind was pulling at my elbow and saying this could grow into something more won-

derful than just another roll in the hay; this could become
the one thing every man wants and which a few men
actually find.

And then I remembered that I had felt that same way
once before not so long ago . . . and right there is where
I stopped thinking.

I took hold of her shoulders and pushed her gently
away. I looked down into that lovely face and said,
"Okay. You figure I took the weight off your shoulders
and you're grateful. The truth is I had hardly anything
to do with getting rid of your troubles. But you're grateful
and that's nice and I'm grateful for the way you are
grateful."

She stared at me with her mouth open, as though her
ears were a pair of damned liars. And then she leaned
her forehead against my lapels and began to laugh. No
hysteria this time; just soft everyday female laughter that
was nice to hear.

"You f-fool!" she gasped. "You crazy delicious hard-
boiled fool! And you call it gratitude!"

She pushed abruptly away from me and turned and
went into the bedroom and closed the door without looking back. I walked over to the portable bar and poured
myself some more Scotch, and if my hands were shaking
a little I didn't blame them.

Almost at once she was back, a dark green velvet wrap
over one arm. Her face was made up again, the tear
streaks and caked powder gone. She gave the wrap to
me and I held it while she slipped her bare arms into the
sleeves. There was a gold diamond clip set high on one
shoulder; it matched those in her hair. She looked like
a million dollars. Why shouldn't she? Her stepfather had
a million dollars.

She left me standing there and crossed over to the
ivory grand piano, picked up a brocaded bag and looked
inside, clicked it shut and put it under one arm and came
back to me.

"I'm ready, Paul."

"Are we going somewhere?" I asked politely.

"Of course, you lug! Out to see the bright spots. Remember?"

"Now I do."

She laughed cozily and brushed a smear of powder off one of my lapels, tucked a hand under my arm and out we went.

Downstairs, I started to steer her toward my heap waiting at the curb, but she said her Packard was parked around the corner and didn't I think it would be more comfortable. I admitted that it probably would and we went around the corner and stepped into eighty-five-hundred dollars' worth of custom-built metal and plush and plate glass. Calling it a car would be the same as calling Buckingham Palace a home. With its instrument panel and a ham sandwich I could have flown a tennis racquet to Belgium.

Behind the wheel, with Leona Sandmark close beside me, I stepped cautiously on the starter. An old contented mother cat began to purr under the hood and I shifted gears and let her roll.

Once I was used to turning corners from the middle of the block, I said, "Where shall I drive modom?"

"Oh, I don't care much. The Peacock Club would be nice. It's on Rush Street."

We went to the Peacock Club.

·15·

We went into the silk-drapery and crystal-mirror elegance of a foyer crowded with people in evening clothes waiting for tables. Beyond red-velvet ropes strung across an arched opening was the same semicircular swath of tables about the glistening dance floor.

Music with plenty of brass and a barrel-house piano, blended with the clatter of tableware, the murmur of voices and the slither of dancing feet to form a curtain of sound like the backdrop of a stage. They had Nod Noonan and his orchestra for the summer months, and a lot of people came to hear Nod and his C-alto saxophone.

"Looks like either we wait or go someplace else," I said, running an eye over the crowded foyer.

Leona flicked me with an amused glance, said, "I never wait for anything, pet." She put her hand under my arm and eased me over to the arched opening.

A man in a dress suit with tails, his face the color of wet lime, bowed to us and said, "Good evening, Miss Sandmark." He curled a lip at my tuxedo, and pushed aside a flunky and unhooked the velvet rope for us himself.

We followed him right down an aisle and around to the right to a table for two bordering on the dance floor. He slid Leona's chair under her with a flourish, removed her wrap with a flourish, whisked a "Reserved" card off the table with a flourish and handed us wine cards—

with a flourish. He jerked his chin up and around, like
Mussolini on a balcony, and crooked a lifted finger at a
passing runt of a waiter and it stopped the little guy as
if he'd run into a wall.

While we were waiting for our drinks, Leona leaned
forward and put her hands on the table for me to hold.
"I'm glad we decided to go out, Paul. I'm too happy to
want to do any thinking."

"You picked the right spot for not thinking," I said.
"After an earful of the noise in this place, your brains
crawl down and hide behind a vertebra."

She crinkled her nose at me. "Dance with me, darling."

I sized up the packed floor. "Dance . . . no. But I'll
like putting my arms around you."

When we came back to the table, our drinks were
waiting. Leona gulped hers, emptying the glass before
putting it down. She caught the small waiter's attention and ordered another. They were brandy cocktails,
which are all right if you are young and can sleep late
the next day.

We drank and danced and drank some more. After a
while they dimmed the lights and put on the floor show.
I drew my chair around beside her and held her hand
while we watched the acts.

When the lights came on again, Leona picked up her
purse and went out to powder her nose. I watched the
dancers for a moment, finished my drink and made a
brief visit to the john. When I came back, there was a
little man with a round patient face and a dinner jacket
sitting at my table. Leona Sandmark was nowhere in
sight.

I sat down across from him and said: "What's the
idea, sweetheart? Tired of tailing me from a distance?"

He put his bright little eyes on me and said, "He wants
to see you. I wouldn't know why."

"D'Allemand?"

"Yeah."

"I'm having me a social evening," I said. "Tell him to give me a ring at the office tomorrow."

His smile was empty. "You know better, peeper."

"I'm with somebody." I began to get sore. "Where is he?"

"Upstairs. It won't take long."

"I hope to spit it won't," I said. I called the little waiter over and told him to tell the lady I would be back in a few minutes. Cleve got out of the chair; and sure enough, his dinner jacket was a size too small across the hips. I followed him across the room and we went into a small elevator behind the checkroom, like before, up one flight and along the corridor to the same door foxy Andrew had steered me to earlier in the week. Cleve rapped lightly on the panel and the buzzer clicked and we went in.

The room hadn't changed any since the last time I was there. D'Allemand was sitting behind the kneehole desk. He was smoking a long thin cigar that looked as though it had been rolled from soft gold. He had on a midnight-blue dinner jacket that did a lot of flattering things for his barrel chest. He waited until I was in front of the desk before he said, "Good evening, Mr. Pine."

"It was," I said hotly, "until I found your stooge crawling out of a crack in the table. Let's get a couple of things straight, fat boy. You paid me five hundred bucks. That five hundred buys my services. It does *not* buy my pale white body. It does *not* buy you the privilege of hauling me in every time you feel talkative. It does *not* give you the right to stick a tail on me. I don't like tails; they make me mad and—all right, what do you want?"

He took the cigar out of his mouth and rested the hand holding it on the desk in front of him. The soft indirect lighting in the room winked from polished fingernails the size of half-dollars and from a five-carat diamond in a platinum setting on his little finger. Smoke from the cigar tip floated lazily up and formed a tenuous blue curtain before the collection of planes and hollows that made up his face. Away back in their sockets his dark eyes brooded at me.

He said, "I am a bit disappointed in you, Mr. Pine. I paid you to furnish me with information. I am not getting it."

I waited to hear some more.

"There is an item in the late papers," he continued, his voice even dryer than I last remembered it, "an item about a dead man. His name was Clyne and he had been murdered. The item did not say who discovered the body, but I learned that by telephoning my friend at police headquarters. . . . Were you about to say something, Mr. Pine?"

"I was breathing," I said. "I do a lot of breathing."

"Of course. However, I think it time you did some talking. Why didn't you tell me Clyne was dead?"

"I had no reason to tell you."

"You were paid——"

"Certainly I was paid. I was paid to learn who killed Marlin, and to learn what he was up to that earned him bullets in the back. I was not paid to come running to you every time I found a lead."

"True. But Clyne's death is linked in some way with that of Marlin. Don't you agree?"

"It sounds reasonable," I said.

"Do you know who killed Clyne, Mr. Pine?"

"It's possible."

He hadn't expected that. He stiffened and the hand holding the cigar jerked slightly. "Who?"

I shook my head. "No. It's nothing but a theory and there are holes in it. Theories don't mean a thing. I could give you several that would fit in a loose sort of way."

He put the cigar slowly between his lips and tightened them around it with a kind of careful savagery. "I have always been interested in theories. Let me hear one of your better ones, hole and all."

"Okay," I said. "Jerry Marlin was working for you.

He tried to give you a cross on some deal and you had him shot. I happened to be around when he got it. That bothered you for two reasons: I might be able to finger the killer, and I must have had some reason for being there in the first place. So a complicated deal was worked out whereby I would be grateful to you for saving my life—grateful enough to answer all your questions.

"But I wasn't that grateful, so you hired me on the pretext that you wanted to know who had killed Marlin. That way we'd be in contact often, and eventually I might spill the reason for my original interest in Marlin."

He sat there and smoked his cigar, his expression that of polite interest. When I paused, he put on a wintry smile and said, "There surely is more to it than that, Mr. Pine. There would almost have to be."

"Not a great deal," I said. "But you're welcome to it. I located Clyne. You were never sure of Clyne because of his friendship with Marlin. He might have known about the cross Marlin was trying to hand you. It would never do for me to learn about that, so Clyne was beaten to death with a blackjack.

"That made two guys that had been sapped: Clyne, fatally; me, once over lightly. You've got an ape called Ownie, who packs a sap and would rather use it than eat.

"Put it all together and it adds up to a theory—a theory with holes, like I said."

He sighed microscopically. After a while he said, "I'm afraid you've turned out to be stupid, Mr. Pine. Also you have imagination. An unfortunate combination . . . and a dangerous one. Such combinations have destroyed empires built by intelligent men. . . . I won't detain you any longer, Mr. Pine."

He looked past my shoulder and nodded in a small way. I turned my head carefully and there was Cleve, an arm's length behind me. He didn't appear especially alarming; he never would unless he added some inches and got rid of those hips.

He said: "Let's go, peeper."

"I'm agreeable," I said.

At the door I glanced back. D'Allemand hadn't moved. He was knocking a quarter-inch of cigar ash carefully into an ash tray. He looked like a man who wanted to be alone with his thoughts for a while. . . .

Leona Sandmark was at the table. She looked sharply at me as I sat down. "I was beginning to worry, darling. The waiter wouldn't say anything except that you would be back. Where were you?"

"Getting threatened at," I said. She had ordered a fresh drink for me and I drank half of it very quickly. "I talk too much. I always have. Not only that but I say things to make people sore at me. So I got threatened at."

" 'Threatened at.' 'Threatened at.' " She repeated the words aloud, listening to them intently. She was a little tight, but only enough to make her sparkle. "It doesn't sound just—quite—right, darling."

"Why not?" I said. "It's a verb, or something. Like shot, or thrown. I could say I got shot at, couldn't I? Or thrown at. But not me. I got threatened at."

She crinkled her nose at me and laughed a little and leaned forward to pick up her glass. The crease between the soft swell of her breasts deepened and stirred, and there was no other place for my eyes. . . .

I wet my lips and my smile wasn't any too certain. "You can talk me into another dance," I said.

"No." Her face had the soft warm look of a woman with drinks under her waist and a man within reach, and the glow in her cheeks hadn't come out of the brocaded bag lying next to her arm. "No, Paul. I want to go for a ride. A long ride, away from people, out of the city, along the lake, where the wind can get in my hair and your arm can go around me. I want your arm around me, Paul. You see, for the first time in a long, long time, I am very happy, dear."

She sighed and smiled and ran the tips of her fingers

lightly along the back of my hand where it lay on the table.

"Can we go now, Paul?"

"Yes," I said.

At that hour there was no traffic to speak of. The Packard drove itself, but I sat behind the wheel in case I needed something to lean on.

We skimmed along the avenue until we passed the Drake, made the bend there and rolled on north, keeping the Oak Street beach on the right.

Leona sat next to me, almost stiffly so, both feet on the floorboards, her head back and her eyes closed. The cool fingers of the night wind slid in and fumbled with her hair and strands of it came loose and swept my cheek and put the smell of tar soap where my nose could reach it.

I switched on the radio and a dance band came in and played for us. Leona stirred, murmured, "That makes it perfect," and hummed a few bars of what was being played.

And out across the restless reaches of the lake an occasional buoy light winked red and white and red again and overhead the circling silver sweep of a beacon endlessly sought the horizons.

"Where are we going, Paul?"

"Just . . . north."

"I don't really care, you know?"

"I know."

"Do you like me a little, Paul?"

"I like you a little," I said.

"Why do you like me—a little?"

"Oh . . . I don't know. You're pretty and your legs are nice."

"Lots of girls are pretty and have nice legs."

"Yeah. I suppose they do, all right."

"Why else do you like me?"

"Well, you've got a rich stepfather. . . ."

"That wouldn't make any difference to you, and you know it!"

I gave the wheel a casual touch and the Packard went around a curve as though it was on tracks.

"You know something, darling?"

"Umm?"

"You have brown eyes."

"Is that good?"

"Unh-hunh. Mine are gray."

"Blue."

"Sometimes they're green."

"Especially when you get mad," I said.

"Or when I want to be kissed."

"Somebody must have told you that."

"Yes. . . . You don't mind, do you, Paul?"

"I don't think so."

"I think I'd like it better if you did. Mind, I mean."

"It could grow into that."

"You're sweet. . . ."

She began to sing an accompaniment to the music from the radio. She sang very soft, in hardly more than a whisper, but in perfect pitch. I let about three grams more of gas into the carburetor and damn near went out the back window. I throttled down in a hurry and my fingers were shaking slightly as I groped for a cigarette. She wanted one, too, and I lighted both with the dash-board lighter.

We talked . . . wandering, pointless talk that had meaning only for the moment. We both sang with the radio a time or two; nobody complained and the only laughter was our own.

And all the time, the convertible ate miles like a kid eating peanuts. Past the city limits at Howard Street, through Evanston, Wilmette, Kenilworth and Winnetka, where people live in homes like magazine illustrations and vote the Republican ticket. Overhead the branches of huge cottonwoods and oaks and elms made the boulevard an unending tunnel where light standards and traffic signals were jewel-tipped stalagmites against the night.

By the time we were passing the huge, walled estates in Glencoe it was nearly two-thirty in the morning. Leona Sandmark came out of a silence that had lasted for two or three miles, to say, "You can turn back whenever you like, Paul."

"All right."

"You must be tired of just sitting there holding the wheel."

"Is there something else you would like me to hold?"

Her laugh wasn't much more than a contented murmur, and she gave me one of those twisted answers. "It's too bad we can't see the lake from here. It must be beautiful."

I said, "It just so happens the next through street leads down to the lake. Okay?"

"That would be lovely," she said, like a well-mannered child.

So a couple of minutes later I made the turn and rolled east along a quiet, night-shrouded street with a high stone wall on one side and an almost equally high hedge on the other. After two blocks the headlights showed a curving cement railing that blocked off the street end. I coasted up almost to it and put on the brakes and turned off the lights and the motor. Beyond the railing, the ground dropped abruptly in a wooded slope to a sandy strip of beach and the steady, sullen slap of surf beyond.

I said, "You spoke just in time. This is the only place within three miles you can get this near the water. The big estates along here have made it a private lake, just about."

Her face was a pale blur in the darkness. "This is glorious, dearest. No noise, no people. Just you and I . . . alone."

There was only one answer to that. I gave it.

I let loose of her, finally, and gasped some breath into

my lungs. She took one of my hands and leaned her cheek against it and didn't say anything. I could feel all the muscles in my body sort of stretch out and relax, and the knot of bitterness I had carried just below my ribs for almost a year seemed less tight now and the pain of it was hardly more than a dull ache. A woman had put that knot there—a woman a great deal like the one now beside me. . . .

Pretty soon a tree frog or two started rubbing their wings together, or whatever they do to make that high skirling note. That and the rhythmic pound of the lake waves were the only sounds. Outside the car windows the darkness hung like black-velvet curtains, and away off to the south a single pin point of light marked a building of some sort. It probably was the nearest building to us.

"Paul, dear."

"Umm?"

"Nice?"

"Very."

"Just . . . one-kiss nice?"

I settled that point.

" . . . Paul."

"Yeah?"

"Are you married?"

"Hell of a time to ask that."

"Well, are you?"

"Nope."

"Were you ever?"

"Still nope."

"Why not?"

"Nobody likes me."

"I . . . like you."

"I couldn't keep you in cotton drawers."

"I don't wear them!"

"Shame on you."

"I mean cotton, you pig!"

The radio said, "This is station WXYZ, Denver. At this time we leave the air, to return——" I leaned over and clicked the switch. The sudden silence seemed almost to have substance.

"We'll miss the music," I said inanely.

Almost as an answer Leona Sandmark turned on the seat until her back was to me, then she let herself drop across my legs. My arms went around her and I bent and put my mouth against hers. Her lips parted and her breath came quick and uneven, and when my hands slipped beneath the folds of the green wrap, she stiffened a little, then let herself go limp and yielding. . . .

I lighted cigarettes for both of us. The dashboard clock read three-ten. I said, "Not that I want to be a cad, lady, but it will take quite a while to drive back."

She drew deeply on her cigarette and her face stood out sharp and clear in the brief light. "Not yet, my darling." Her voice was deeper than usual, soft and caressing. "This is perfect . . . a moment that must never end. I've never been so completely happy, so . . . well, happy."

"I must be pretty good," I said, grinning.

She caught my hand and hugged it to her, embarrassing me a little. "You are, darling! You'll never know *how* wonderful!" Her breath caught slightly in a gasp and she giggled suddenly. "Oh, I don't mean——I mean, part of it probably is because you took away my fear that John had killed my father. The fact that my real father killed some stranger isn't important. I never knew him, so it doesn't make any difference, does it?"

"The stranger, or your father?"

"Either. Both. All I know——"

The car door next to me jerked open and a flashlight beam smacked me square in the eyes. A quiet, half-familiar voice said: "All right, Romeo, pile out!"

The startled gasp belonged to Leona; I was too petrified to do more than goggle my eyes at the hot lance of light in my face. I turned my head to get the thing out of my eyes and said: "Okay, copper. Take it easy."

"This is no pinch, Romeo." The words made me even more sure that I had heard the voice before, and at the back of my mind a couple of gray cells were trying to figure out where. "You could call it a stick-up. Now get out, before I blow a hole in you."

The light came down just far enough to let my eyes go back to work. The man behind it was no more than a black hulk, but the dark metal of an automatic was clear enough in his other hand.

"Come on! Out of there, you bastard!"

"Wait!" It was Leona's voice—high-pitched with fear. In the light from the torch I saw her hand scoop up the brocaded bag from the seat. "I have money! I'll give it to you!"

She snapped open the bag and took out a small gun and shot the man three times squarely in the face.

The heavy automatic went off while he was getting the second bullet. The floorboards developed a jagged hole between my feet, but the man was crumpling forward even as it happened. Leona said something like "Ugk," and the gun fell from her fingers. Then she jerked her head around and half out the window and was sick—very sick.

I said, "Jesus Christ," shakily. It was a prayer, nothing else. I got out of the car by stepping over the body, and picked up the flashlight and the automatic. When the light found the dead man's face, there was enough light and enough face for me to recognize him.

C. L. Baird. The man who wanted to pay twenty-five G's in phony dough for the release of his business partner.

"Paul! Darling! Are you all right?"

I looked up and let the light flicker across Leona Sandmark's face as she sat huddled in the far corner of the seat. The face was still beautiful but a trifle green.

"You gave it to him, all right," I said.

"He—is he—?"

"Very," I said. "This was no stick-up, Leona. This guy was after my gizzard. He trailed us out here and tried to knock me off." I stared at her curiously. "That was fast thinking—and fast shooting. Do you always carry a gun, baby?"

"I—I thought we might do some gambling at the Peacock. I usually take a gun with me when I do that. I never know when someone might try to hold me up on the way home."

"That's all right," I said. "The law will want to know. That's why I asked."

She began to tremble. "What will they do to me, Paul?"

"The police will love you," I said. "The papers will have a field day. This guy was a hired killer—and hired killers almost always have records."

"How do you know he was a hired killer?"

I shrugged. "He had no personal reason to want me dead. I never saw the guy in my life until a couple of days ago. So, he must have been hired to get rid of me."

"But who in the world would want to do that?"

I didn't answer her. I was thinking of a fat guy behind a kneehole desk—a guy who didn't want his empire messed up. It seemed he didn't like the kind of theories I went around handing out, so he put a man on my trail when I left the Peacock Club—a man who had a job to do, a man who had come damn near doing his job.

Well, the cops could do the digging into that angle . . . if the cops found out about it. They wouldn't find it out from me, though; as far as I was concerned the dead man had tried a Lovers' Lane stick-up and walked into bullets instead of money.

"What shall we do, dear?"

Before replying, I stooped and took hold of Baird's coattails and yanked him out of the doorway and let him flop into the street. I said, "Okay, beautiful, here's what you do. Get behind the wheel and drive back into Glencoe and find the local police station. Get hold of whoever's in charge and tell him exactly what happened. I'll wait here to keep anyone from stealing our prize."

She shrank back against the upholstery, her face stricken. "No! I can't go—not alone! Why must you stay here, Paul?"

"Do it my way," I said wearily, "and quit asking questions. If the body should be found with neither of us around, and an alarm get phoned in and we get picked up before reporting what happened—well, the police could get the idea we were trying to skip out without letting them know things. . . . Go on, get moving. And answer their questions and tell the truth and don't babble. Just keep in mind that neither of us ever saw this guy before. After you get back here, I'll do the talking."

She pulled in her lower lip and bit it indecisively. Then she nodded in a petrified way and slid behind the wheel and started the motor. The headlights flashed on and she turned the car around, clashing the gears some, and drove away.

I lighted a cigarette and looked down at the loose heap of meat and cloth that had been a man a few minutes earlier. It would keep me from being lonesome. I didn't plan on being appreciative.

· 16 ·

They came in an ambulance—a nice white one that probably had a siren but it wasn't being used at three-twenty-five in the morning. The people who lived in the estates around there paid too much in real-estate taxes to have their sleep disturbed at that hour.

There were two of them, in plain clothes. One wore a dark panama; the other was bareheaded. They hopped out after the ambulance pulled up three feet short of where the body lay in the sharp glare of the headlights. The guy in the panama came up to where I was standing and peered at my face. He could see mine because of the headlights, but his back was to them so that he was only a collection of shadows. He said, "You Pine?"

"Yeah."

"I'm Royden, chief of detectives."

I nodded without saying anything. Royden turned around and said, "Okay, Milt, get the stretcher."

His companion went around behind the ambulance and swung back the big door and came back with a rolled stretcher. Royden left me standing there while he and Milt went over the vicinity with a flashlight. They said a word or two to each other that I didn't catch, then between them they got Baird's body on to the stretcher and into the ambulance and closed the door.

Milt got in behind the wheel, and Royden said, "Okay, Pine, there's room in front for all of us."

I got in between them. Milt turned the wagon nice and

quiet and we went with a soft rush back up the street, turned south and into the main part of Glencoe.

We pulled in at a curving asphalt driveway that went past a square white-stone building of two floors, and around behind it to a long low garage large enough to hold a dozen cars.

Royden got out and I followed him through a rear screen door into the white-stone building. We went along the tan linoleum of a narrow corridor and into a large room divided lengthwise by an oak railing. There were green-shaded bulbs hanging on cords from the ceiling, a few desks and chairs and three tall brass spittoons on black-rubber mats. The place was clean and smelled strongly of Lysol. An elderly man with a fringe of white hair around a pink scalp was pecking out a report form on a Royal typewriter with most of the finish chipped off

I followed Royden through a swinging gate in the railing and over to an oak door. He rapped his knuckles against it once, and a heavy pleasant voice on the other side told us to come in.

It was a fairly large office, with three windows along one side covered with heavy black screens. A bank of green metal filing cabinets stood against one wall, and there was a long heavy glass tank containing water and tropical fish under the windows. A picture of ex-President Herbert Hoover, in a dark walnut frame, hung above the filing cabinets. The people of Glencoe had probably put the police chief into office on the strength of that picture.

Behind a plain oak desk sat a large, fleshy man in a pair of gray flannels and a loose-weave shirt of the same color. The shirt was open at the throat, showing a thick clump of coarse black hair that matched the close-cropped growth above his square, heavy-featured face. In one corner of his strong mouth was an amber-stemmed pipe with a straight stem and a silver ring around the bowl.

As Royden and I came in, the man behind the desk took the pipe out of his mouth and pointed the stem at an empty oak armchair. "Sit down, Mr. Pine. I'm Myles Abbott, chief of police."

I sat down and lighted a cigarette. Royden went over and leaned against the wall next to the aquarium.

Abbott leaned back, getting a complaining squeak from the springs of his oak swivel chair. He studied me through a pair of small deep blue eyes and puffed a time or two on his pipe before he took it out to say:

"It's a long time between killings in Glencoe, Mr. Pine. This is a quiet community, and some of the wealthiest and most respected citizens have residence here. Our police force is small but efficient—highly efficient. We don't like criminals to come into our community, and we don't like crime—especially murder."

I said, "Where is Miss Sandmark?"

That hurt his feelings. He had another paragraph or two of preface to get through before talking business. He said shortly, "She's here. I've heard her side of it. Let's hear yours."

I told him the truth, but I left out everything that had names in it. He might have heard about Leona Sandmark's connection with Jerry Marlin's death, but I didn't mention it and neither did he. I didn't talk about the first time I'd seen Baird, either. There was no point in complicating matters.

While I talked he sat dreamy-eyed and puffed at his pipe and rocked himself gently in the swivel chair. When I was through, he took his pipe away from his teeth and rubbed a square palm thoughtfully against the bowl and nodded. He said, "The young lady said you were a private detective. Show me."

I passed over my wallet and he looked through my cards. He tossed it back to me and said, "Are you carrying a gun, Mr. Pine?"

"Not in these clothes."

"Then the gun used was Miss Sandmark's?"

"I told you that."

"You don't mind my asking again?" He was polite, with steel in it.

"I don't mind. It was her gun."

"Rather an unusual thing for a young lady to carry with her on a date, I would say."

"It was her first date with me. That probably explains it."

It was worth maybe a small smile but I didn't get even that. Abbott said, "Miss Sandmark gave me an explanation for having the gun. She also told me, almost word for word, the same story you've given me. Perhaps that's why I'm wondering a little. I've learned to distrust identical stories, Mr. Pine. They sound too rehearsed. Too pat."

"That's true," I said, to make him feel good. "Of course, ours isn't a long story and it wouldn't be complicated. Anything short and simple would have to sound pretty much the same, no matter how many people told it."

He worked his lips in and out and watched his hand rub around on the pipe bowl. He was thinking. When he was through thinking, he put his small blue eyes back on me and said, "I wonder some about a private cop running around with an heiress. There's usually a reason for something like that . . . other than an ordinary date, I mean. I'm curious, Mr. Pine."

"It's a shame," I said, "that I can't figure out some movie stuff to make it a more interesting story. But I thought you might like some unvarnished truth. That alone should make this situation unique."

He took a deep breath and let it out and pushed himself back away from the desk. He fumbled open the middle drawer and took out a gun and put it down on the bare wooden surface in front of me. He said, "Is this the gun Miss Sandmark had in her bag?"

I looked at it without peering and I made no move to touch it. It was either the same gun Leona had brought with her to my apartment three days before, or one exactly like it. A Colt .32, small, compact, deadly. Nice for a woman's handbag. A gun a woman could shoot. It wouldn't stop an elephant, but Baird hadn't been an elephant.

"It might be," I said. "This is the first time I've had a look at it."

There was a knock at the door behind me and a uniformed man came in and put some papers and a brown alligator billfold in Abbott's hand and went out again.

The police chief took his time digging through the stuff. There was quite a thick slab of bills in the money compartment of the wallet; also some identification cards. The papers were two or three envelopes, with enclosures, and a couple of invoices or bills. I could have known more about it if Abbott would have handed them to me, but he didn't.

Some pencil marks on the back of one envelope caught his eye and he looked at them for a full minute. He kept working his thick lips in and out; probably a trick he'd picked up from reading Nero Wolfe mysteries. He was built for the part, all right.

He lifted up his blue eyes and gave me a Keen Stare. "This is very strange, Mr. Pine. Very strange indeed."

"Not so far, it isn't," I said.

"What," he asked heavily, "do you think I find written in pencil on this envelope?"

"You'll have to tell me," I said. "My crystal ball is a little cloudy this morning."

"Written here," he went on, as though he hadn't heard me, "is your name and address on Wayne Avenue in Chicago; also another address—office, I suppose—on East Jackson Boulevard."

I didn't like that but there was very little I could do about it.

"In that order?" I asked. "I mean, is the Wayne Avenue address first and the office address second?"

He put the envelope down and continued to stare at

me, his expression puzzled and a bit angry because he was puzzled. "Exactly. Why do you ask that?"

I held my cigarette stub between a thumb and forefinger and looked around: man hunting for ash tray. Abbott scowled, but he opened a side drawer and took out a glass tray and shoved it over to me. I leaned over and ground out the stub and sat back again and looked interested.

The chief held his temper but it wasn't easy for him. "Why did you ask that, Mr. Pine?"

I shrugged. "It seemed the kind of question a smart detective would ask."

He put his hands slowly on the desk top, palms down, and anger began to color his square face. "Don't try my patience, damn you. I'm chief of police in this town and don't you forget it. You're involved in a murder, Mr. Pine. I'd talk kind of small if I were you."

I was beginning to get a little fed up with this. "I'm not you and it's not murder. If you're a policeman, for Chrisakes act like one with some sense. Miss Sandmark and I were parked near the lake and somebody came along and tried a boost and got bullets instead. That's not murder, even if you sit there and sweat off fifty pounds trying to make it murder. The fact the guy had my name and address may make it something more than attempted robbery. I don't know that and you don't know that.

"The thing for you to do, if you're on your toes, is to fingerprint the corpse, get them classified and call Central Station in Chicago to see if they've got something on the guy. You've got papers from his pockets; even from here I can see there are names on them. Central may have him under those names. Get the guy identified, find out if he has a record, *then* start calling Miss Sandmark a murderer."

Before the chief could let loose at me, somebody knocked on the door. A little guy with glasses and a bookkeeper's face sidled in, said, "Excuse me, Chief

Abbott," in a scared voice and put a sheet of glossy
cardboard in front of the boss, then slid out the door
again.

Abbott smiled smugly and put the cardboard in front
of me. The surface was ruled into ten squares, and in
each square was an inked fingerprint, the print wider
than you'd expect because the inked tip of each finger
and thumb had been rolled on the paper to get a complete
surface. In a ruled box under the prints were the symbols
giving the classification.

I used one forefinger to push the sheet back to him.
"Nice timing," I said. "I sit here and tell you your
business, while all the time you're way ahead of me."

He liked that. He liked it so much he wasn't mad at
me any more. In fact, he was so pleased that he reached
for the phone on his desk and went ahead and followed
out the rest of my suggestion. Maybe he had intended
to do that all along.

It wasn't more than a minute before he was talking to
somebody in the identification bureau at Central Station
in Chicago. The chief gave his own name and position
and said:

"We've had a little trouble out here, Sergeant. I wonder if you have any record of a man calling himself—"
he squinted at one of the envelopes from Baird's pockets—"Charles L. Hogarth. Address given: 2996 East
Fifty-eighth Street, in Chicago. . . . I'll wait, sure. Incidentally, I have an F. P. classification on him. . . .
All right."

He put the receiver down on the desk and dug through
his pockets until he found some matches to use on his
pipe. He got it going and picked up the receiver and
said, "Hello," just to make sure no one was waiting on
the other end, then settled back in the chair. He closed
his eyes and sat there, the receiver propped against one
ear, clouds of blue smoke floating up from the pipe
bowl. . . .

"Yes." He opened his eyes. "Wait a minute." He

found a pencil and a scratch pad in the middle drawer. "Go ahead. . . . Yes. . . . Yes. . . ." The pencil was working all the time. "Michigan State Penitentiary. . . . Yes. . . . Fine." He picked up the fingerprints. "Go ahead. . . . Check. He's the man, all right; that agrees with the classification I have here. That will do it, Sergeant. I'll give you a report on my end of it later in the day. Thanks again."

He put back the receiver and looked at me. "The man Miss Sandmark shot is known as Charles Hogarth. He was a criminal of the worst sort. He served a sentence in Michigan for stealing cars, a sentence in Atlanta for counterfeiting, a sentence at Joliet for robbery with a gun. He had been booked on suspicion of grand larceny, of operating a confidence game, of murder. None of those last charges resulted in a conviction, but it seems pretty certain some of them should have. His last sentence was a short one at Michigan, and he was paroled April 28, this year. He had a string of aliases as long as the Atlantic cable."

I nodded. "Now what?"

"Well . . . ." He pulled on the pipe. "I'm pretty much satisfied. Your story and that of the young lady match up, as I said before. We tested her hands for nitrates; she fired a gun all right. But in view of the dead man's record and the more or less obviousness of the case, I'm inclined to allow Miss Sandmark and you to return to Chicago. The inquest won't be before Saturday; I'd like you both to be here for that. Miss Sandmark is socially prominent and the daughter of a very wealthy man. There's no point in causing her or her father any unnecessary embarrassment."

"Besides," I said, "you never can tell when they might move to Glencoe."

It took him a minute to figure out what I meant by that. When he did, it wasn't anything he was fond of. He pressed a buzzer and the uniformed man put his head in at the door.

"Have Miss Sandmark step in," Abbott said.

A moment later the door opened and Leona came in. She crossed over to me as I stood up. "I want to go home, Paul."

"The chief says we can leave," I said.

"Why, of course we can leave. We've done nothing wrong. It isn't against the law to defend yourself against a criminal."

Abbott said, "It turns out you've done the country's police quite a service, Miss Sandmark. The man was a hardened criminal, with a staggering record. The only thing I must ask you and Mr. Pine to do is attend the inquest. We'll notify you both in time."

She gave him a smile I wouldn't have minded getting myself. "Surely. And I want to say that I've never met an official as intelligent and understanding as you have been."

He did everything but loll out his tongue. "Just my duty, Miss Sandmark. Just my duty."

He took the .32 off the desk and handed it to her. "I took the liberty of firing a test bullet from your gun, Miss Sandmark. Routine, you know."

"That's quite all right," she said carelessly. She dropped it into the bag and snapped the catch. "May we go now?"

Abbott punched the buzzer again. When the cop outside looked in, the chief ordered the Packard brought around to the front of the station.

He went out with us, opened the car door for Leona and bowed her in. I opened the door on the other side myself and nobody bowed me in. But I was satisfied.

There were stains on the floorboard just inside the door next to the driver's seat. I closed the door and said good-by in a polite voice, started the motor and stepped on the gas.

We were three blocks out of Glencoe before I took my first deep breath since Baird had been shot.

· 17 ·

The first time she spoke was when we were well into Evanston. "I was scared to death they would call John, darling."

"It wouldn't have made much difference," I said. "He's bound to learn about it. You'll get a lot more room in the papers over this than you did on the Marlin killing." I chuckled briefly. "You're getting to be a bad risk for suitors, baby. Guns have a habit of going off around you."

"That's not a very nice thing to say."

"You're right. . . . But, as I say, the papers are going to nail you plenty on this one. I don't know of another time when a doll as socially prominent as you ever was mixed up in two homicides within a day or two of each other. So there's no way you can keep John Sandmark from finding out what happened."

"That's not what I meant," she said slowly. "I want to be the one to tell him what happened tonight. Can you imagine the state he would be in if that police chief had telephoned and said I just killed a man? That, on top of the call this State's Attorney's man is going to make on him today, would just about drive him out of his mind with worry.

"But that's all over with now. When the police learn the dead man in the hotel was not my real father, they'll stop bothering John and go after the logical suspect."

I said, "And it makes no difference to you that the 'logical suspect' is your real father?"

"Not in the least," she said calmly. "How could it? I never saw him before that night at the hotel; in fact, I hardly knew his name until the night Jerry told me of meeting him."

"All right," I said. "I can understand that."

For the next few miles neither of us had much to say. It was getting light over to the east. It was going to be another cloudless hot day.

"Paul."

"What?"

"Have you any idea who killed Jerry?"

I sighed. I was tired of Jerry Marlin. "Idea, yes. Proof, no."

"Who do you think killed him?"

"Well, to tell you the truth, baby, you may have avenged Marlin tonight."

She gasped, and I felt her body tense where it touched me. "Paul! Do you mean the—the man I shot—?"

"That's what I mean. You see, I had a run-in with this guy before. His name was Baird."

I told her the story of Baird's call on me, of the phony money, of the very handy arrival of D'Allemand's boys in "time" to keep my head in one hunk. I told her the rest of it too; of Clyne and his death, of my showdown with D'Allemand, connecting the last with the fact that Baird had tried to kill me less than two hours afterward.

What I didn't tell her was the blackmail angle aimed against John Sandmark, and that the deaths of Marlin and Clyne tied in some way with the twenty-five-year-old robbery and murder at the Gannett Express Company. It wasn't time for her to know about those things. It might never be time for her to know.

It kept her thinking until we reached the Outer Drive south of Foster Avenue. Then she said, "That would make D'Allemand responsible for all three deaths, wouldn't it, Paul?"

"What three deaths?"

I knew she was staring at me strangely. "Why, Jerry and Clyne and even this man Baird. I mean, if Baird hadn't been sent out to kill you he wouldn't have been shot."

I said, "You asked me if I had an idea. That's one of them."

"It seems conclusive to me," she said.

"Yeah."

"What are the other ideas, Paul?" she said, a shade too casually.

I moved the wheel about a tenth of an inch, which was enough to follow a tight curve in the road. I said, "My mind gets into some funny places when it hunts ideas."

"What are you getting at?"

"Your stepfather could have hired Baird to get rid of Marlin."

She jerked away from being near me and her voice came closer to being shrill than culture should have permitted. "I thought so! You don't miss a trick, do you, Mr. Detective! Well, let me tell you something! John Sandmark is the finest man who ever drew breath. He would no more hire a killer than he would—would kill *me!* So you can just put that idea where it won't do anybody any harm, you hear me?"

"I hear you," I said. "I could still hear you if I were in Omaha."

That brought her voice down. "I didn't mean to shout," she said sullenly. "But, honestly, you make me so—so darn *mad* at times."

She spent the rest of the ride thinking, and she didn't seem so satisfied any more. Probably, I figured, my remark about her stepfather had gone in pretty deep.

It was ten to five when the convertible rolled to a stop at the curb in front of the yellow-brick apartment building. I got out and went around and opened the car door and helped her out. When we were in the foyer, I pushed the elevator button to bring down the cage, and said, "Well, get some sleep, beautiful. You've a tough day ahead."

She put a hand on my sleeve. "Come up for a drink, dear. I'm all unstrung."

"I'm not much good at restringing."

Her cheeks pinked up but her eyes never wavered. "Please, Paul."

I followed her into the cage and we rode in silence to the sixth floor. She unlocked the door and went in ahead of me and pressed the wall switch, lighting the lamp in front of the mirror in the hall.

I had one foot over the sill when a gun went off in the dark living room and a thin line of fire streaked at Leona Sandmark. She screamed once, slumping to the floor as the gun went off a second time and my fingers hit the switch.

The only light, now, came from the still open door into the outer hall. But there wasn't much of it, and what there was didn't reach where I crouched above the limp body of the girl. The bag with the .32 in it was around somewhere but I wasn't going to move around looking for it. I just crouched down and waited, and the wetness on my forehead wasn't there because the weather was warm.

Silence. They built the pyramids and tore them down and built them over again, and I never moved in all that time. My leg muscles were beginning to complain, but they'd have to do a lot more than complain before I moved them.

Somewhere in the middle of all that blackness a door closed softly, but I heard it. I could have heard an ant with the hiccoughs right then. Overhead, naked feet thudded on a rug and I heard a window being raised up there. The shots must have awakened somebody.

I moved a hand around carefully and found the brocaded bag. I opened it and took out the .32. It was like shaking hands with God. I gave the bag a small flip and it struck against the wall across from me. It made a hell of a noise, or so it seemed; but right then my ears were as sensitive as an ugly girl at a high-school dance.

Nothing happened. I crawled an inch at a time to where I could reach the light switch. I gave it a push and the table lamp went on again.

Nothing happened. Nobody moved. Nobody shot at me. Nobody was around any more except Leona Sandmark's body and me.

She lay in a huddled heap near the wall, her eyes closed, her face as white as a surrender flag. There was blood along her neck and on one bare shoulder and it was spreading as I watched. It wasn't until I bent over her that I saw the slow rise and fall of her breasts under the yellow gown and knew that she was still alive.

There was a shallow groove about half an inch long in the side of her neck just below the angle of her jaw. I swung her up in my arms and carried her over to the sofa in the living room and put her gently down. I laid the .32 on the coffee table, and went into the bathroom and found a towel. I wet part of it and came back and sponged away the blood and put a gauze bandage from the medicine chest around her neck.

She came out of her faint while I was finishing up. For a few moments she lay there without moving, just staring up at me in a frightened way.

I said, "It was close, baby: But you're all right, now."

"Somebody tried to kill me."

"Yes," I said. "This time it was you."

"Did you see who it was?"

"No."

"He got away?"

"If he got stopped, I didn't do it."

"I'm afraid, Paul."

"So am I."

"Maybe he's still here!"

"I doubt it," I said. "But I'll go make sure."

I took the gun from the coffee table and prowled the joint. There wasn't anyone around. The kitchen window had been forced and the door was unbolted and standing open. I closed it and went back into the living room and drew open the blinds and the draperies, letting in the dawn's early light.

She hadn't moved. I wiped off the gun absent-mindedly and put it down on the coffee table again.

"We're all alone," I said, giving her a wolfish leer to cheer her up.

"I think I'd like to sit up. I'm all right now."

I left her mixing a highball and went into the bedroom and closed the door and crossed over to pick up the ivory telephone.

The operator came on the wire and I gave her John Sandmark's number. After several rings, the same middle-aged woman answered the phone and she was just as indignant when I asked for Sandmark as she had been the morning Marlin was killed. But I insisted and she finally went off to get him.

I lighted a cigarette and tapped my foot on the floor and looked at the rose-satin bedspread. It lay smooth and sleek and there were no depressions in it now as there had been that other time.

"Hello." It was the woman's voice again and it was worried. This was like seeing a movie twice, and like a movie, it would be the same all the way through.

"Yes," I said. "I'm waiting for Mr. Sandmark."

"He isn't in, sir."

"You mean he's gone out this early?"

"I don't . . . His bed hasn't been slept in, sir. I——"

"All right," I said sharply. "Does anyone there know what time he went out?"

"I'd have to ask," she said doubtfully.

"Then go ahead and ask. I'll hold on."

The minutes dragged. I sat there and smoked. The ash

fell off my cigarette and I ground it into the rug with my foot. . . .

"Hello." The woman again. "Mr. Sandmark went out shortly after eleven last night and has not yet returned. Is there any message?"

"Did he say where he was going?"

"No, sir. Any message?"

"Let it go," I said. "It isn't important."

I put back the receiver, thought for a moment, then called police headquarters and asked for Lieutenant George Zarr. He was off duty, they told me, and so was Captain Locke. I refused to talk to anyone else and broke the connection, then dialed the State's Attorney's office at the Criminal Courts Building.

A sharp, clear voice answered—a voice I recognized.

"Frank," I said, "this is Paul Pine."

"The hell it is! What're you doing up this time of morning?"

"I'm not very bright, is all. Frank, is Crandall there?"

"Ike? Hell, no—that guy works days. He's too good for the night shift."

"What's his home phone?"

"Hold it a minute."

He was back almost at once. "Berwyn 9902-J."

I thanked him, got hold of the operator and gave her the Berwyn number. After half a dozen rings the receiver went up and a man's voice growled: "Yeah?"

"Crandall?"

"Yeah."

"This is Pine, Crandall. Paul Pine. I hear you got a date to ask John Sandmark and his stepdaughter some questions later this morning."

"What about it, Pine?"

"I don't think it's going to come off, that's all. Leona Sandmark was plugged just a few minutes ago, in her own apartment. And John Sandmark isn't at home. I just called there."

"The hell you say! I *thought* that guy knew a lot more

than he let on. So he killed his own kid to keep her mouth shut! How come you know all this, Pine? Where you at?"

"At the girl's apartment."

"So you had to play smart, hunh? You had to shove your nose into police business. Why, God damn you, Pine——"

"Skip it," I said harshly. "You want the guy, don't you? Then meet me near Sandmark's place as soon as you can get there. You're in Berwyn; that's not far from where he lives. And you'd better bring a homicide man with you. I called the station, but both Zarr and Locke are off duty. Locke lives out north somewhere; maybe you better get Zarr. He's entitled to be in on this."

"Good enough. He's got an apartment in the 4900 block on Washington Boulevard. That's only a few minutes from here. Suppose we meet you at the corner of North Avenue and Kenilworth in twenty minutes."

"I'll be there."

I went back into the living room. Leona Sandmark looked up from the depths of the sofa as I came in. There was a highball glass, half filled, in one hand and a fresh cigarette in the other. Most of the color was back in her cheeks and the strained lines were about gone. The white gauze around her neck showed no blood. Evidently the bleeding had stopped, although she was going to have a stiff neck for a while.

I sat down beside her and took the glass from her hand and drank what was left. It was Scotch and plain water, and very good, too. I said, "You've had it tough, baby, and it's going to get tougher before it gets better. I can be wrong; I hope to Christ I *am* wrong. But get some iron in your guts just in case."

The color began to go out of her face again and fear started to grow in her gray-blue eyes. "What are you trying to say?"

"I've already said it. Now go put on a street dress or something. We've got to go someplace."

"Where?"

"Later."

"Where, Paul?"

"To your stepfather's."

She stared at me uncertainly, opened her mouth to say something; then she got off the couch, dropped her cigarette into an ash tray and went into the bedroom.

I took a deep breath and another drink. . . .

When she came out she was wearing a chartreuse suit of shantung and a white blouse with a high collar to hide the bandage around her neck. I smiled at her and said, "You've got what it takes, honey. No matter what happens before this is over, you won't let it throw you."

We went down the elevator and out to the curb. The sun was up and there were people out on the streets. I helped her into the front seat of my car and went around and got behind the wheel and drove north.

On North Avenue, a block east of Kenilworth, I pulled in at the curb. I said, "In a few minutes a car will pick me up at the corner of Kenilworth. When you see me get in, wait ten minutes—then come to your stepfather's home. I'll be in the library. You have a key to the house?"

"Yes."

"Okay. You think you can drive this pile of junk? I mean, after being used to that convertible——"

"I can drive it, Paul."

"See that you do. Ten minutes."

I got out and walked off up the street, the sunlight stretching my shadow way out ahead of me.

There was a drugstore on the corner. I leaned against one of the window frames where Leona Sandmark could see me, lighted a cigarette and waited. . . .

A black sedan, a Buick, came east on North Avenue at a good clip, cut in fast at the curb and the brakes went on, taking a hundred miles off the rubber. A city car; to hell with the tires.

"Pine." It was Crandall, behind the wheel.

I tossed away the cigarette and went over. Zarr was in front next to Crandall. He said, "This better not be from morphine, Pine. I don't like to get up this early."

I opened the rear door and got in and pulled it shut again. As the car got under way I said, "You've at least been to bed. This is the last out of the ball game, Lieutenant. This is where you find out who sicked the twelve preachers onto that corpse, and get yourself a killer besides."

· 18 ·

A middle-aged woman who looked as though she had made a million beds in her day opened the door to my ring. Her expectant expression fell on the rug when she saw the three of us standing there. Alarm flickered in her pale-blue eyes and her blue-veined hand tightened suddenly on the knob. Almost anyone can recognize a cop, even one in plain clothes. She stood there, tight-lipped, and stared at us across a distance of three feet that might as well have been three miles.

I said, "Good morning. We'd like to see Mr. Sand-mark, please. Right away. It's important."

The faint morning breeze stirred the starched folds of the neat blue Hoover apron, but nothing else about her moved as I pushed one of my feet across the threshold. But when I reached out a hand and laid it against the door, her thin shoulders jerked a little and the alarm in her eyes turned to fear.

Words spilled out of her. "No! I mean, I'm sorry, but—well, Mr. Sandmark isn't in just now. If you will come back——"

My hand under her elbow stopped her there and moved her to one side at the same time. "It's all right, mother. If you don't mind, we'll kind of wait in the library. Tell Mr. Sandmark Paul Pine is here . . . when he comes in, I mean. It won't be necessary to mention these men; they're with me."

Meanwhile I was walking ahead and she was backing

away. When she saw there was no stopping us, she clutched the remaining shreds of her dignity in her trembling hands and said a little wildly:

"I'll tell him the *minute* he comes home! I'll tell him how the three of you actually *forced* your——"

By this time Crandall, Zarr and I were in the shadowy depths of the central hall. I steered them through the library door, leaving the housekeeper outside. "You mustn't excite yourself, mother," I said, and closed the door softly in her face.

Enough morning light came in the French windows to make out the room's furnishings. But it wasn't strong enough for my purpose. I snapped on a couple of table lamps over near the huge fireplace and the room sprang alive under the soft yellow glow.

Crandall shifted his feet uncomfortably in the depths of the gray carpeting and looked around at all the magnificence. "I sure in hell hope you know what you're doing, guy. This could blow up on us in a big way."

"Not any more it can't," I said. "Sandmark's too far out on a limb ever to crawl back. We might as will sit down and wait."

I got Zarr into the depths of a high-armed lounge chair and Crandall across from him on the blue leather chesterfield that faced the hall door. Zarr dug a blunt cigar from the breast pocket of his light-gray suit jacket and stripped off the cellophane wrapper. I pushed an ash stand over where he could reach it and he rolled the cellophane into a little ball and flipped it at the bowl. It overshot the mark and I bent stiffly and took it off the rug and put it in the tray and scowled at him.

"Don't act like a cop all your life," I said. "This isn't a tavern, you know."

He looked at me with a sort of bleak wonder, found a wooden match in one of his pockets and leaned over to strike the tip against the sole of a square-toed shoe. He put the flame to his cigar, turning the weed carefully until it was burning to his satisfaction, waved out the match and dropped it with exaggerated care into the ash tray alongside the ball of cellophane. He said, "What're you so jumpy about, Pine? You act like a rookie making his first pinch."

He was right. I was drawn as tight as a dowager's corset. I ran the fingers of my left hand across the side of my neck and stared at the nails as though I expected to find something foreign under them. Crandall watched me from where he sat, straight and stiff, on the edge of the chesterfield. He seemed nervous and doubtful and a little angry. The last was at me.

I paced up and down a time or two before Zarr said, "How about giving us some of this before Sandmark gets here? Crandall tells me the guy killed his stepdaughter last night. How do you know it was Sandmark? You see him?"

"It had to be him," I said. I sat down on the arm of the chesterfield and lighted a cigarette and threw the match in the fireplace. "You see, I was out with his stepdaughter last night and I got quite a bit of information out of her before she ran into that bullet.

"This thing goes back twenty-five years. It goes back to San Diego and two guys working for an express company out there. But I told you about all that. Let's get down to this year.

"About a month ago Raoul Fleming, Leona Sandmark's real father, came to Chicago. He came here to see his daughter. He got in touch with her through her current boy friend, Jerry Marlin. He asked Marlin a lot of questions, but ducked out when Marlin wanted him to talk to the girl.

"A day or so later Fleming went out to Leona's apartment to call on her. She wasn't home, so he left a note in her mailbox. Sandmark got hold of that note and it scared him. It scared him because that old San Diego beef against Fleming had been a frame, and he figured Fleming had come to town to even the score.

"Meanwhile Fleming got in touch with his daughter

and asked that she come to his hotel and see him. She agreed and went out to the Laycroft to meet him. But he was expecting a second visitor by this time and got rid of his daughter in a hurry. And the next day Fleming was found dead in his room—murdered.''

Ike Crandall stirred uneasily. He said, ''The girl tell you this, Pine?''

''That's right.''

''How do you know it's the truth?''

''Something has to be the truth. This sounds more like it than anything else. You want to hear the rest of it, or what?''

He scratched his ear and blew out his breath and said to go ahead.

I got up and went over and dropped some ash into the tray next to Zarr. I stood there, talking to both men.

''The girl was no fool. She knew Sandmark, guided by that missing note, had gone to the hotel and killed Fleming. What she didn't know until later was that Jerry Marlin had followed her to the hotel and had seen Sandmark go in after she left. It seems she broke a date with Marlin earlier that night, acting so funny about it that he got suspicious.

''It was Marlin's chance. Millionaire murders old enemy—what a setup for blackmail! He started putting the bite on Sandmark. The old man didn't like that, so one rainy night he shot Marlin full of holes.

''He was sure no one could touch him now. But he was wrong. Marlin had let his pal Ken Clyne in on the deal. Not all the way—just enough to give Clyne the idea of taking over the extortion job. Clyne tried it—and went out with a skull full of blackjack.''

They were listening, which was fine. They were nodding, which was even better. Crandall wasn't sitting stiff any more; he had leaned back and was smiling a little. Zarr was staring dreamily at the ceiling, watching the heavy layers of cigar smoke moving in the light from the windows.

I had never really realized what a deadly thing circumstantial evidence could be. . . .

"Sandmark," I continued, "was all set. The only one who could hurt him now was his stepdaughter, and he knew damn well she'd never give him away unless the cops somehow got onto the pitch and started sweating it out of her. But there weren't any unsnipped ends that would lead the cops to Leona Sandmark.

"But there was something he didn't know about . . . and this will interest you, Zarr. It appears that Fleming was a wealthy man himself. From what he told Marlin, he had cleaned up a mintful in Africa, or some such place. When he was found dead and couldn't be identified, he was headed for a pauper's grave and God knows what would happen to all the money of his back on the Dark Continent."

Zarr pushed himself up from the chair depths to knock some more ash into the tray. He scowled a little and said, "Why should this part of your story interest me particularly? Do I get some of this Fleming's dough?"

"I don't know about that," I said. "But you were all hot and bothered about me being at that screwy funeral. This is where you get the answer to why it took twelve preachers to bury the old man."

The lieutenant's heavy brows went up. "Damned if I hadn't forgotten about that! Don't tell me Sandmark was the one who hired all those parsons and paid for the funeral!"

"Certainly not," I said. "He'd be the last one in the world to stir up interest in the dead man. Nope, there was only one person who would have a reason for making a circus out of that burial."

"Who?" Zarr growled.

"Jerry Marlin."

They sat there and blinked at me. My bombshell was a dud; the fuse had been too short.

"Okay," I said wearily, "I'll draw you a picture." I glanced at my wrist watch; not much time left. "Marlin had quite a hold on Leona Sandmark. If it could come out who the Laycroft corpse was, all that dough would go to the daughter and make her a nicely curved gold mine. Without it, she would still be nicely curved but not much use from a dollar-and-cents standpoint, since her only income came from her stepfather.

"But, Marlin reasoned, if he should tip off the cops to who the dead man was, they might find out that Sandmark was mixed up with Fleming. That could result in bringing out the very facts that Sandmark was paying Marlin not to spill, thereby ending *that* source of income.

"So Marlin schemes a scheme: he will hire a bunch of preachers to bury Fleming, send money to the coroner for a private funeral; in other words, put on a circus ceremony so fantastic that the newspapers will be bound to get interested. That way Fleming's picture is certain to be circulated all over the world, and somebody will recognize it as a picture of an African millionaire and identify him. Millionaires, I hear tell, have a wide circle of people interested in them. Eventually Fleming's right name would come out and his daughter would get his fortune. Meanwhile, enough time would have elapsed to bury any clues to Fleming's murder so Sandmark would not even be suspected of doing the job.

"Understand: I'm not saying it was a perfect idea. I'm not saying it was a good idea. Nobody ever accused Marlin of being overly smart. But there's your answer to that screwy funeral."

Lieutenant Zarr was pleased—so pleased that I could see three gold fillings in his upper left bicuspids. "I'm satisfied," he said, nodding. "It fits right in there. You're okay, gumshoe; remind me to like you from now on."

"That's good of you," I said, and if right then I recalled his fist in my face the day before, my expression didn't tell him so. . . .

"Anyway," I went on, "I got to snooping around, hunting for Marlin's killer, and I dug out a lot of this story. Over at Clyne's I thought things over and made up my mind to let you boys in on it.'' They grinned at each other but I ignored it. I could afford to now. ''Anyhow, Crandall, you went out to see Sandmark and let out just enough to scare him. Then, when you said you wanted to talk to his stepdaughter *and* him the next day . . . well, he went off the deep end. Leona Sandmark was bound to crack; she was a girl; how could she outsmart the law? Leona Sandmark had to die.

''It wasn't as if she was his own kid; she was Fleming's brat. His neck was worth more than hers. So early this morning . . .''

My voice trailed off. Through the closed door we could hear quiet feet coming along the hall outside.

I whispered: ''This is the pay-off, boys. You got a gun, Crandall? Get it out. . . . Slump down, Zarr, so you can't be spotted right away.''

They followed orders. They were trained to follow orders. I moved over and stood next to where Crandall was sitting. He had a Smith & Wesson .38/.44 Heavy Duty revolver in his right hand, resting it lightly on his knee. He seemed casual enough but his jaw muscles were tight with strain.

The steps came up to the library door. They were light, uncertain steps. The steps of a man walking toward something he didn't understand and probably wouldn't like.

The knob turned. You could see the light glint on it as it turned. The door opened. Leona Sandmark came in.

Ike Crandall saw her first. He hadn't been expecting a girl. His eyebrows went one way and his jaw the other. Zarr, whose back was to the girl, took hold of the chair arms and pushed himself up a ways and turned his head toward the door.

I flashed a hand down and grabbed the gun from Crandall's slack fingers, leveled it, and said, ''Don't move, you son of a bitch.''

· 19 ·

The whole thing hadn't taken six seconds. Leona Sandmark, a few steps inside the room now, stopped short and stared at me. Ike Crandall and George Zarr were staring too. But they were not staring at me. They were staring at where the gun was pointing.

It was pointing at George Zarr.

The silence was so thick you could have walked on it. Zarr's mind was trying to catch up with his eyes; by the time it succeeded it would be too late. It was already too late. There was a gun under his coattails, but even with a few second's warning he would never have been able to get to it quick enough. Not while he was sitting in that high-armed chair—which was why I had wanted him there in the first place.

Crandall croaked, "Hey, that's *my* gun!"

Nobody laughed, although I have never heard anything funnier.

I said, "Come here, Leona," without taking my eyes off the petrified police lieutenant.

When she was where she could see all three of us, I said, "Take a look around, baby. Do you see——"

I didn't have a chance to finish. Her eyes were on the frozen face of George Zarr. Her lips sagged and she gasped one word:

"Father!"

It broke the ice on Zarr's muscles and he came out of the chair as if he had been shot out of a bazooka. His hand darted for his hip——

I yelled at him. Not words; just a yell. It stopped him like one of Medusa's snakes. I said, "In the kneecap, flattie. Not where it will kill you. Hell with that noise. You got a date with the fireless cooker."

His eyes would have burned holes in Superman. He let himself slowly back into the chair and he laid his fingers gently and carefully down on the arms and he kept on looking at me.

Crandall had his lips close enough together by this time to put out the point of his tongue and wet them. He said hoarsely, "What *is* this? What *is* this? Will you for Chrisakes tell me what *is* this?"

Leona Sandmark was still standing there in a sort of unhinged fashion, staring at Zarr's murderous expression. She said, "Father," again, with the toneless lack of inflection of a village idiot. "Father, what——"

I said, "No, Leona. He's not your father. He's a guy called George Zarr. Only he's not George Zarr, either. His name is Jeff Ederle."

That meant about half as much as nothing at all to her. It couldn't have meant anything to a girl who had never been allowed to hear the details of something that had happened when she was in rompers.

But it meant something to Ike Crandall. He said, Ederle? Wait a minute, Pine. That's this express-company guard you mentioned out at Clyne's yesterday, isn't it?"

"That's it," I said. "But hold up a second; I can talk better when I know this guy isn't heeled. . . . Stand up, Zarr. Slow."

He stood up as though he had bolts for joints and iron rods for bones. I circled around him and pushed the Smith & Wesson against his spine and snaked a hand under his coat and took the .38 he had there. I slipped it into my side pocket and ran my hand over him to make sure there wasn't another one around; then I got clear and in front of him and said, "Okay, sit down again."

When I was back near Crandall, I said, "This is too

big for the two of us to handle, Ike. I think we better
get a squad over here to take him.''

He shook his head—not for no; just to clean out the
cobwebs. ''But, Pine—I thought we were here to pick
up Sandmark. I thought you said the stepfather had
killed this girl. Why, you built up a case against him
that——''

''Leona.''

She looked at me with glazed eyes. ''Yes . . . yes,
Paul?''

''Get on the phone. Call the Oak Park police and tell
them to get a cruiser out here to pick up a guy who's
been disturbing the peace. Don't say any more than that;
we don't want any reporters in this for a while yet.''

She started for the phone on the desk. I said, ''No.
Make the call from another extension. There's a reason.''

She hesitated, frowning at me in a mixture of wonder
and worry, then turned and went over to the hall door
and disappeared.

I sat down next to Ike Crandall and used my free hand
to get out a cigarette and start it going. I blew a shred
of tobacco off my lip and my breath moved the thin
streamer of smoke rising from the ash stand where Zarr's
forgotten cigar smoldered.

I said, ''You're right, Crandall. Sure I built up a case
against Sandmark. You could probably have fried him
with it too. That should teach you a lesson, but I know
damn well it won't. . . .''

There was a vise slowly squeezing the back of my
head: the beginning of a headache brought on by lack of
sleep and no lack of strain. I put up my hand and rubbed
my left temple a little. I looked across to where Zarr sat
behind the stone wall that was his face, and then I looked
down at the gun in my right hand. I wondered if I couldn't
join a union and go on strike and sleep through the
negotiations. . . .

''There wasn't any other way I could play it, Ike,'' I

said. "When you called Zarr at his apartment a little while ago and told him Sandmark had killed his daughter and that the three of us were going to make the pinch . . . from that moment he was suspicious. He knew we weren't going to do anything of the kind, but he did think that maybe you and I *thought* that's what we were going to do.

"Every word I said up until Leona Sandmark came in here was aimed toward taking away his suspicion by making him believe I saw things the way he wanted them seen. The more evidence I piled up against Sandmark, the less on guard Zarr became. And right at the moment when he was breathing easiest . . . that door opened and the last person in the world he expected walked in!

"That paralyzed him. Honest to God, Ike, nobody ever took a worse jolt than Zarr did right then! I'll bet I could have gone out and bought a gun and come back and pointed it at him before he could come unstuck from the shock of seeing Leona Sandmark—*the girl he had killed*—walk in that door!"

Crandall said slowly, "You're a permanent smear on the police blotter if you can't make this stick, my friend."

"You think I don't know that?" I snarled. "Let me give you this thing, Crandall. Let me show you the whole picture of it.

"Let's go back twenty-five years. Three guys are working in San Diego, for the Gannett Express Company—Raoul Fleming, John Sandmark and Jeff Ederle. One night there's fifty grand in the company safe. Sandmark figures out a pitch where he can get that dough, frame the job on Fleming and get rid of him so he can take over Fleming's wife.

"Around this time Jeff Ederle, a guard at Gannett's, has got himself tangled up with some married woman and has to leave town. His fingers get to itching for those fifty G's; with it he can go somewhere and live in style.

"So let's reason it out this way: Ederle goes down to

the office that night, knocks off the watchman and is about ready to clean out the safe, when Sandmark comes in. Ederle is scared off, leaving Sandmark to find the dead watchman.

"That makes it perfect for Sandmark. He calls Fleming from the office and gives him some wild story to get him down there. When Fleming shows up, Sandmark maybe tricks him into shooting at what appears to be a prowler in the darkened office. Then Fleming turns on the light . . . and there is the dead watchman!

"A moment later in comes Sandmark—obviously having just arrived. He says something like, 'My God, Raoul, you've killed the man! Lam out of here, you fool; I'll cover you somehow until this can be straightened out.' So of course Fleming, rattled as hell, takes a powder. That's all Sandmark wants; he crosses Fleming like a T, gets his wife and his job and, eventually, the express company."

Crandall pursed his lips and began to shake his head before I finished those last few words. "Hunh-uh, Pine. No 'cutor's going to make a case out of that many guesses. Christ, I could ride sidesaddle through some of the holes in your story."

"No prosecutor will have to make a case out of it," I told him impatiently. "Naturally I don't know the details. I don't have to know them and neither do you. We don't have to hang that old job on Zarr. He gets his for murder—for a couple of murders—right here in town and during the last month."

Crandall looked over at the motionless man in the lounge chair. He looked at him with a kind of obscure curiosity, as though seeing Zarr for the first time. He said, "What about all this, George?"

What George said was not for nice ears. Most of it had to do with my parents' morals, and my teeth began to ache a little from the pressure I was putting on them. But none of the words gave Crandall anything he could use.

I think that did more than anything I had said to convince the State's investigator. He tightened up around the mouth and eyes, and the faintly yellow cast to his skin seemed to deepen. He turned back to me and said, "What's the rest of it, Pine?"

The door opened and Leona Sandmark came back in, still walking in her sleep. She said, "They're sending somebody right away."

I smiled at her and said, "You better go upstairs and lie down awhile, baby."

If she heard me, she showed no sign of it. "Hilda says John isn't home. Have you any idea where he is, Paul?"

"No. He's big enough to be out by himself. Go on to bed."

She didn't like that. Her face turned red and her eyes blazed at me. "Well! I'll do nothing of the kind!"

"It won't do, Leona." The gentleness in my voice startled her. "I can't say what I have to say if you're here."

She worked up a smile but it wasn't much of a success. "Now you've made me curious, Paul. I'm staying."

Crandall cleared his throat and moved his feet on the rug. "Let her stay. Her stepfather's in the clear, you said. Let's hear the rest of it, Paul."

Calling me "Paul" was his way of indicating he was on my side now. I could use that.

I shrugged. "Have it your way. . . . Okay—we're back in San Diego. Zarr—I can't get used to calling him Ederle—skips town that night, thinking he'll be wanted for the watchman's murder. When he finally reads about it he is amazed to learn the San Diego cops want Raoul Fleming for the murder *and* for some missing money. Now Zarr knows damn well he, himself, killed that watchman. Maybe, he reasons, the law is using the story about Fleming and some stolen money as a blind, figuring Zarr will grow careless and get himself picked up.

"So he comes to Chicago, changes his name and gets—of all places—on the local police force. Back in those days fingerprints weren't so widely used and Zarr's weren't on record.

"He works his way up until he's a lieutenant on homicide. Then here about a month ago a gambling joint is raided and some of the customers brought in, among them Leona Sandmark.

"Zarr, on duty that night, sees those customers brought in. Naturally he doesn't recognize Miss Sandmark, here, but when her stepfather arrives to bail her out . . . well, Zarr recognizes him and gets panicky. If Sandmark pegs him as Ederle—ouch! And Zarr hasn't changed so much since the old days that he can't be recognized.

"So Zarr decides to keep an eye on Sandmark. He checks on him, learns what Sandmark's setup is here in town. He finds out Sandmark's daughter is running around with a shady character named Jerry Marlin. And right there is where he gets an angle.

"If, reasons the lieutenant, he can get something on Sandmark or the daughter, then he won't have to worry about being turned in if Sandmark ever does run across him again.

"Sandmark himself doesn't seem to be the kind of guy who does anything he can be nailed for. But the daughter—that's something else again. A girl who gambles and runs around with the wrong kind of people. Sounds like she's the best bet."

I heard Leona Sandmark gasp faintly at this point, but I avoided meeting her eyes. I turned my head just far enough to locate the fireplace and tossed the small stub of my neglected cigarette past the huge brass andirons.

"Zarr," I continued, "spends some time watching Miss Sandmark and Marlin. And one of those times he sees Marlin with none other than Raoul Fleming!

"That really gets Zarr excited! Fleming is the one guy who can tell him if the West Coast bulls actually want him for the watchman's murder. If not, then Zarr has nothing to fear from Sandmark or anyone else! So he tails Fleming, learns the old boy has a room at the Lay-croft and goes up to see him one night.

"Well, something goes wrong—I don't know what—and Zarr beats the guy to death with a sap. Maybe Zarr said the wrong thing and accidentally let Fleming see who *had* bumped that watchman. Or maybe Zarr found out he was carrying around the hatful of diamonds Fleming told Miss Sandmark he was going to cover her with. Your guess is as good as mine and neither of them matters.

"Anyway, while Zarr is standing in Fleming's room, the dead man on the floor, there's a knock at the door. I'll bet Zarr damn near had a stroke right there! What can he do? Refuse to answer? No, he's been moving around and whoever's outside may have heard him.

"He shoves the body into the closet, opens the door . . . and there is Leona Sandmark. He knows her right off; he saw her at police headquarters the night of the gambling-house raid.

"But she doesn't know him; and before he can say anything, she says something like, 'Father? I'm Leona.'

"Right then it's all clear to him. This girl has never seen her real dad because he skipped out while she was still an infant. Zarr, thinking fast, passes himself off as her old man, and gives her a fast line of patter and a faster brushoff. A couple minutes after she leaves, he gets out of there too.

"When Fleming's body is found, Zarr takes over the case. He handles it carefully and without any show. He'll be the happiest guy alive once the time comes for the body to be stuck in a numbered grave out in Oak Forest.

"And right there is where he runs into a snag. For a couple of days before Fleming is due for a Cook County burial, Marlin gets *his* brainstorm, and all those screwy funeral arrangements take place. The papers get going on the thing and Zarr begins to worry that somebody will identify the body.

"And he's got other troubles, too; don't ever think he hasn't! There is always the danger he'll run into one of the Sandmarks and get recognized. Maybe Sandmark himself wouldn't do anything about it; but think of him running into the girl and having her yell, 'Father!' at him, like she did a few minutes ago."

Zarr's face was like the death mask of a very old man. He seemed unable to speak, to move a muscle, to do anything more than sit there and stare at me with killer eyes.

But Crandall was thinking now. He glanced to where the girl was sitting in a small pull-up chair and said: "Miss Sandmark, how does what Pine has said connect up with your knowledge of this thing?"

She put a hand slowly up to her mouth and looked stonily back at him. "Father—I mean John Sandmark—knew where Raoul Fleming was staying. I knew Fleming hated him. This man—is the man I saw in room 318 at the Laycroft that night. He said he was my father. I had every reason to believe him."

There was nothing of indecision in Crandall's eyes or expression now. He said, "I guess maybe we'd better hear from you, Zarr."

"You always were a sucker for a fancy yarn, Ike." It was the first quotable thing he had said since I flashed Crandall's gun on him. "I'll do my talking to a lawyer."

That showed his training. He was too old a hand at the business to make any admissions, no matter what the evidence against him.

Crandall grunted. "If it turns out you're Ederle, you're done for, Zarr. Particularly when Miss Sandmark has already identified you as the man in her father's room the night of the murder."

He waited for Zarr to say something more, but the police lieutenant had gone back to hating me with his eyes.

To me, Crandall said, "When did you start measuring Zarr for all this, Pine?"

"Not until just a few hours ago," I said, "although little things were piling up all along. I guess the first one was on the second morning after that nutty funeral. Zarr came to my office and gave me a song-and-dance about how he might lose his job because of all the attention the funeral would get. It sounded a trifle too farfetched for me, although I didn't attach any importance to it at the time.

"The second item was when he fed me knuckles over at Clyne's that afternoon. Just before he clipped me, he said, 'I told you I don't like coincidences.' That crack referred back to a remark he had passed to me when he was asking about my being mixed up in that funeral. It showed Zarr tied up the funeral with Clyne's death, something he had no business knowing about.

"Another point: A few minutes after he smacked me, Zarr mentioned, in your hearing, the name of the Gannett Express Company. Since I hadn't given him the company's name up to that time . . . *how did he know it?*

"Another: Zarr refused to go with you to see Sandmark when you suggested it that day. Why? Well, now you know. Sandmark would have put the finger on him right then and there as Ederle. Yet this morning Zarr had no hesitation about coming here once you told him Leona Sandmark was dead.

"Of course, the real clincher was when Miss Sandmark described her 'father' to me. It was Zarr she described; and you know, Ike, even with all the points I've told you about, I *still* didn't realize it was Zarr she saw in that hotel room. Not until after he tried to kill her awhile ago, and I learned Sandmark hadn't been home all night, did I wake up enough to learn the score."

But Crandall was shaking his head. "There's a big hole right there, Paul. Zarr didn't object this time to coming here. How could he be sure he wouldn't run into John Sandmark and get recognized?"

I didn't say a word. I just looked him in the eye and waited.

Leona Sandmark saw it first. She stood up slowly, her mouth trembling, her eyes stricken. "No! You don't know what you're saying! How can you—?"

I went over and pushed her gently back into the chair. "I told you things were going to get rough, baby. You've no choice but to take it."

Ike Crandall was still groping. "I don't see this at all. What are you getting at?"

I said impatiently, "Can't you get your eyes past the end of your nose? John Sandmark is dead."

That rocked him. It rocked Zarr, too. His face got even bleaker and his hands clenched and straightened spasmodically.

"How do you know that?" Crandall demanded harshly.

"He's got to be dead. Otherwise Zarr would never have agreed to come here. I say Zarr killed Sandmark last night. He called him out and took him somewhere and killed him. I'll eat my 1928 deputy-sheriff's star if he didn't."

Suddenly Leona Sandmark put her head down on her knees and began to cry with a sort of agonized restraint that was tougher to listen to than the wildest kind of hysteria. Crandall and I looked wordlessly at each other and then at George Zarr, who sat there and stared at his hands and kept what he was thinking off his face.

Crandall went over and stood there staring at the lieutenant's bowed head. He said, "By God, George, you do get around! Four dead in hardly more than a month. Fleming, Marlin, Clyne . . . and now John Sandmark. Are you out for a record, or something?"

I said wearily, "No, Ike. Only two of them belong to Zarr. Fleming and Sandmark. But that will be enough to burn him."

That cut him adrift again. He rubbed the side of his jaw with uncertain fingers and gaped at me. "Will you for Chrisakes quit playing detective? What about Marlin and Clyne, then?"

"The guy that got them," I said, "has already paid his bill. He was a man named Baird. He died outside of Glencoe just a few hours ago, while he was getting set to beat the top of my head in."

That was when I gave him the story of what had happened on that dark side road out along the North Shore. I gave him only the action, naming no names and making no mention of the call Glencoe's police chief had made to Central Station. Abbott, I thought, would appreciate that.

It interested Crandall, all right, but it didn't satisfy him. Not that I had expected it to satisfy him. He said, "How do you know this Baird killed Marlin and Clyne?"

"Marlin," I said, "was double-crossing a certain party. So Marlin was taken out of there. Clyne knew too much about the connection between Marlin and that certain party. Now Clyne is no longer with us. Then I started shooting off my mouth, and I was slated to leave this life. Miss Sandmark kept that from happening—for the time being anyway."

"And who," Crandall said slowly, "is this 'certain party'?"

"No," I said. "The man I'm talking about is a man you couldn't touch in a thousand years. It seems he has friends in the high places around town—friends who would not take kindly to being embarrassed. If I gave you his name, the only thing that could come of it would be my body in a ditch, and I do not want my body to be in a ditch.

"The man who killed Marlin and Clyne is worm meat, just as they are. Retribution is a good word: why not respect it?"

Crandall shook his head doggedly. "I want his name, Pine."

"You want my testimony against Zarr, too, brother. I forget important details when I get pushed around. And for all I know, I may have another gunman out to get me, now that Baird is gone. And for the same reason he had.''

While Crandall was chewing that over, the door chimes sounded and the housekeeper let in a couple of cops in Oak Park harness. They came into the library and stood just inside the door looking uncomfortable.

Crandall said, "Okay, George," to Zarr. "I'm going to have to take you in and book you. From there on it will be up to you."

Zarr's expression had nothing to say. He got up, waited while Crandall told the cops enough to satisfy them, then went out the door between them.

"Paul," Crandall said, "you and Miss Sandmark better come along with me. I'll have to take statements from both of you."

"You'll have plenty of time for that later on," I said. "What do you use for a heart—your gallstones? This girl has been through enough to put gray hairs on a plaster bust; and my throat hates my tongue."

He nodded reluctantly. "Fair enough. Get some sleep, both of you. But I want the two of you at my office around five this afternoon."

When he was gone, leaving Leona and me alone in the library, I said, "Try to get some sleep, Leona. Maybe a sedative will do it. I'll pick you up around four. We'll have to do what Crandall wants, and the sooner it's over with, the sooner you can start living again."

She sat there, her shoulders bowed, her eyes fixed on nothing at all. "Is he really dead, Paul?"

"I'm sorry, kid. But there's not a chance that he's alive. Go on to bed."

She looked at me dully. "No. I can't stay here. I couldn't bear to stay here. Take me home, Paul—to my own apartment. Please."

"If that's what you want," I said. "Come on."

· 20 ·

She gave me her keys and I unlocked the door to 6A and flicked the switch, flooding the tiny reception hall with soft light. Daylight through the windows bathed the living room in a warm glow and we went in there.

She crossed over to the windows and leaned against one of the frames, letting the early morning breeze from the east cool her skin. The harsh light showed lines around her eyes and mouth—lines that were not there before. They did not surprise me; what she had gone through during the past eight hours would put lines in the Washington Monument.

I mixed two drinks, using Scotch, soda and ice cubes. I took one over to her and leaned against the opposite side of the same window frame.

"Here's to you," I said, lifting my glass in salute.

She nodded. "To you," she repeated soberly and touched the rim of her glass to mine.

We drank. Deeply. She lowered her glass and stared down into it as though the future was there for her to read.

"What's left for me, Paul?"

"Probably fifty years," I said. "And you'll need less than one of them to get over what tonight has done to you."

"I loved him, Paul. He was the only man who was ever good to me."

I said, "Look. You've taken an awful wallop and it

hurts. But it won't kill you and it won't hurt forever. A right kind of guy would hold your hand and pat you on the back and let you cry into his shoulder padding. But I'm not the right kind of guy. I'm tired and I'm sleepy and my feet hurt. Suppose you go on to bed, and about three-thirty I'll phone you to be ready at four. Okay?''

She looked out the window without seeing anything. "I wouldn't be able to sleep. I don't think I can ever sleep again.''

"I know. You'll be thinking that while you're snoring.''

She ran a finger slowly up and down the side of the glass in her hand. "You're a funny person, Paul. You seem so—so calloused. Hard. Bitter. Why are you that way?''

She wanted to talk; and, like most people when they've taken a bad jolt, she wanted to talk about personal things. Like what makes you tick and why are you the way you are. I figured another ten minutes wouldn't ruin me and maybe she would feel better. So I said:

"I don't think I'm hard or calloused or bitter. At least I don't mean to be. I get wet-eyed in the movies once in a while, and I think kids are wonderful.

"Maybe I give the impression you get, Leona, because my work makes me see people as they actually are. Oh, I used to be a trusting soul. I thought people, even the shoddy ones, would give a straight deal if they got one themselves. And I used to go to bat for them, right down the line.

"But after a few years of being lied to and cheated and double-crossed—well, I quit handing out halos. Too many of them were turning out to be tarnished instead of glowing; red instead of gold . . . halos in blood.''

There was a brooding wonder, a thoughtful curiosity in her eyes. And then she smiled a little, although she was not amused. "I think,'' she said softly, "that if you ever fell in love, you'd go back to seeing things in their true perspective.''

I stood there and looked at how my thumb curled around the glass I was holding.

"You were in love once, weren't you, Paul? I mean really in love?"

"You could call it that."

"Tell me about it."

"I'll tell you nothing about it."

"Why?"

"That would be telling you about it."

She lifted her glass and drank the rest of her highball, then turned and walked slowly over to the lounge chair, sat down and put her head back and closed her eyes.

I straightened, put my glass down on an end table and said, "I'll be running along. See you late this afternoon."

"Stay with me, Paul."

She had not moved . . . she just sat there with her head thrown back, her eyes closed, the words coming out without her having anything to do with them.

I said, "You've got to go to bed, baby."

Her eyes opened slowly—and they were green again. "So do you, darling."

A minute ticked away while we looked deep into each other's eyes. I said, "Just like that?"

"Yes." She said it so softly I barely heard her.

"You," I said, "are a woman, by God! You've shot a man, been shot at, seen a man proved a murderer, learned your stepfather is dead--all within a few hours. And now you want to be slept with. I give you a bow, damned if I don't!"

Her gaze never wavered . . . and very slowly her lips curved in a smile. It was the kind of smile that was already old when Eve was born—a patient smile, a confident smile, the smile that comes to a woman when she looks upon the man she wants and means to have—and who knows at last that she belongs to him.

"I love you, Paul."

My hands began to shake. "How do you know who

you love? You're as punchy as a cauliflower ear. You couldn't be anything else after last night.''

"This is different, darling. This is real. I love you . . . and you love me.''

"I do like so much!'' Every cell in my body was crying for me to go over and get down on my knees beside her and put my arms around her. "You're just another beautiful woman. You're rich and spoiled and hard as nails. I don't love you. Why should you think I love you?''

She was smiling and holding out her arms to me. "Please, sweetheart. I want you near to me. . . .''

And then she was in my arms and her body was pressed against me and her eyes were large and luminous and her breath was warm against my mouth. . . .

I put her away from me abruptly and went over to the liquor cabinet and made two fresh drinks. I came back and sat down on the arm of her chair and gave her one of the glasses and lighted cigarettes for both of us. I said:

"Before retiring, a lady and gentleman always share a drink and a cigarette. It wouldn't do for us to treat tradition lightly.''

We drank, smiling into each other's eyes. She said, "John would have approved of this, darling. I only wish he could have lived to see it.''

She watched the smoke spiral up from the glowing end of her cigarette and went on talking, her mood pensive now. "Think how many have died, Paul. My real father, and Charles, and Jerry, and this man Clyne whom I never knew . . . and John. And I suppose that police officer will be executed for his part in what happened.''

She sighed softly and rubbed her cheek against my sleeve and her lips curved in a slow smile. "But I'm not going to think of death any more. I'm going to think of living . . . with you, Paul.''

I finished my drink . . . and if my hand shook a little, it had a reason for shaking. I got off the chair arm and set the glass carefully on the coffee table and turned my back on Leona Sandmark and went over to the wall and stared at a framed print hanging there.

Just one word. But one word too many. Now I knew the truth—and no truth was ever more bitter: I looked down at my hand and it was a fist and I was not surprised. . . .

I turned around then and looked at Leona Sandmark. She was still sitting there smiling at me. She was still beautiful—she would never be more beautiful. But it wasn't beauty to me now. It was just some meat, with patches of hair here and there—nothing I wanted any more. I said:

"It seems I closed the books a little too early, baby. You see, one more will have to die. That will happen the day they put you in the electric chair and throw the switch."

She sat there and looked at me, the smile frozen on her lips. And it seemed that very slowly the face behind that smile began to wither and fade away, leaving the smile hanging there. Just as slowly one of her hands came up and she put her fingers against her cheek.

"What are—you saying, Paul?"

The muscles bunched under my jaws. " 'I love you, Paul; come sleep with me.' Why, you two-bit little tart, I ought to feed you a sap until you spit buckshot. So it was you who murdered Jerry Marlin . . . you who killed Clyne. But I couldn't see it because your face and your body were so beautiful I couldn't see past them."

It wasn't until she tried a second time that her shock-stiffened lips parted enough for her to speak.

"You're mad! Mad! How can you *say* such a thing! You know I didn't kill them. You yourself saw a man kill Jerry while he was with me. You must be insa——"

I said savagely, "Shut up, you bitch! You're through lying to me. If you can't *tell* the truth, then by God you'll *hear* it.

"The day I called on John Sandmark he told me of

some of your love affairs. He told me of a high-school boy, of a married man . . . and of a crook. A crook who was a confidence man, a gunman, a phony-money passer. He never told me this crook's name, but now I know it.

"His name was Charles Hogarth. Another of his names was C. L. Baird. He got out of the pen lately and he came back to the hot little hunk he used to run around with in the good old days. He found she was in trouble: a guy named Marlin was putting the bite on her. Marlin was getting five hundred a month from her because he thought she had killed a man at the Laycroft Hotel.

"So she talked Hogarth—Baird—into killing Marlin. And when Marlin's pal, Clyne, tried to take up where Marlin left off, he got it, too. Meanwhile a private dick by the name of Pine started to sniff around and find things out, so Hogarth had to get him as well. The first time he tried it, D'Allemand's boys interrupted him. So Hogarth and his girl friend worked out another plan. She would date this private eye and take him out to a lovers' lane—tailed by Hogarth—park there and let Hogarth come along and bump him off.

"But the girl hadn't been paying blackmail because she had killed the man at the hotel. She was paying it because she thought her stepfather had done it; and rather than refuse to pay Marlin and have the facts get to the police, she paid off . . . until Hogarth came along and took care of the blackmailers.

"But the night this nosey snooper was to get taken care of too, the girl found out that the man murdered in the hotel was not Raoul Fleming. That's what she thought, anyhow, when she saw that newspaper clipping.

"That put an entirely different light on the matter. If the dead man was not her father, then John Sandmark was not the killer.

"And so the girl had a beautiful idea. She reasoned that the only person alive who could cause her any trouble, the only one who had anything actually on her, was not the private dick—oh, no. It was *Hogarth*—the man she had hired to get rid of Marlin and Clyne.

"So she let things ride exactly the way she and Hogarth had planned. Let them ride right to the point where Hogarth was on the edge of killing the private dick. Then she yanked a gun out of her purse and killed Hogarth!

"Beautiful? Brother, I hope to tell you it was beautiful! The supposed stick-up man had a mile-long record, he was shot while engaged in a criminal act . . . and no one, except John Sandmark, would suspect the girl had ever seen Hogarth before that night.

"Yes, it was perfect. Hell, I thought all along that D'Allemand had hired Hogarth to get rid of all three of us: Marlin, Clyne, Pine. It wasn't until just a minute ago that I saw the whole stinking picture.

"For *you* told me, baby! You told me while you were listing the men who died while this thing was going on. You named Fleming and Charles and Marlin and Clyne and John Sandmark. Get it, sweetheart? *'And Charles'!*

"How could you know Baird's real name was Hogarth? You weren't in the chief's office in Glencoe when Abbott first learned the guy's name. I was with you all the time afterward, and nobody mentioned that name. Hogarth was a man who dabbled in counterfeit bills; so was the guy you used to run around with!

"And so you turn out to be a murderer, baby. Not only because you arranged to have two men killed, but because you deliberately shot another man to death yourself."

I walked over in front of her, my arms dangling loosely at my sides. She shrank back in the chair, her face twisted with fear . . . and *guilt*. It was there to see, and I saw it. Nobody could have missed seeing it.

"Murder is a matter between you and the State, baby. But when you try to lock the door permanently by running a love affair with me, selling me on how much you love me and how much I love you, laying me open for a kick in the teeth even bigger than the one I was just getting over—that is where it becomes a personal matter—a matter between you and me.

"You've got until five o'clock this afternoon to get out to Crandall and tell him the truth. I'll let *you* tell him; I'll like that. And maybe you won't burn after all. Your legs are too nice and you stick out in front too pretty for that. A smart lawyer may get you off with a small sentence; maybe no sentence at all.

"But that won't mean much to you, beautiful. A bloodstain soaks too deep. It does something to you. It takes something from you that you can't go on without, and it puts something in its place that you can't go on with. You're finished, baby. You're all washed up. You're done for."

For another moment I stared down at her face—a face no longer beautiful but a hundred years-of-hell old. Then I turned and started for the door.

"Wait! Paul, for God's sake, wait!"

She was out of the chair, across the room, at my feet, her arms holding desperately to my legs.

"It's true—all of it! I couldn't help it . . . I couldn't help it! I was so afraid John had killed my father. I was insane—crazy with worry. And then when Charles Hogarth came back, I took the only way out I could see. But things kept twisting and turning and closing in. . . .

"Oh, my dearest, haven't I suffered enough? I love you, Paul, I love you! Don't do this terrible thing to me!"

I drew back my arm and brought the back of my hand down across her face with all my strength. The blow knocked her away from me, drove her into a huddled heap on the floor. I said, "Before five this afternoon, you hear me? Either you tell it or I do."

She lay there, staring up at me. I turned and went into the reception hall, opened the door and closed it behind me.

The elevator was somewhere below. I put my finger on the button.

It was very quiet there in the small corridor. The only sound was the faint whine of the ascending cage. It came up slowly—too slowly for me. Yet I could wait. I knew how to wait. I could wait forever.

I was opening the elevator door when the sound came from behind the closed door to 6A.

It was a single sound. A sharp, brittle sound. The sound of a Colt .32. A man named Charles Hogarth had died with that same sound in his ears.

I got into the cage and rode down to the first floor and went out into the hot clean light of a new day.

Also Available in Quill Mysterious Classics: